"You don't need to see us home."

"Thought maybe I could help you put those young'uns to bed."

She laughed softly. "You mean you want to be sure the cattle rustlers didn't take advantage of our day in town to steal my few head of cattle."

He grinned. "That, too."

"I do appreciate it, but you don't need to watch over us." She had a strange longing for that exact thing, but with Uncle's threats hanging over her, she didn't dare lean on Edmund.

"Me?" He put a hand on his chest and gave her a mock-wounded look. "Watch over you? The independent, capable Mrs. Lula May Barlow?"

Hmm. Maybe he wasn't so guileless, after all. But at least she knew he meant her no harm. She rewarded his little performance with another light laugh and the skeptical arching of one eyebrow.

And was rewarded with that chest-deep chuckle she'd come to like far too much.

* * *

**LONE STAR COWBOY LEAGUE:
THE FOUNDING YEARS—
Bighearted ranchers in small-town Texas**

Florida author **Louise M. Gouge** writes historical fiction for Harlequin's Love Inspired Historical line. She received the prestigious Inspirational Readers' Choice Award in 2005 and placed in 2011 and 2015; she also placed in the Laurel Wreath contest in 2012. When she isn't writing, she and her husband, David, enjoy visiting historical sites and museums. Please visit her website at blog.louisemgouge.com.

Books by Louise M. Gouge

Love Inspired Historical

Lone Star Cowboy League: The Founding Years

A Family for the Rancher

Four Stones Ranch

Cowboy to the Rescue
Cowboy Seeks a Bride
Cowgirl for Keeps

Ladies in Waiting

A Proper Companion
A Suitable Wife
A Lady of Quality

Love Thine Enemy
The Captain's Lady
At the Captain's Command

Visit the Author Profile page at Harlequin.com for more titles.

LOUISE M. GOUGE

A Family for the Rancher

HARLEQUIN® LOVE INSPIRED® HISTORICAL

If you purchased this book without a cover you should be aware that this book is stolen property. It was reported as "unsold and destroyed" to the publisher, and neither the author nor the publisher has received any payment for this "stripped book."

Special thanks and acknowledgment to Louise M. Gouge for her contribution to the Lone Star Cowboy League: The Founding Years miniseries.

Recycling programs for this product may not exist in your area.

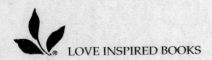 LOVE INSPIRED BOOKS

ISBN-13: 978-0-373-28370-5

A Family for the Rancher

Copyright © 2016 by Harlequin Books S.A.

All rights reserved. Except for use in any review, the reproduction or utilization of this work in whole or in part in any form by any electronic, mechanical or other means, now known or hereinafter invented, including xerography, photocopying and recording, or in any information storage or retrieval system, is forbidden without the written permission of the editorial office, Love Inspired Books, 195 Broadway, New York, NY 10007 U.S.A.

This is a work of fiction. Names, characters, places and incidents are either the product of the author's imagination or are used fictitiously, and any resemblance to actual persons, living or dead, business establishments, events or locales is entirely coincidental.

This edition published by arrangement with Love Inspired Books.

® and TM are trademarks of Love Inspired Books, used under license. Trademarks indicated with ® are registered in the United States Patent and Trademark Office, the Canadian Intellectual Property Office and in other countries.

www.Harlequin.com

Printed in U.S.A.

You have not chosen me, but I have chosen you and
ordained you that you should go and bring forth
fruit, and that your fruit should remain:
that whatsoever ye shall ask the Father in my name,
he shall give it [to] you.
—*John* 15:16

Enjoy the adventure!

Louise m gouge

Writing this Lone Star Cowboy League continuity series with Renee Ryan and Regina Scott has been such a delightful experience for me. Not only are these lovely ladies two of my favorite authors, but they made my story better with their input. I can only aspire to reach their heights of talent and success. I would also like to dedicate this story to my daughter and granddaughter, Jane and Savannah Reese. These two horsewomen supplied me with the information I needed regarding Lula May's horses. As always, I am grateful to my dear husband, David, who is my biggest encourager and loving supporter. Most of all, I thank my Lord Jesus Christ, from whom come all things pertaining to salvation, life and godliness.

Chapter One

High Bar Ranch
Little Horn, Texas
June 24, 1895

"The very idea, Mr. McKay. You think I don't know my fence needs repairs?"

Widow Barlow stood in her kitchen, fists posted at her waist, shoulders hunched high as she glared at Edmund McKay, looking a whole heap like an angry, ruffled-feathered brood hen protecting her nest. Looking a whole heap like Edmund's ornery widowed cousin, Judith, who'd raised him. Which made his unexpected visit all the more difficult for him. Behind Mrs. Barlow in the dim kitchen light of a kerosene lamp, Edmund could see her two teenaged stepsons and her own three smaller children watch him with wary expressions, like he was a grizzly bear about to attack their mama.

"You don't need to worry that my horses will wander over into your pasture, because we always keep an eye on them." Mrs. Barlow waved a hand toward the kitchen window that faced out that way. The sun was just appearing over the horizon, chasing away night shadows as it rose. "I've ordered the barbed wire, and it will be in at the general store any day now."

"Well, ma'am—" Edmund swallowed hard, partly to get past the mouthwatering aromas of fresh baked bread, bacon and coffee filling this room—this family had just finished eating breakfast, and the remains littered the kitchen table—and partly to hide his vexation. He didn't know much about women, but Mrs. Barlow's defensive, self-sufficient attitude puzzled him, just as his cousin's meanness always had. And Mrs. Barlow sure wasn't anything like his sweet, compliant sister-in-law, who always acted real pleased when his brother Josiah offered to help her. Not only did Mrs. Barlow not want any help, she didn't even dress like other women. Instead of a dress, she wore some sort of mixed skirt and trouser getup, probably to make it easier for her to do a man's work on her horse ranch, seeing she no longer had a husband to do it. If this woman was always so disagreeable, Edmund couldn't imagine why Frank Barlow had married her in the first place.

Great hornets, if Edmund had known Mrs. Barlow would get all in a huff, he never would have mentioned the weakened fence. So much for the guilt he felt for not looking in on this little widow woman right after Frank died last winter. He blamed his neglect on his preference for being a loner, a man who loved his freedom and solitude. On the other hand, the Good Book said folks should take care of widows and orphans. Loner or not, he'd failed in his Christian duty, and now look what he got for it.

"I just thought—"

"Never you mind." The lady spoke in a snippy way, just like Judith used to do. "Calvin's been riding fence lines since he was eleven, and he let me know about the problem over a week ago. As you can see, we manage just fine."

As if to emphasize her assertion, sixteen-year-old Calvin gave Edmund a decisive nod as fierce protectiveness smoldered in his eyes.

"Yes, ma'am. I'm sure you do." Not given to a temper, Edmund felt more foolish than angry. Did the older boy really think Edmund would harm his stepma? Didn't this family know about the hard-won respect and trust most other local folks gave him? If he'd suspected they didn't trust him, he never would have come. Edmund never went where he wasn't wanted.

Once was enough for that. When he, Josiah and their brother, David, were just little mites, their parents died, and they were each sent to a different relative. The cousin who raised Edmund was a strong-willed, bossy widow who hadn't welcomed another mouth to feed. Forced to take his meals in the kitchen while the family ate in the dining room, Edmund always felt like an outsider, so he hit the trail as soon as he turned sixteen, Calvin's age. If not for an old cowboy taking him under his wing, Edmund could well have ended up an outlaw. Hunger can do that to a man. These Barlow young'uns might have lost their pa, but they still had each other, and they still had a strong ma to hold them together. He could almost envy them that, if envy weren't a sin.

Mrs. Barlow kept on looking at him with her light brown eyebrows bent into a frown. He shuffled from one foot to the other and rolled his brown Stetson in his hands. Maybe he should just apologize for living and go back home.

Nope. He needed to tell Widow Barlow why he'd bothered her this early in the morning, so he cleared his throat.

"Um, well, I didn't come about the fence. I came over to invite Jacob—" he gave the ten-year-old a slight nod and was rewarded when the boy's eyebrows shot upward with surprise and his lips formed a lopsided grin "—that is, you may know that after John and Helen Carson's barn burned down, CJ Thorn came up with a plan to teach local boys about ranching. CJ calls them the Young Ranchers' Club and says they were a big help to Molly's folks in cleaning up the place after the fire and getting the new barn built." Maybe invoking his friends' names would influence Mrs. Barlow. "What with CJ and Molly newly married, I'm gonna have the boys over to my place this week. The Forester boys and the Gillen boys and a few others are the regulars. Jacob would fit right in—" That was a mighty long speech for Edmund, and he was beginning to feel worn out despite it being first thing in the morning.

Mrs. Barlow's blue eyes narrowed, and her frown turned into a scowl. "Jacob learns everything he needs to know about ranching right here at home, and it's past time for him to start doing his chores." She glanced toward the door, a clear invitation for Edmund to leave.

Edmund would be glad to do that, but he couldn't let his nephew Adam down. "Yes, ma'am, I'm sure you're teaching him a whole heap. But Adam will be there, too, and he'll be disappointed if his best friend can't join the group." A tiny bit of guilt crept into his mind. Using CJ's name to add credibility to his invitation was one thing, but he shouldn't blame Adam for this intrusion into her world. Jacob's surprised look turned to excitement as he glanced between Edmund and his ma.

"Adam?" She blinked those big blue eyes, and her entire countenance changed from antagonism to something a lot more pleasant, almost a smile. In spite of her grouchiness, she was a nice looking woman any day, but a smile made her right pretty. "Hmm. If Adam will be there—" She glanced at Jacob, who chewed his lip and pleaded with his gaze. She relaxed her stance and gently pulled him forward. "You want to go?"

"Yes, ma'am." Full-on happiness shone on the boy's face, giving Edmund a kick of satisfaction in his chest.

Mrs. Barlow heaved out a sigh. Was it relief or defeat? "All right, then." She ruffled her son's hair. "You may go. We'll shift your chores around with your brothers so everything gets done."

To their credit, not a hint of grumbling or disapproval came from either Calvin or Samuel. Not even from little Daniel, who was a mite young to join Jacob and the others.

When Mrs. Barlow turned back to Edmund, he caught a hint of worry—or was it fear?—in her eyes that didn't seem to have anything to do with Jacob. Not knowing much about women, he had no idea how to figure it out. Still, he was pleased she'd let Jacob join the other boys. He'd saved the best part until last.

"You'll be glad to know Pastor Stillwater will cart the boys back and forth each day."

"That's not necessary. Jacob can get there by himself." She posted her fists at her waist again. "And I have only one condition for him to join."

Edmund's chest tightened. Now what? "Yes, ma'am?"

"I want you to bring him home every evening and have supper with us. That'll repay you for your efforts."

"You don't have to repay—"

"If you won't come, he can't go." She crossed her arms over her chest and lifted her chin.

Now that Edmund had a little bit of her trust, he didn't want to lose it. But supper with this big family? Not something he'd ever seek, even with the fine breakfast aromas tempting him just now. She was probably a real fine cook. For a brief moment, he let himself admire her pretty face with its upturned little nose sprinkled with freckles and eyes that seemed not to miss anything going on in her domain. He had no place for women in his life, especially not peevish women, but he could admire them from a distance.

"Well?" She tapped one foot on the broad board flooring and raised one eyebrow.

Suddenly, he felt like a schoolboy being scolded by the schoolmarm. Yet he had to admit, if only to himself, that he was tired of his own cooking and the occasional bland fare served up by Mushy, his cowhands' cook. Maybe he should give it a try.

She was standing there waggling those fine eyebrows expectantly, and he bit back a chuckle. "Yes, ma'am. That'll be fine."

"Good."

Good? Maybe so, maybe not. Edmund wasn't so sure. Sitting down with a large family when he was used to eating in peace and quiet…and alone…might prove to be more of a challenge than teaching young boys about ranching.

Mrs. Barlow sent the other children off to do chores while she went to help Jacob get ready. Alone in this spotless kitchen with all of its tempting smells, Edmund felt both pleased and a bit frustrated by her behavior. Women! Who could understand them? He'd stick with what he did know, running a cattle ranch. He'd worked with cowboys all of his adult life, so he felt confident he could wrangle the young boys in his charge. In a way, it would be payback to kindly Old Gad, the cowboy who'd mentored him both in his job and in his spiritual life. When he'd tried to repay Old Gad for his kindness, he'd told him just to pass it on. That's what he was trying to do now, what he always tried to do.

And in the back of his mind, he felt the Lord's nudge challenging him to figure out ways to help his pretty, stubborn little neighbor take care of her ranch…without her knowing it, o'course.

Once Lula May and Jacob were back in the kitchen, she tied a clean red kerchief around the neck of her oldest birth child. She made a final inspection of his fresh tan shirt and brown trousers and his well-brushed, hand-me-down boots. Nobody could say she didn't take care of her children or, as they grew up, that she didn't teach them to take care of themselves. "There. All ready to go."

"Yes, ma'am." Jacob's bright blue eyes sparkled with excitement, the most joy she'd seen on his face since his pa died last January. She and the children had all grieved Frank's passing, still grieved it, but for some reason she'd yet to figure out, Jacob seemed to take his pa's death the hardest.

"Go on, then." She waved a hand toward the kitchen door where Mr. McKay stood waiting, hat in hand. "Get your horse."

The man gave her a quick nod and an almost-grin. She'd never known what to make of her quiet, somewhat aloof neighbor. Frank had called him a good person, and she'd always respected her husband's judgment, but now she was on her own deciding whom to trust. Besides, being a good person didn't mean this man would teach her son properly.

"Let's go, cowboy." Mr. McKay clapped a hand on Jacob's shoulder, and the two of them exited the house through the narrow mudroom off the kitchen. On the way out, Jacob grabbed his well-worn hat from a peg by the door.

Doubt darted through Lula May. Exactly what would Mr. McKay teach Jacob? She should have asked. She hurried out the door behind them, passing the man's horse ground-tied a few yards from the house. Nibbling at a clump of grass, the stallion stayed in place, a good sign, because she kept her broodmares in a nearby field. The stallion not taking off in that direction meant he was well trained not to move once his reins hit the ground.

"I'll help you saddle up," the man said. "Which one's your horse?" He looked across the corral where a dozen or so of Lula May's quarter horses awaited their morning feeding.

"It's in the barn," she called out. "And he can saddle his own horse."

Mr. McKay turned, surprise registering on his face. Or was it annoyance? Never mind. If he was going to teach her son anything, she had a right to know about his methods.

"Go on, Jacob. Get Buster."

Her son hurried obediently into the barn while Lula May joined Mr. McKay at the corral fence.

With one boot on the lowest rail and his arms resting on the top one, the rancher appeared to be studying her stock. Was he interested in buying? She could use a sale right now to pay for that barbed wire when it came in. Raising cow ponies wasn't as lucrative as cattle ranching, but it was a business she and the children could manage without having to hire cowboys.

"You need a horse?" She followed his gaze, which seemed to have settled on the paint gelding Calvin had raised to sell.

"No, ma'am." Still studying her horses, Mr. McKay left it at that.

Lula May felt a scratch of irritation at his brief answer. "I don't know what you're planning to teach my son, but don't you baby him. He learns quick. You'll see when he brings Buster out of that barn all saddled and ready to go."

"Yes, ma'am."

Was that all he had to say? Wouldn't he tell her about his plans?

"Well?"

"Ma'am?" He stared down at her from his considerable height, his face crinkled with confusion.

Being tall for a woman, she usually didn't have to crane her neck this way to look up at a man. An odd, giddy feeling tickled her insides. Shame on her. Frank hadn't even been gone a year, and here she was reacting to this man like a schoolgirl.

"Just exactly what are you going to teach the boys?" Her words came out harsher than she intended. Mr. McKay didn't deserve rudeness. "I mean, well, what will they be doing? Does Jacob need to bring a dinner pail?"

"No, ma'am. My bunkhouse cook'll fix vittles for them." He brushed away a horsefly trying to light on his clean-shaven cheek, and the mild scent of leather and soap wafted toward Lula May. "This morning, I'll test 'em, find out what they know. Go from there."

The way he clamped his mouth shut told Lula May that was all she'd get from him on the subject. At least she didn't have to worry about Jacob getting hungry while he worked. She tried to think of something to chat about while they waited for her son, but this man just about defined what it meant to be taciturn.

His unexpected visit this morning had miffed her more than a little, but now that she understood he hadn't come to complain about the weak fencing between their two properties, she could relax a little.

Not that she could ever truly relax. Her children and her ranch were her whole life, and she had to be vigilant every moment to be sure everything went well. When Frank fell ill three years ago, he'd urged her to hire a cowhand to help out, but that would have meant turning control over to someone else, some man who might take advantage of the situation. Instead she'd taken up the reins of running the place and kept his illness quiet right up until a week or so before he'd gone to Glory.

She hadn't needed help then, and she didn't need it now. What she hadn't learned about the care and training of horses in childhood from her uncle's groom, Tobias, she'd learned from Frank. She'd learned all she needed to know about cooking from Tobias's wife, Annie. Along with her five children, Lula May raised exceptional cow ponies and worked toward the day when the High Bar Ranch became a respected quarter horse supplier that drew cattle ranchers from all over Texas and beyond.

She looked up at Mr. McKay again. He was one of the most competent cattle ranchers in the county, if his success was any indication. That hat looked fairly new, and his boots, too. She hadn't been able to afford new boots for some time, but at least she managed new garb for the older boys, and they handed things down to the younger ones. No shame in that. Even more prosperous folks with half a brain passed clothes down to save money.

"Ma'am?" Mr. McKay gave her a quizzical look, and she realized she'd been staring at him. Those green eyes briefly widened before shuttering down. Here was a man who didn't let people into his life, a practice she knew all too well.

Before she could respond, a fat mouse darted from a crack in the barn wall, with one of the barn cats in pursuit, straight toward Lula May. She raised a boot to stomp the mouse, and it must have seen the danger of its course, because it hopped about a foot into the air and turned its frantic flight toward the corral. The yellow tabby didn't miss a beat but scrambled under the fencing, chasing his quarry in a haphazard path among the milling horses and out the other side and disappearing around the corner of the barn. How both critters avoided those hooves, Lula May couldn't guess.

"Good mouser." Mr. McKay chuckled, a pleasant resonant sound low in his chest.

An unexpected ache touched something deep inside of Lula May's own chest. She missed the sound of a man's laugh, a man's conversation. In truth, she missed the sound of any adult conversation. If not for the ladies' weekly quilting bee and church on Sundays, she'd be hard-pressed to remember how to talk to other grown-ups.

She offered a small laugh of her own. "We have a few dozen cats. You need one? Or two?"

"Thanks." He shook his head. "Got a passel of 'em myself." He went silent again.

Lula May withheld a huff of frustration. Jacob would be in the barn a few more minutes, and it felt so awkward to just stand here.

"Mr. McKay—"

"Edmund." He gave her a shy, crooked smile.

Why, he *was* shy. And probably not used to talking to women. Bless his heart. Maybe she could bring him out a bit. She gave him a bright smile.

"All right, then. And I'm Lula May."

He nodded and touched the brim of his hat. "Yes, ma'am."

"You have any favorite foods I can cook up for you?"

He stared off for a moment. "No, ma'am." When he looked back at her, his broad face was creased thoughtfully, his head tilted to the side in a charming way, which he probably had no idea was charming. "Maybe no beans."

She ached to laugh at his confession, delivered in such an honest, boyish manner, like one of her own boys might say it. But she knew better than to laugh at any man or boy. "I'm assuming you mean pinto beans. I got string beans ready to pick." She hooked a thumb over her shoulder in the direction of her kitchen garden near the house. "Is that all right?"

He grinned, a real, true grin. "Yes, ma'am."

Also grinning from ear to ear, Jacob emerged from the barn leading Buster. "I'm ready to go, Mr. McKay."

Mr. McKay…Edmund…gave a low whistle, and his stallion lifted his head. "Come, Zephyr." The tall bay animal, equal parts Thoroughbred and quarter horse, and easily sixteen hands high, walked purposefully toward his master, with his reins dragging between his forelegs. Arriving at his destination, he lowered his head and accepted a carrot Edmund had pulled from his back pocket. "Good boy." Edmund scratched the animal's forehead and ran a hand down his neck. Zephyr leaned into Edmund as a child would to his father, a bonding gesture Lula May knew well from her own favorite mare, Lady.

"Wow." Jacob watched wide-eyed as the stallion munched his reward.

Lula May knew just how he felt. If Edmund could train this magnificent animal with such obvious gentleness, she could set aside her worries. He wouldn't teach Jacob to break a horse, a practice most cowboys employed.

With some difficulty, she squelched the urge to hug Jacob goodbye. He'd started resisting hugs some time back, just as Calvin and Samuel had at this age. She wouldn't embarrass a single one of them by forcing such attentions on them just to satisfy her maternal impulses. At least Pauline and Daniel still needed her hugs.

"Go on, now. And you listen to Mr. McKay." She couldn't resist saying that, even though Jacob always listened well.

Jacob and Edmund mounted up, said their goodbyes and rode off. For several minutes, Lula May stood and watched until all she could see was the dust stirred up by their galloping horses. Even as her heart filled with gratitude toward Edmund, it ached for her son.

Dear, sweet Jacob, firstborn of her three birth

children. She sincerely loved Calvin and Samuel. Yet Jacob's birth had truly opened her heart to what motherhood was all about. Still, Jacob had lived his entire ten years in the shadow of his two older half brothers. They weren't unkind to him, but they did treat him more as a pesky puppy. Even eight-year-old Pauline, a "little mother" to all four of her brothers, bossed Jacob around more than she did the others.

At first, when Edmund invited Jacob to join his Young Ranchers' Club, Lula May had been insulted, even more than when he pointed out that her fence needed mending. But as she'd prayed to control her temper, Edmund had mentioned Adam, and the Lord whispered in her mind that maybe this was just the thing to help Jacob come into his own. Since his only pal would be there, and Adam treated Jacob as an equal, she gave in, even though it was hard.

As she walked back toward the house, she thought of Frank. What would he say to her letting another man teach his son? As if to answer her question, sixteen-year-old Calvin met her at the back door.

"You did right, Ma." He chewed on a biscuit covered with butter and strawberry jam. "It'll be good for him."

"You think so?"

"Yes, ma'am." He polished off the biscuit and swiped his hands across his trousers. "I'm headed out to feed the stock."

"All right." Satisfaction warmed her heart. As with Jacob, she resisted the urge to hug her very capable eldest stepson. Calvin always knew just what to do around here. Although she'd never confess it to anyone outside of the family, without him and Samuel, she never could have managed the ranch this far.

She'd pretty much reared Calvin and Samuel since they were six and four, and they'd always called her Ma. Yet she couldn't help wondering whether they wished, like their father always seemed to, that their birth mother hadn't died. Her own mother and father died of a fever when Lula May was twelve, and at twenty-nine, she still missed their loving ways.

"Ma, Daniel won't make his bed." Eight-year-old Pauline awaited Lula May in the kitchen, her fists firmly at her waist in imitation of Lula May's customary scolding pose.

Six-year-old Daniel peered around his sister, pulled his thumb from his mouth, and grinned.

Lula May had a hard time giving her youngest child a stern look, but she somehow managed. He sure was full of vinegar. "Daniel, mind your sister and make your bed."

"See there." Pauline shot her brother a triumphant look.

Unlike Jacob, who withered under the mildest scolding, Daniel giggled and scampered off to obey. Pauline huffed out her impatience as she set about washing breakfast dishes. Oh, how Daniel liked to get his sister's goat. Lula May tried not to laugh. It wasn't wise to set one child against another. They all needed to work together from before dawn till late into the night.

"Here's the firewood, Ma." Samuel came in the back door and dumped a large armload of fuel into the wood box. "One more trip, and it should carry you through fixing supper. Then I'll muck out the barn."

"That's fine, Sammy." She watched her fourteen-year-old stepson hurry back outside. As with all of her children, she felt a surge of affection as she watched him working so responsibly.

Maybe she wasn't being fair to her stepsons in thinking they missed their mother. And she shouldn't compare their lives to her own because their upbringing had been so different from hers. After Emily's death, they'd been able to stay with their own gentle father in the home they were born in. When Lula May's parents died, she'd been sent away from all she'd ever known and to her uncle in Alabama, a cruel man who'd made it clear he resented her being there. Made it clear he found her incapable of doing or being anything important. He was forever comparing her to the "delicate, well-mannered Southern belles" in their church. She ran away from his controlling ways at eighteen and came to Texas to marry a kind widower with two sweet little boys.

She never regretted it for a minute. Frank had been a good husband, if a bit distracted most of the time. One thing that always hurt, although Lula May had never told him, was that he'd never put away the wedding picture of Emily and him that hung over the parlor mantelpiece and one of Emily on their bedroom wall. Nor had he ever asked Lula May to sit for a photographic portrait. Being a young bride, she'd lacked the self-confidence to suggest storing Emily's pictures, or at least moving them to the boys' room. And now she couldn't make a change for fear of hurting Calvin and Samuel.

To be honest about her own feelings, while she'd been deeply fond of Frank, she'd never felt for him the kind of love her parents had shared. Still, she and Frank had had a good marriage, and she was sorry he was gone. One of the last things he'd said to her was what a good wife she was and he knew she'd manage the ranch just fine. Even though she'd already been managing it by herself for three years, she appreciated his faith in her. She loved the ranch and everything about running a horse breeding business. Not that it wasn't sometimes complicated, even frustrating. But the rewards outweighed the complications, and if trouble didn't come visiting, she'd have a legacy to hand down to the children.

Problem was, she did have one big worry. Not that she'd tell the children unless something came of it, but last week, she received her first letter ever from Uncle. "I hear you married an old widower and he up and died on you. I would imagine you need some help with that farm he left you, being that you never amounted to much when you lived with me." That was just like him to send an insult. She could almost hear his condemning tone as she read the words. "I am concerned for you, girlie, so it is my responsibility to see what I can do for you." That was nothing short of a threat that he intended to impose himself back into her life. Well, she wasn't having any of it. She'd run away from him at eighteen to avoid being forced into marriage to one of his wealthy friends, a disgusting, hard-drinking, cigar-smoking old carpetbagger. So she wasn't about to have anybody in her life who'd try to control her.

My, my. What on earth had set her off thinking about these things? She needed to quit cogitating on bad memories. She'd deal with Uncle if and when he came around bothering her. For now, she must plan a special meal for Mr. Edmund McKay. Feeding him supper was a good idea. It was the least she could do for him for taking Jacob under his wing.

Why on earth had she been so rude to Edmund? That wasn't her way. But if he was anything like Frank, a hearty meal would be the best apology she could serve up.

So, what should she fix that would be a worthy repayment for his kindness to Jacob? Beef stew? Chicken and dumplings? She had a ham in the smokehouse that would go well with pinto beans, but she'd promised no beans. Her other favorite way to serve ham was with sweet potatoes, but it was too early in the season to dig them up. And she wasn't about to serve him sandwiches after his hard day of riding herd on a posse of young boys. It would be hard to get through six nights without serving some sort of beans. Maybe one of these nights she could add just the right seasoning to some black-eyed peas so Edmund wouldn't mind eating them.

She'd make a lemon cake, of course. And while she was at it, she would make a second cake to take to Nancy Bennett. The poor dear was feeling poorly, and Lula May knew Lucas would appreciate a dessert.

Nancy was the closest friend Lula May had because they'd both been mail-order brides. Nancy had married

Lucas last year, and Lucas had made sure to introduce his new wife to Lula May. Just in time, too, because with her midwife and nursing experience, Nancy had been a big help during Frank's final days. Even Lucas had made several trips to visit Frank, and he'd been the first to offer his condolences when Frank died. He'd asked about each of the children, as though understanding the loss of their father, and had asked Lula May if she needed anything.

"Mama." Pauline pumped cold water into the dishpan and added some hot water from the tank at the back of the stove. "That Mr. McKay sure is tall. His head just about reached the ceiling." An odd little twinkle beamed out from her blue eyes. What mischief was she up to?

"Yes, he is, sugar. Now be sure to use enough soap chips to get all the grease off the dishes. Make 'em shine." They'd need to make soap one day soon, once the lavender came to full bloom and she could add it to the saved up ash and fat to give them a nice fragrance.

"Yes, ma'am." Pauline scrubbed a plate, gently slid it through the clear water in a rinse pan and set it on a tea towel on the counter beside the white porcelain kitchen sink. "He's handsome, and he's got broad shoulders, too."

Lula May paused in gathering ingredients for tonight's stew. What *was* this child up to? Best to ignore whatever it was. "Uh-huh." She dug into the vegetable bin and retrieved two large onions.

"Yep, he just about filled this kitchen, didn't he, Daniel?"

"Huh?" Daniel walked into the room, snatched up a tea towel and began drying the dishes.

Lula May would leave it to her daughter to explain. She had some important meal planning to do, and she needed to decide which chicken to kill and pluck. Oh, wait. She'd decided on beef stew. Oh, dear. What was wrong with her?

While she *stewed* over the stew, she couldn't help overhearing Pauline and Daniel discussing Edmund as if he were some splendid knight who'd appeared in their home right out of the pages of their Brothers Grimm fairy tales storybook.

She'd allow that Edmund McKay truly had filled this kitchen, being tall and strong and broad-shouldered. She'd allow that when he'd stood there looking at her, she'd noticed his intense green eyes and that fine shock of thick sandy brown hair. She'd even allow that he was a handsome man, as Pauline had made a point of saying. And—

Oh, my. Why was she letting her small children lead her on this way? She refused to have anything to do with any man. After all, she'd run this ranch with only the children's help for three years. She didn't need a man to tell her what to do and how to run her life. Not Uncle. Not Mr. Edmund McKay. Nobody. And that was that!

Yet off and on throughout the day, her ruminations alternated between her cruel, controlling uncle and the quiet, handsome rancher next door. Neither one seemed to think she was capable of taking care of her family good and proper. Proving them both wrong was a challenge she would gladly undertake.

Chapter Two

⌒

"Hey, watch out!" Edmund yelled at Jacob Barlow about a second too late to keep the boy from jumping from the barn loft into the haystack below.

Edmund's heart almost stopped. If Jacob broke his neck under his care, how could he face Lula May? Injuries often happened in the daily routine of working on a ranch, but this boyish foolishness posed an unnecessary danger.

Jacob landed safely, with Adam jumping down right behind him, and Edmund heaved out a sigh of relief. The two boys rolled off the hay, laughing all the way, and began to wrestle like a couple of playful puppies.

"Get over here." Edmund beckoned them with a brisk whip of his hand. He hadn't expected them to horse around like this while they waited for the other boys to arrive. *Lesson number one in teaching: have a plan before you start.* Tomorrow he'd have a job for each boy upon arrival.

These two promptly obeyed him, but they kept

laughing and shoving each other. Using his height to advantage, he stood over them, hands fisted at his waist, and scowled. "Adam, you're my kin, so I expect you to set a good example. Understand?"

Looking deceptively innocent, Adam blinked his brown eyes. "Yessir." He slid a mischievous grin toward Jacob.

"And you mind me." Edmund directed his order to Jacob, who looked a heap more apologetic.

"Yessir." Jacob chewed his lower lip and stared down at his boots.

Edmund would have to be careful with this one. Unless he was playing with Adam, he was like an orphaned colt, a mite skittish and uncertain of being accepted, especially around anyone older. Edmund would have to figure out a way to build some confidence in the boy, as Old Gad had done for him.

"All right." Edmund pointed to the barn door and gentled his voice. "Get in there and take the horses out to the corral, fork out some hay for them and then muck out the stalls." As the boys dashed away to mind him, he added, "And no horsing around."

Only Jacob called "Yessir" over his shoulder.

Edmund shoved his hat back from his face. He sensed a potential dustup with Adam, and he'd have to pray about how to handle it. He hadn't been around young'uns very much, but he did know there was a difference between outright mischief and harmless horseplay. Exactly how that difference showed up in each boy would require some thought and lots of prayer.

What had gotten into these two to set them off? Was

it excitement about what they'd learn today? Or just excitement about getting to spend time together on a day other than Sunday after church? Edmund figured he'd be learning a good deal about boys over this next week. He'd never had much of a childhood himself and couldn't call to mind a time when he'd ever truly played with a friend or even his brothers because they'd been separated when Edmund had barely learned to walk and Josiah had just been put in long pants. Josiah, who remembered more about Edmund than the other way around, even claimed they had a baby brother named David. If Josiah hadn't come looking for him a few years ago, Edmund might barely recall that he had a brother, much less two.

An empty feeling nudged its way into his chest. A longing, in truth, that he had no idea how to identify, much less to satisfy. And not all that different from the odd little pang he'd felt when he stood in Miss Lula May's kitchen with all of those mouthwatering smells of bacon and fresh-baked bread floating around him. The pleasant family scene had taunted him because it was something he'd never had, never could have.

He gave himself a mental kick. Self-pity never solved anything. Besides, he had some boys to ride herd on, so he needed to concentrate on that. Better still, he didn't have to cook his own supper tonight. And tomorrow night, he'd be meeting with CJ and the other ranchers to discuss the association they'd decided to establish to protect folks from the cattle rustlers who'd been stealing cattle over the past month or so. Too much to think about in the here and now to waste time ruminating on his own personal past.

The preacher, Brandon Stillwater, drove his wagon into the barnyard, and seven more boys piled out. In addition to the Forester and Gillen brothers, Edmund recognized Charlie Donavan, the ten-year-old brother of Sheriff Fuller's brand-new mail-order bride, Stella. The other two seemed familiar, maybe from church. Time to get busy. He hollered at his two hands who'd offered to help with the boys, and they came running.

"I expect you'll be wanting me to pray for you." Stillwater's silvery eyes sparked with good humor. "This is quite a herd you're taking on."

Edmund responded with a laugh, but in truth, he did have a few busy grasshoppers in his belly. "I always appreciate prayers, Preacher."

"Well, I'll leave you to it. See you at about four o'clock."

"Sounds good." Edmund waved to his friend and then turned to the task at hand.

Once he corralled all nine youngsters, lessons began, from taking care of horses and their tack to discussing the basics of branding, which was already done for this year, to learning how to lasso a long-horned steer without getting gored. All the time in the back of Edmund's mind, he couldn't stop thinking about supper with the Barlows. While a tasty meal was a mighty powerful draw in that direction, he also couldn't help but look forward to seeing Lula May again.

Edmund had learned from his brother that a gentleman held a lady's chair at the supper table. Lula May seemed a bit surprised when he attended to that duty.

While Edmund was enjoying that lilac smell she wore, her young'uns grinned at each other. At her instructions, he took his place at the other end of the table.

"How'd he do?" Lula May bent her head toward Jacob, on her left, while she ladled up a bowl of fine-smelling beef stew from a big fancy china serving dish. She passed the bowl to the right, to her daughter, who passed it to Calvin, who passed it to Edmund.

Once it was set in front of him on the white linen tablecloth, Edmund could well have dug his fork into the bowl. Would have done so if not for Josiah and Betsy showing him the manners Old Gad had neglected to teach him. While his mouth watered, he tried to keep his mind on her question. He glanced at Jacob, whose face was lit with confidence after a day of besting the other boys at almost every task, even though the other boys had already been working with CJ for some time.

"He did fine." Edmund punctuated the compliment with a curt nod.

Jacob grinned until Samuel snickered and elbowed him. Doubt crossed his face, and he chewed his lip, something he hadn't done since morning. Lula May was too busy serving her children to notice the exchange, so it was up to Edmund to fix the damage. Like chickens in the barnyard, cowboys on a trail ride, young'uns in the school yard, boys liked to keep a pecking order. Most meant no harm by it, and Edmund could see Samuel didn't intend meanness. Yet Jacob didn't seem to notice the fondness in his older brother's eyes that showed he was teasing.

"Yep, Jacob bested the other boys in riding and roping, even the older ones who've been working with CJ." Edmund would give the boy a pat on the shoulder if Samuel weren't seated between them. "And he can saddle up faster than any of the others."

Jacob rewarded him with a renewed grin.

"I'm glad to hear it." Lula May's face looked all the prettier for the pride beaming from her eyes. After serving everyone else, she filled her own bowl and then folded her hands in her lap. She looked down the table toward Edmund, and for a moment, he feared she would ask him to pray. He'd never prayed in front of other people, rarely ever prayed out loud. To his relief, she said, "Jacob, will you please bless the food?"

"Yes, ma'am." The boy straightened, folded his hands together and bowed his head. "Dear Lord, we thank you for this family and for this fine day, for Ma's good cooking and for livin' in the USA. Amen."

His rhyming prayer didn't lack reverence, but Edmund still came near to chuckling at its singsong beat. Then, when everyone else added a solemn "amen," he quickly reined in his humor. Maybe this was a traditional family prayer. Tradition and family, two things he knew nothing about. Even after spending time with Josiah and his brood, Edmund still had no idea how to act around them, how to feel connected to them. He sure couldn't let himself feel a part of this family.

A wretched, useless feeling of loneliness tried to rear its ugly head like a rattlesnake, but he quickly stomped it out. For one thing, he enjoyed his solitude too much ever to marry. But most of all, he had no idea how to get on with women, an important first step. While he was here, he would enjoy this tasty cooking. Nobody expected him to participate in the conversation now buzzing around the table, and that was just fine with him. He never liked to talk much anyway.

Josiah had taught him to wait until the lady of the house took the first bite before starting to eat, so Edmund watched Lula May. Good thing she didn't waste time, because all the young'uns looked as hungry as he was. She lifted her fork in a refined way and began, with everyone else following suit.

At last! He took his first bite, a mannerly sized chunk of beef that had caught his eye the moment the bowl was set before him. As he chewed, the flavor burst throughout three of his senses. He'd already been enjoying the aroma. Now the tasty seasonings started his mouth to watering, while the perfect density of the meat reminded his teeth what they were there for. His jaw ached with the pleasure of it, and he closed his eyes to enjoy a kind of food bliss such as he couldn't ever remember feeling before.

"Now, Mr. McKay, I mean, Edmund." Lula May chose that moment to level a critical eye on him. "I have some things to discuss with you."

He gulped down the partially chewed bite and took a swig of coffee to keep from choking. "Yes, ma'am?" Had he done something wrong? Long forgotten feelings of inadequacy filled him, reminding him of the way Cousin Judith had criticized almost everything he'd ever done, no matter how hard he tried to do right.

* * *

Lula May's mind had been churning with ideas all day long. This morning she'd been a bit concerned about how to lead the conversation over supper, as a good hostess should do. But it didn't take long for her to come up with more topics than one meal would provide time for. Good thing she had all week to cover them. But which to start with? Maybe the most serious one.

"I need to know what's going on in regard to the cattle rustling." She should probably clarify that. "I was mighty sorry to hear you lost about twenty head or so even before the Carsons' fire. Today, when I was up at Nancy Bennett's, she said Lucas said you men plan to form an organization so you can work together to put a stop to the thefts. What can you tell me about it?" She gave him an expectant look and took a bite so she wouldn't talk too much, as she often did with other adults. She'd confessed her bad habit to Nancy, and her friend had offered several pieces of advice, one being to just stop talking and give the other party a significant look. From the appealing confusion spreading over Edmund's face, she wondered whether they would just be sitting here staring at each other down the length of the table.

"We had our first meeting after church the other week, and we decided to meet on Tuesday evenings, starting tomorrow." He seemed to think he'd answered the question, because he concentrated on his bowl and took another bite.

"Who?" She'd seen the men gathering but figured it was none of her business. With no women among the group, she wouldn't have dared to approach them and ask what it was all about. Now that she knew, she had to find a way to get reports about their meetings.

He blinked, clearly still confused by her questions. This man was so frustrating. A woman would offer endless details without prompting. But then, Lula May had always needed to prod Frank for more information, no matter what the topic. Maybe most men were just that way. Not Uncle, of course. He'd never let Lula May talk much at all except to say "yes, sir" and "no, sir."

"Who's meeting?"

"CJ Thorn, Clyde Parker, Sheriff Fuller." He crinkled his forehead thoughtfully. "All the local ranchers."

"All? I wasn't informed about the meeting." She hadn't meant to raise her voice. Yet it stung her sensibilities to know they'd left her out entirely.

Edmund blinked again, as if he'd never considered her, either. Didn't anybody know she was here? It was a wonder he'd remembered to invite Jacob to join the other boys today. And even that was Adam's idea.

"Well, ma'am." Edmund crinkled his forehead again. She wished he wouldn't do that, because it gave him an appealing, boyish look. "First thing we gotta do is catch the rustlers, a mite too dangerous for a lady."

In the corner of her eye, Lula May noticed Calvin's frown. He hadn't been able to hide from her his fast-draw practicing behind the barn, and she'd done nothing to discourage him. A man had to know how to shoot. But Calvin was still too young to ride with the grown men after rustlers. If she insisted on taking part in the meeting of the men, would he insist upon joining her?

"You run just five head of cattle, and you keep them close by." Edmund's expression turned solicitous. "I doubt the rustlers will bother you."

Any other time, she'd take that dismissal as an insult. Now, with her concerns about Calvin, maybe she'd better turn the conversation. "Nancy says the rustling's not all you plan to discuss. Now that Little Horn's incorporated, you're going to make plans for the community."

A brief nod. "Could be." He went back to eating.

If that was all he was going to say, maybe she should have left a few seasonings out of the stew so he wouldn't be so taken with it. He'd already finished his first bowl, and she passed the tureen down to him so he could help himself to a second one.

"Lots of needs around here." To her surprise, he kept talking as he ladled more into his bowl and helped himself to another roll. "The Carsons' fire, the rustlin', a couple of widows who need looking out for." He gave her a tiny grin and a slight shrug.

A tide of heat surged up her neck. "You can't mean me." She could hardly keep from sputtering out her indignation. "Just you look around this place." She waved a hand in an arc as if she were outside and showing off her whole spread. "We're doing just fine."

His jaw dropped, and his eyebrows shot upward. "I meant no insult, ma'am."

"No, of course not." What was it about him that appealed to her one moment and got her goat the next?

"What I should have said was I'll be happy to help with whatever you're doing." She couldn't keep from repeating, "We're doing just fine, and we should share our blessings with those less fortunate."

His face relaxed a little, but he seemed hesitant to take another bite, giving Lula May a twinge of regret. Maybe having a man in the house after so long had put her nerves on edge. What a poor example she was setting for her children. She waited until he finished his next bite before asking her next question.

"Where will you be meeting?" She offered a bright smile and sipped her coffee.

"At the church tent."

"Hmm. I suppose that's the only place large enough to accommodate everyone." She had some ideas about that, too, but maybe she should change the subject. After a moment or two of sorting through her cogitations of the day, she said, "Who all came out to join Jacob and Adam today?"

Another blink. Oh, my, she wished he'd quit doing that in response to her questions. Every time he did it, she felt a funny little tickle near her heart.

"Charlie Donavan, Donny Carson, Pete Smith, the Gillen and Forester brothers."

"I see." She knew several more boys around Jacob's age. "Other than Adam, they're all ranch boys and probably know most of the things you're teaching them. Have you considered inviting some of the town boys?"

Jacob scowled, but he knew better than to interrupt adult conversations with his objections. Once she'd started questioning Edmund, the children had quit talking, as they'd been trained to do.

Lula May had an idea she knew what had upset Jacob, and it was all the more reason to press Edmund to include the others. "How about Elgin Arundel, Georgie Henley and Alec Green. They're all about the same age as Jacob and Adam."

"Hadn't thought of 'em." Edmund reached for another roll, maybe his third.

Did he really like her cooking, or was he just extra hungry from riding herd on those boys all day long? Not something she could actually ask him.

"Just think of it." She put a bit of wonder in her voice, hoping he'd catch her vision. "Town boys learning hands on about ranching. That would teach them about what keeps their parents' businesses running. Why, they probably don't even realize that the entire economy of the county is based on the cattle business. They need to know the hows and whys of that." And along the way, maybe those town boys would learn not to be so snobbish toward the ranch boys, but she'd keep that thought to herself. Saying it out loud would make it gossip.

"Sounds good." Edmund's shoulders had relaxed. That must mean he didn't mind her sharing her ideas.

"And then when you're done at your place, you could take the boys into town so they can appreciate what business owners experience. Both ranch boys and town boys can see how everyone contributes to the community." She sent Jacob a meaningful glance, but he stared down at his empty bowl.

Edmund, on the other hand, wore his bemused face again. Maybe he was in a hurry to get shed of the boys and didn't want to extend his involvement. Time to change the subject again.

"Now, about tomorrow night's meeting." She gave Pauline and Daniel a nod, and they began to clear the empty plates from the table. "If only men are getting together, you'll need some refreshments. I'll do some baking tomorrow and you can take it." She eyed Samuel and slid her gaze to the lemon cake sitting on the sideboard. He quietly retrieved it, along with dessert plates and forks. While Lula May served generous slices for everyone, she watched Edmund. "What do you think the men would like for refreshments?"

He grinned as he took a healthy bite of cake. "Hmm-mmm. Can't beat this."

"All right. Lemon cake it is." She tapped her chin, counting the ingredients left in her larder. She might need to make a trip to town tomorrow. A picture formed in her mind of the men seated on the benches in the church tent and eating her cake. "You know, I've been thinking."

A low chuckle came from the other end of the table. "Yes, ma'am?" My, my, he was handsome when he smiled. Never mind what that deep voice did to her emotions.

"It's just too bad we don't have a proper church building. Not just for Sunday services but for prayer meetings, community events, all sorts of gatherings, like the ranchers' meeting." The ladies of the quilting bee had raised some money by selling quilts at the

Founders' Day celebration, but it was soon evident the project couldn't fund much more than a single load of lumber. "Could you bring that up tomorrow night?"

"I could."

She beamed her best smile his way. "Nancy told me you men were planning to collect dues for joining the organization." She wouldn't mention that Nancy feared Lucas wouldn't have any money to contribute. She didn't say why, but Lula May suspected Lucas might be saving up so they could afford to have a baby. "Why not use those dues to build a church? What with beef prices being steady right now and roundup coming, soon everyone will have some money set aside for things like this. What better project than building a church?"

"Well." Edmund cleared his throat. "The plan was to have funds to help people in need."

"Seems like there should be enough money to get everything done." Lula May knew how to pinch a penny, but she'd noticed some folks were a bit more careless with their finances. "And who's going to be in charge of the collection?" It had better be someone she trusted, or she wouldn't donate a dime.

Edmund finished his cake and set down his fork. "Why don't you do it?"

"What?" Lula May was speechless. For about half a second. "Why, I'm not even invited to the meeting."

There was that grin again. "I'm inviting you."

If it wasn't the worst of bad manners to laugh at a lady, Edmund would give in to a hearty guffaw at the look on Lula May's face right now. Shock, surprise, a hint of a smile that was growing by the second.

"You're inviting me?" She blinked those big blue eyes, and he had to swallow hard not to fall right into them.

Great hornets, she was a pretty woman, especially in that blue dress she now wore, which was a sight prettier than the getup she'd worn that morning. *Oh, no.* Those thoughts had to stop. He had no intention of being lassoed by a woman, especially not one so much like his strong-willed cousin.

"Yes, ma'am." He couldn't see any reason to leave her out, especially since she had so many good ideas and backed them up with a well-run ranch.

She sat there looking at him for a few seconds and then glanced around the table. "Children, time for evening chores."

As all five got up to obey, she gave each one a motherly smile that hit Edmund right in the chest. These young'uns were mighty blessed to have such a loving mama, something he couldn't remember having, though Josiah claimed their mama had heaped a lot of love on the three brothers before she died. Maybe she'd been just like Lula May, who, after a long day of ranch work, cooking, baking and visiting Nancy Bennett three miles away, still had a smile left in her for her children. And for him, though he couldn't attach any meaning to it other than her fine manners. His cousin had doled out a fair amount of affection to her own four children, but never had anything left for Edmund.

He'd come here expecting to eat a quick supper and

then to head on back to his own place. Now, with two big bowls of stew, three buttered rolls, a large slice of cake and several cups of coffee under his belt, he couldn't move if he wanted to.

He'd say he'd been a captive audience for all of Lula May's chatter, but that wouldn't be fair. He liked what he heard. Liked what he saw. Not just Lula May, but the young'uns. They sat respectfully through the whole meal while the adults talked. They obeyed their ma, even when she just gave them a look or a tilt of her head. Now they were out in the kitchen cleaning up the dishes without bellyaching about it. Edmund couldn't exactly say why, but he enjoyed it all, even though for him it wouldn't last past this week.

"All right, puppy, let's go."

Edmund could see Calvin through the wide doorway talking to Jacob.

"Get the bucket. Let's see if you can milk a cow as well as you can rope a heifer."

Jacob's shoulders slumped as he minded his oldest brother, trudging after him with bucket in hand. The bright-eyed, confident boy Edmund had brought home had faded quickly when his brothers called him a puppy. But it wasn't Edmund's place to correct them, so he'd keep his concerns to himself. And he'd try to figure out how to make Jacob's confidence stick.

"About tomorrow night's meeting." Lula May stood up and waved Edmund toward the parlor.

He managed to get to his feet and follow her, one hand on his overstuffed belly. Maybe he should walk home rather than ride to work off that large meal. As he followed her, the scent of lilacs hit his nose again. If she was anything like Betsy, she probably made her own perfume from those bushes at the back of the house.

"Have a seat." With a brisk wave of her hand, she ordered him to sit in Frank's chair, which stood near the stone fireplace.

Didn't seem right, but he wouldn't embarrass her by refusing. Besides, the worn but fancy settee looked a mite fragile for a big man like him. He settled into the comfortable overstuffed leather chair and blew out a long breath. Tomorrow night, he wouldn't eat so much, no matter how good her cooking tasted. He glanced around the room, noticing the frilly cotton curtains over the windows and the crocheted doilies on every flat surface. The main room at his house couldn't even be called a parlor, much less boast such homey furnishings.

"I've been thinking about it, and I'm not going."

Edmund opened his mouth to object, but she silenced him with another one of those brisk hand gestures.

"No, it's best this way." She picked up a sewing basket beside her rocking chair and started sorting through a small box, sizing buttons to a shirt that looked like it would fit little Daniel. Didn't this woman ever get a chance to rest? "I appreciate your invitation, but I want you to ask the other men what they think about my coming."

"I don't think—"

"Because the last thing I want is to show up and be told it's no place for a woman." She bit off a length of thread and aimed it through the eye of a needle. "I can just see Lucas Bennett or Clyde Parker saying my ranch is too small for the rustlers to bother with. Never mind that I have a stake in the community as valid as anybody else's. I want, no, I *need* to be a part of decisions that will affect the community where my children will grow up and live their lives." She huffed out a long sigh like she was real tired.

Edmund felt a bit tired himself just from listening to her. No, that was a mean thought. With all of her responsibilities, no wonder she felt a mite protective. A whole lot protective. And she might not think she needed anything, but looking around this place, he could see a few things that needed fixing. Like that broken transom over the parlor door into the hallway and the buckled floorboard by the piano. He could do both of those in one afternoon and at the same time teach Calvin and Samuel how to do such repairs. Before he'd left his cousin's home, he'd had to teach himself that sort of work on his own.

"So, tomorrow night, would you ask around and see whether the men have any objections to my attending? If they put up a fuss, I'll just have to depend on somebody else to tell me what's going on. If they say I can come, I'll be there next week." She folded the shirt and set it in her lap. "What do you think?"

Edmund hesitated. Was it really his turn to talk? Again he scolded himself for the uncharitable thought. "I'll ask 'em. Shouldn't be a problem."

"And don't you go making it sound like we're in need. As I said a while ago, I'll be happy to help anybody, but we're doing *just fine*." She glanced at the transom as if she'd noticed him studying it. "Come winter, we'll catch up with things like that, just like everybody else does. You hear?"

Her tart tone of voice stung, and he struggled to answer politely. Great hornets, she sounded like his cousin. Not everything she said, but enough to annoy him to no end and bring back some decidedly unpleasant memories.

"Yes, ma'am." Yes, that was *just fine* with Edmund, to use her favorite words. Stubborn woman. How could a man help somebody who refused to see she needed help? And why should he care? He was a loner, and he wasn't about to give up a piece of himself and start caring too much about anyone else, no matter how much he'd enjoyed this family supper.

Yet as he rode Zephyr home in the deepening twilight, he sensed the Lord reminding him of the importance of being charitable to widows. After throwing in with Old Gad and coming to faith in the Lord, he'd learned early on not to ignore the Almighty's prompting. If He wanted Edmund to watch out for Lula May, he would do it. He could endure her scrappiness so he could eat some more of her tasty cooking. He chuckled to himself. What could she serve that could equal that fine beef stew and those fluffy biscuits? He couldn't wait to find out.

After Lula May saw Edmund to the door and watched him ride away, she felt a flush of embarrassment over her excessive talking. Try though she might, she couldn't hold her tongue, not when she had so many important topics to talk to him about. Being here with the children all week, she rarely got a chance to talk with other adults. Even joining the ladies' quilting bee hadn't turned out to be the outlet she'd hoped for, because most of the other members chattered about women's issues and left the ranching and business discussions to their husbands. Not having a husband, she didn't have that luxury and wouldn't want to do it anyway. She'd loved being involved with everything about the ranch even before Frank took sick.

Still, she continued to attend every other meeting or so just to get away from her regular work routine, and she truly loved participating in the many good works the ladies planned. Maybe she should try talking with them more so she wouldn't unload all of her chatter on her poor bachelor neighbor.

She laughed to herself at the memory of his bemused expression as he tried to follow her jumping from one subject to the next. Frank always used to sit in his chair in the parlor and nod absently while reading his newspaper. At least Edmund had listened. At least he respected her enough to invite her to join the other ranchers. That respect meant a whole lot to her. Not that she could put any personal store by it. Edmund was just being polite. As for those foolish, pleasant little pinches she'd kept on feeling in her chest whenever he'd look at her, well, she'd just keep on ignoring them. She had enough to deal with without thinking about matters of the heart. The last thing she needed was to fall for Mr. Edmund McKay, no matter how attractive the man was.

Chapter Three

"Now don't you forget what I told you." Edmund set his hand on Jacob's shoulder after they dismounted from their horses outside the Barlows' house late the next afternoon. "Your big brothers aren't tryin' to whup up on you. They just like to pull your leg. The more you let them get to you, the more they'll do it. Over time, you'll learn how to give back as good as you get."

"Yessir." Jacob stared up at him, his blue eyes round and bright with confidence after a day of showing the newly invited town boys what ranching was all about. "Teasing's different from mocking and just goes to show they're including me."

"Right." Edmund had learned that lesson from Old Gad, but it hadn't been easy to believe. He'd grown up under a constant barrage of criticism from his cousin and her young'uns. Nothing he'd ever done had been right in their eyes, even though he'd borne the brunt of chores and the carpentry upkeep of his cousin's rickety old house. Old Gad was the first person to treat him with respect, the first one to say "well done" when he'd worked hard to learn something new. Not until Edmund had gained some confidence had his mentor started teasing him, mostly about his height. When he'd passed six feet, Old Gad, just five foot four on a good day, had called him string bean, lamppost or whatever foolishness came to mind. Edmund grinned just thinking about it. He sure did miss the old fella.

"Well, it's about time." Grouchy as usual, Lula May came out the back door wiping her hands on a fancy embroidered tea towel. "Supper'll be ready shortly. There's a cowboy having a look-see at my stock over at the corral, so I have to find out if he's seen anything he likes." She hung the towel over the hitching rail by the back door and strode toward the barn. "Want to come along?"

"Yes, ma'am." Edmund and Jacob spoke at the same time and then shared a grin as they fell in beside her.

Lula May glanced from one to the other. "You men have a good day?"

Again they chorused "yes, ma'am," which earned them one of her sweet smiles.

Today she was back in her skirt-trouser getup, but she didn't really look any less ladylike than she had in that frilly blue dress last night. Edmund could see the importance of her wearing this outfit for horse trading. Made her look like she meant business so that cowboy couldn't ride roughshod over her in case he was inclined to do so. As they neared the corral, where the man stood and studied the stock, Lula May's smile went from sweet to businesslike. Edmund looked forward to seeing her in action.

"So what do you think?" She stopped a few yards away from the wiry man somewhere in his thirties.

Edmund recognized him from the area. Worked at the Ogdens' spread, if he wasn't mistaken. The way the cowboy looked Lula May up and down, much like he'd looked at the horses, caused an unfamiliar sense of protectiveness to rise up inside Edmund. He noticed Calvin and Samuel standing in the barn door, the expressions in their eyes mirroring his own feelings, and reminded himself that she didn't need his protection. He'd woken up this morning not quite as certain about the Lord's direction in that matter.

"If not for all the white among the spots and that pink nose, the paint would be a fine horse. Probably gets sunburned in this heat. I'll do you a favor and take him off'n your hands for twenty-five dollars."

The offer was an insult. Calvin gave out a fake cough, and Samuel snorted. They had no intention of letting Lula May get cheated, so Edmund could mind his own business. He kept his expression impersonal when the cowboy cast an uncertain look at him.

Lula May clicked her tongue. "Zeke, Zeke, what am I going to do with you? That horse is worth a hundred dollars to somebody who knows how to take care of him, and you know it. Besides, I have another buyer for him, so you're too late." She pointed at a brown mare. "Now, Circe here is a grand little cow pony, seven years old, well trained and a bargain at sixty-five dollars."

"Sixty-five?" Zeke sputtered and coughed. "Why, I can get a better horse at any ranch around here."

"All right, then." Lula May clicked her tongue again. "You have a good evening. I've got work to do." She turned toward the house.

"Now, wait just a minute." Zeke shot another look at Edmund and lifted his hands like he was asking for help.

Edmund gave him a deflecting shrug and shook his head. No way was he a part of these negotiations, not when Lula May was doing such a fine job.

"Forty dollars for the mare," Zeke shouted.

Lula May stopped and slowly turned back. "Fifty-five."

"Fifty-five? That's more'n five months' pay." Zeke ripped off his hat and slammed it to the ground. "Fifty, and that's my last offer."

A wily smile crept over the lady's face. "Sold."

Edmund caught the smothered grins on Calvin's and Samuel's faces. They must have seen their ma do this before. For his part, Edmund thought Zeke was getting a bargain. The mare was a fine-looking animal.

While Lula May retrieved a bill of sale from the house and Jacob tended his horse, Samuel led the mare out of the corral and removed her lead halter. Zeke saddled her up with his own tack, which he'd carried on his shoulders when he'd walked to the ranch, and soon the sale was completed. He might have huffed and puffed, but as he rode away, his relaxed posture and instant bonding with Circe showed he considered those fifty dollars well spent.

After watching her in action, Edmund's admiration for Mrs. Lula May Barlow shot up about nine yards. Looked like nobody would ever be able to take advantage of her.

As they all trooped back toward the house, Calvin nudged Jacob. "You lose any mavericks today, puppy?"

Jacob glanced at Edmund and grinned. "Nope, but I did send a rattlesnake to its final reward."

"What!" Lula May stopped and gripped the boy's shoulders, her face growing pale beneath those scattered freckles. She glanced at Edmund. "What happened?"

Edmund shrugged. In addition to the lilac perfume she wore, he'd caught a whiff of some sort of fine-smelling chicken meal that stirred his appetite, and he'd hoped they could talk about this around the supper table. "You tell her, Jake."

Jacob copied Edmund's one-shoulder shrug. "Nothing much to tell. A rattler slithered in from the range and tried to get into the henhouse. I saw him first, so Mr. McKay let me use his six-shooter to finish him off."

Edmund wouldn't tell Lula May that he'd had to steady the gun for the trembling boy while he fired it. No sense in discounting the real courage Jacob had shown in overcoming his fears.

"Well!" Lula May shook her head and gave Edmund a grateful smile. "My, my."

"Good job, pup." Calvin grabbed his little brother around the neck and ruffled his hair.

"Woof, woof." Laughing, Jacob wriggled free and

raced into the house, followed closely by Calvin and Samuel.

Lula May set a hand on Edmund's arm. "Thank you." Her eyes were rimmed with red like she was about to cry. "Just two days, and look at the confidence you've given him."

Edmund wanted to shrug again and say something real smart like "aw, shucks." He wasn't used to dealing with grateful mamas. Grateful, pretty women. Lula May blinked those big blue eyes, and he felt a considerable disturbance in his chest. Swallowing hard, he managed, "Do I smell chicken?"

Lula May watched with satisfaction as Edmund dug into his second bowl of chicken and flat dumplings, one of her specialties. Tonight, instead of assaulting the poor man with all of her new ideas or insisting the children eat quietly while the adults talked, she reined in her mouth and initiated the family's usual supper conversation. Each person took a turn holding the large "talking feather," an eagle's feather Calvin had found out on the prairie years ago. Each one shared something special that happened in his or her day and some blessing received from the Lord. No one was permitted to talk without the feather.

Pauline, Daniel and Calvin had already had their turns, with a mixture of laughter and groans in response to their stories, and the feather had reached the far end of the table.

"You don't have to participate, Edmund." Lula May hadn't thought ahead about how this favorite family activity would affect their guest. Maybe Edmund would be too reticent or even too embarrassed to talk in front of her family.

Calvin started to pass the feather across the table to Samuel, but Edmund intercepted it.

"Not so fast, cowboy." He took the black-and-white feather from Calvin and studied it for a moment. A slow grin came over his face clear up to his bright green eyes. "Can't think of a bigger blessing than this fine meal. Best thing to happen to me today." He held the feather out to Samuel, obviously finished.

Jacob snickered. "'Specially after what Mr. Mushy served us for dinner. What was that, exactly, Mr. McKay?"

"Best not to ask, Jake." Those green eyes twinkled, and Edmund sucked in his cheeks, probably to pucker away a smile.

Everyone else laughed with loose and free guffaws such as none of them had since Frank died. For Lula May's part, she felt as if the weight that had been sitting on her chest for three years was finally starting to lift. When her turn came to share her day, she was ready.

"Any day when I sell two horses is a good day, and I thank the Lord for His provision."

"You sold two?" Calvin had been out in the far pasture working with some of the younger horses when her first customer came by, and she hadn't had a chance to give him the good news.

"Yes. Lucas Bennett wants that paint Zeke was so keen to buy. He said he'll be back late next week with the money." She wouldn't try to figure out why Nancy said her husband might not be able to pay his dues for the cattlemen's group and yet now wanted one of Lula May's most expensive horses. But then, while Frank had taught Lula May about horse ranching, he hadn't shared money matters with her until he became ill and took to his bed. Then he'd taught her everything he knew. Not all husbands would be so willing to do that. Not many men. And thinking of the other ranchers, she quashed the urge to remind Edmund of his promise to ask them about her attending the meeting next week. If it was meant to be, she wouldn't have to remind her neighbor like a nagging wife. Oh, dear. Where had that thought come from? Best to quash that, too.

To her relief, as Edmund took his leave of her right after supper, he brought up the subject.

"You sure you don't want to go tonight? The men'll want to thank you for these." He held up the paper sack of oatmeal cookies she'd made instead of lemon cake because they were easier to serve.

After such a pleasant supper, her heart couldn't have been any lighter, but now it soared. He remembered his promise to her. "No, but thank you." She laughed softly. "And if they think those cookies are a bribe to let me come next time, tell 'em they're right."

Edmund chuckled in that chest-deep way of his, and her heart tumbled all over itself. She really had to stop these pathetic reactions to his manly ways. She'd been around men all her life and had learned early on that nothing good ever came from giving in to giddy emotions they stirred up. Still, it was awful nice to see Edmund come out of himself with her, with her family.

And the value of what he was doing for Jacob's self-confidence couldn't be measured.

Letting her son take part in the Young Ranchers' Club had been a good decision, she silently told Frank. Even as she did that, she knew she was being unfair to her late husband. He'd always been kind to her, much like her father had been and nothing at all like her cruel uncle. But he always seemed distracted, and she'd come to the conclusion that he was always comparing her to Emily, always missing his first wife.

Now, for just that reason, as Edmund rode away, she reminded herself that she didn't need a man in her life. Edmund might be attractive and mannerly, even a bit shy and self-effacing, but he was probably just as controlling as most men when it came to women. Sure, he'd invited her to the meeting, but he also had one of the most successful ranches in the area. That took a powerful lot of control. She would never again submit herself to being under any man's control. *Never.*

That night, Edmund met some resistance from the other ranchers, but in the end, after they'd eaten the oatmeal cookies, more men agreed to Lula May's joining them than objected.

On Wednesday, he looked forward to giving her the good news that evening, not to mention enjoying another one of her fine meals. He couldn't remember ever having such a good time as he'd had during supper last night. A man could get used to that sort of thing.

Whoa! Gotta stop thinking that way. He didn't need a woman in his life. Didn't need a ready-made family.

Sure, he enjoyed teaching ranch skills to the boys who came to his place each day. Had enjoyed the relaxing talk around the Barlows' table the past two evenings. Yet he missed the quiet of his own thoughts after a long day of work, times when he sorted life out, read a good book and made decisions for expanding his spread and protecting it from more cattle rustling.

Funny how he couldn't keep those thoughts in mind that evening when Lula May served up ham and black-eyed peas like he'd never eaten in his life. And on the side, tasty turnip greens with a dash of tangy apple cider vinegar and corn bread dripping with fresh-churned butter, not to mention chocolate macaroon cookies waiting on the sideboard for dessert.

As he'd figured, Lula May was pleased at the vote in her favor. Maybe she didn't seem as enthusiastic as he'd expected, but that just went to prove how unpredictable women were. To be fair, during supper he noticed an odd shadow cross her face from time to time. Maybe she had some sort of worry that was none of his business. Yet, after thinking on it for half of the meal, he couldn't keep from blurting out, "Lula May, are you doin' all right?"

She blinked those big blue eyes and put on one of her pretty smiles that didn't seem quite real. "Why, yes. Everything's just fine."

If she was one of his hands, Edmund would know how to coax or demand an honest answer from her. But as little as he knew about women, he did know not to bully them. Wouldn't even want to. Bullying destroyed trust. Before he could think of a way to crack open her protective shell, Calvin spoke up.

"Say, Mr. McKay, would you stick around after supper and play a game of checkers with me? Ma and my brothers don't give me much of a challenge, but I believe you could."

Something in the boy's eyes said more than his invitation. Did Calvin also notice his ma's mood and hope for some help from Edmund? Not that he felt he could help, but he'd go along with Calvin instead of his own better judgment that told him to hightail it out of there after dessert.

"Sounds good to me." In fact, he hadn't played checkers in a while and would enjoy a game or two. "That is, if your ma doesn't mind." He sent Lula May a friendly, questioning look.

"No." Her voice had a bit of a squeak to it. "No, that's fine. Calvin, get your chores done first." She commenced to giving orders to the young'uns, and they hopped to it like they were going to a party. "Mr. McKay and I will be waiting for you in the parlor."

In the few minutes it took for Edmund to settle into Frank's chair and Lula May to take up her mending, she'd managed to paste on a more relaxed face.

"Would you mind telling me more about last night's meeting?"

"Sure." Edmund had already told her over supper about some of the discussion. "What would you like to know?"

"Did they like my idea? I mean about using some of the dues to start building a church?"

"I didn't mention it." Her wounded expression provoked him to hurry on. "I thought you should bring it up when you come next week."

"Oh." She still frowned. "So you don't agree with me?"

"No, ma'am. I mean, yes, ma'am, I agree that we need a church building. I just think that sort of project is more appropriate for the ladies' quilting bee."

"I disagree."

Of course she disagreed. Edmund kept his expression neutral and tried to appear interested as she went on.

"Most men handle the finances for their homes, so they'd have more resources to draw from than their wives would. Besides, we sold and raffled off quilts at the Founders' Day celebration and couldn't raise near enough to build a shed, much less an entire church. The men should take on this project."

"Yes, ma'am, but putting that on the cattlemen's association is a bit impractical." Edmund felt cornered. He sure didn't want to start an argument. "The men will be busy figuring out how to protect their ranches from those rustlers. They don't need to add such a big project to the agenda."

"Big *and* important. When winter comes and when the spring winds blow, you'll be glad to meet in a sheltered building instead of a tent."

Edmund groaned inwardly. How did he get out of this dilemma? "Tell you what. If you feel strongly enough about it, you can bring it up to the other ranchers and see whether they agree with me or you. Besides, you had the idea, so you should tell 'em."

"Oh." She blinked those pretty blue eyes in an appealing way.

"And if you come up with an idea I like, I'll let everybody know."

Now she smiled, and that made Edmund's chest warm up even more than the ham and black-eyed peas had. "All right then, because I'd hate to embarrass either of us with talking too much in front of the other men. Most of them prefer for the ladies to keep quiet, if their behavior at church socials is any indication." She poked her needle through a hole in a white sock. "If you think they'll like any of my ideas, well, then..." She gave a little shrug. "I know the other men respect you, so you can make sure my ideas are actually put into action."

"I can try." If anybody else pulled such a trick on him, he'd feel used. Yet the conversation had shown him something new about this spunky little widow. She claimed not to need anything, but if nobody listened to her ideas, she did need someone to speak up for her. "I should tell you that George and Robert appreciated your idea about including their sons in the Young Ranchers' Club, and I hear Mercy Green did, too. Pastor Stillwater brought the new boys out these past two days, and they're all starting to get along real fine." He paused to enjoy her smile. "I did tell 'em that was your idea."

A real happy look bloomed all over her face. "That was nice. Thank you, Edmund."

Edmund had to swallow hard to keep from telling her how pretty she was when she smiled that way. Such talk should be reserved for courting, and he was *not* courting Widow Barlow. Had no plans to court her or anybody else. Had no idea *how* to court. Didn't want to. No, sir!

Pretty soon the young'uns came in, filling the room with their chatter. Little Pauline served out those mouthwatering chocolate macaroon cookies. Calvin set out the checkerboard, and he and Edmund started their game. The other three boys, even little Daniel, looked on with interest, each one insisting on a turn. Edmund could tell he'd be here for a spell. Funny, the idea didn't bother him in the least. It was a mighty homey scene with Lula May and Pauline sitting nearby mending socks and humming a little tune in harmony. A man could get used to... *No.* No, he couldn't. Wouldn't. His freedom was too dear.

Besides, Lula May kept glancing toward her office just off the parlor, a worried look returning to her face. The last thing Edmund needed was a moody woman in his life, happy one minute, worried the next and peevish at the drop of a hat.

Even so, he couldn't get shed of the thought that she had a problem. Nor could he ignore the Lord's familiar prompting. Maybe he should try to get her mind off of whatever was troubling her.

"Say, Lula May, I've been meaning to ask you." He

jumped two of Calvin's checkers and reached the other side of the board. "Crown me."

Calvin groaned as he did it and then studied the board for his next move.

"Yes?" Lula May stared down at her mending, which was a good thing because Edmund didn't want to get caught up in those big blue eyes.

"Did you sell any more horses today?" He'd planned to talk to Lucas Bennett about the paint, but the man hadn't shown up at the meeting. He'd sent his foreman, Hank Snowden, instead. Edmund sure hoped Lucas came through with the money for the horse so Lula May wouldn't be let down. Especially since she might have been able to sell the paint to that cowboy yesterday.

"Not today. In a good month, I sell one or two." For a talkative lady, she didn't seem inclined to say more.

How was a man supposed to draw more out of her? Maybe he should try talking to her like he would to a man. "Do you sell to just anybody?"

Now she looked up. "You got somebody in mind?"

"No." Maybe this was a bad idea. He hadn't meant to get her hopes up. "But if anybody asks, I'll send 'em your way. Any good man, that is."

"I'd be much obliged." She grinned when Calvin took three of Edmund's checkers in one move. "You'd better watch out there." She slipped the milky-white glass darning egg out of the sock she was working on and inspected her work. "I only sell to folks who'll treat my horses right."

"I admire that practice." It probably cost her some

sales, but some things were more important than money.

Edmund eyed Calvin. He needed to win this first game to gain the boy's respect, but not too easily. He nudged his crowned checker over one square and eyed his opponent before looking back at Lula May. "Where'd you learn so much about horse training?"

From the guarded look on her face and the hunching of her shoulders, he could tell he'd stepped over a line. Then she relaxed. "Down in Alabama where I grew up, an elderly former plantation groom taught me." She paused and chewed her lip like Jacob used to do. "How about you? Did you grow up on a ranch? Is that where you learned to raise such prime cattle?"

"Nope." He waited his turn, then took the rest of Calvin's checkers.

Even though he groaned over losing, Calvin shook Edmund's hand like a man and moved over so Samuel could play.

While they reset the board, Edmund considered how much he should tell Lula May about his life. With her growing up on a plantation, she'd probably had most everything she needed in life, even after the ravages of the war. What would she think of his humble beginnings? He reminded himself that Old Gad always told him there was no shame in being an orphan. Once he got started, though, he found himself telling the whole yarn: his parents' deaths, being separated from his two brothers, being on his own at sixteen. He left out the part about his disagreeable cousin. But he did tell her about the old cowboy who found him one day walking down the road all hopeless and hungry and turned his life around. He was rewarded with those pretty blue eyes getting all red around the edges. He supposed a woman's tears were all right when a smile went along with them.

Having stayed later than he'd planned, he rode home in the dark. This had been the best evening so far. Good food, good games of checkers—just for fun, he'd let little Daniel beat him—good conversation. Just sitting in Frank's chair in that nice little parlor with all of them around him had stirred up some of those vague longings inside him again.

No, he needed to quit entertaining such foolhardy thoughts. They'd bring him nothing but grief. How could he get them to stop? With three more days—and evenings—ahead to complete his bargain with Lula May, how was he going to guard his heart against misery when it stopped? After all, why would a lady raised on a Southern plantation want to have anything to do with a simple rancher who'd learned everything of value in life from an ordinary old cowboy?

In spite of his reservations, he couldn't stop feeling something was out of line, and that annoying sense of protectiveness came back, as sure as anything a prompting from the Lord. He recalled the uneasy glances Lula May cast toward her office from time to time. Was she worried about the cash she'd collected yesterday from her horse sale? If Zeke mentioned to anyone that he'd bought from her, the rustlers might hear of it and try to rob her. Or maybe it was something else. Edmund could have pressed her about whatever was bothering her. But he'd probably just mess it up, and she'd probably get her feathers ruffled like she did on Monday morning and claim he was sticking his nose in her business. Best just to keep quiet and not let her know he was keeping an eye out for her. Yep, that was the best way to go about it. The best way to stay out of trouble.

"That all right with you, Lord?" He aimed a glance up toward the starlit sky.

Silence, both inward and outward, was all he heard in reply. Zephyr, on the other hand, shook his head from side to side. If Edmund didn't know better, he'd think his stallion was a mind reader.

Once Lula May saw Edmund to the door and watched him ride away, she was surprised by how empty the house felt, even though the children were making the usual amount of noise as they got ready for bed. Just getting the taciturn man to talk about himself—a self-defensive move she'd employed to keep from blurting out too much about her own life—had brought about something special. Knowing he'd been an orphan like her, one who'd had a kindly old mentor, again, just as she had, moved her deeply. Maybe the day would come when she could tell him the truth about her past.

Even as she thought it, her heart plummeted to her stomach. It was time to face the bad news about that past. After hearing the children's prayers and tucking in the younger ones, she made her way to her office and dropped into the leather chair behind Frank's large oak desk.

As she pulled Uncle's newly arrived, unopened letter out of the top drawer, a feeling of dread washed over and through her. After all these years, what could that cruel man possibly want from her?

Chapter Four

Well, girlie, you've had plenty of time to answer my letter, so there are either of two situations keeping you from employing the common courtesy I taught you. Either you have chosen to ignore your poor old uncle, your only living relative, who did so much for your ungrateful self when you were growing up like a weed. Or you are in some kind of trouble, and you need my help. As you well know, I always see to my duty, no matter what it costs me, so I am packing my bags and coming out there to find out what your problem is.

I understand you have two stepsons, who no doubt resent you for taking their mama's place, and two sons of your own. With their pappy dead, they are likely all hard for you to handle, so I'll do what I can to straighten them out. As for that girl, I can see to it she does not turn out like you, although it might be too late for that.

You can look for me to arrive next Monday, July 1, on the three-thirty afternoon train. I will expect you to pick me up at whatever run-down station you folks have out there. Bring a buggy that can carry luggage because I am bringing a trunk so I can stay until I solve all of your problems. I will also expect you to return to me the property you stole from me when you ran away like a cheap floozy to marry that run-down old man and abandoned all the good sense I tried to teach you.

Your loving Uncle Floyd

Terror ripped through Lula May. He truly was coming, and the reality of it made her feel as if she might lose her supper right into the wastebasket beside Frank's desk. Worse, Uncle seemed to know all about her children, but how? After his first letter, she hadn't bothered to try to figure out how he'd found her. But now she realized most any cowboy who'd ridden through the area would have heard about her because of her horses being available for sale. Knowing Uncle, she had no doubt he'd hired someone to search for her and, once he found out where she was, to learn all he could about her and the children. And yet none of her friends had mentioned anybody asking such nosy questions. The local ranchers might have been reluctant to let her join their cattlemen's association, but not a one of them would tell a stranger details about her family. She trusted their integrity without a doubt.

Good thing she put off reading this horrible letter

until Edmund left and the children were in bed. What with preparing a big dinner and doing other chores, she hadn't had time to read it, even though her mind wandered in that direction from time to time while she mended socks, each time stirring a hiccup of concern in her chest. Now that she'd read it, the bad news was worse than anything she'd expected. What was Uncle talking about when he said she'd stolen something of his? She'd never stolen anything. According to Frank's will, this ranch was hers and everything on it, with provisions for each of the children when they reached adulthood.

When she'd run away eleven years ago—escaped, actually—from Uncle's cruel control of her life and his plans to marry her off to that horrid old man, she'd packed very little in her small handmade carpetbag. Only a change of clothes and a few mementos of her parents, none of which held any monetary value. She searched her mind for what he could be talking about.

Ah. Yes. There was something. She'd taken the pearl-and-diamond necklace her mother had left to her, one of the few things she'd carried with her when she was forced to move from Ohio to Alabama after her parents' deaths. Mama had inherited the jewelry from her own mother. When Lula May arrived at Uncle's house as a twelve-year-old, he'd rifled through her few belongings and had laid claim to the necklace. He argued it was his by rights because his mother's will stated she had disinherited Lula May's mother for marrying a Yankee. But Lula May contended that Grandma gave Mama the necklace when she turned sixteen, four years before the marriage. Uncle claimed Lula May was lying and locked the necklace in his safe. She hadn't seen the jewelry during the six years she'd suffered under Uncle's tyranny.

Then, as she'd made her plans to run away, Lula May had tried to think of what she would need to survive alone in the world. Mama's necklace was the only thing of value she could take honestly. While Uncle's cook, Annie, plied him with her tasty fried chicken, Tobias had found a way to open Uncle's safe, and Lula May had helped herself to the jewelry. Even after she'd answered Frank's advertisement for a mail-order bride and moved out here to Little Horn, just having it tucked away had given her a sense of security.

Now, in the event that some lawyer or judge decided the necklace did belong to Uncle, Lula May couldn't give it to him. Three years ago, when Frank became ill and money got scarce, she'd taken it to a jeweler in San Antonio and sold it to save the ranch. While she still had some of the money in the bank in town, it wouldn't be enough to satisfy Uncle. Maybe he'd try to take the ranch away from her. What would she do then? He'd probably threaten in all sorts of horrible ways and carry out those threats if she didn't comply with his orders. If she understood the law correctly, a male relative could demand custody of children from a widow. The thought of Floyd Jones raising her children sickened Lula May.

She folded her arms on the desk and laid her forehead against them. In all these past eleven years, even when Frank became ill, she'd never felt so helpless. Or frightened. She had no doubt Uncle would do anything to gain control of her. Of her ranch. Her children. But one thing was sure. She must not let the children know either how afraid she was or the danger they all were in. Just as when Frank fell ill, just as when it became clear that he would not recover, she would keep this matter to herself. Frank had been a private person, so he'd let her manage the ranch without hiring a cowhand to help, as he'd wanted her to do. She'd never have done that anyway. Besides, there wasn't a single person in the world she could turn to. The men who'd been so reluctant to let her join the cattlemen's association because she was a woman would likely muscle in and take over simply because she was a woman. It all seemed so hopeless. How in the world would she manage these next few days until Uncle arrived? How would she manage to protect the children with him in this house?

After a few minutes, she sat up and huffed out an impatient breath. That was enough self-pity for one day. For one calamity. She would manage this situation just as she had everything else in her life, and protect the children while she did it. In another year or two, Calvin would be old enough to shoulder some of these burdens with her, but for now, it was up to her to do it alone. She'd smile and be cheerful and hope for the best. That attitude had gotten her through Frank's illness and death. It would carry her through whatever trouble Uncle brought her way.

Tasty fried rabbit, creamy mashed potatoes and gravy, and buttery string beans couldn't distract Edmund's attention away from the dark circles under Lula May's eyes. Last evening he'd failed to learn what troubled her, and with her too-happy smile and strained laughter, he doubted she would open up to him tonight, either. Even so, he had to try. Had to obey the Lord's prompting to help her whether she wanted him to or not.

When supper ended and the children began cleanup, he just short of invited himself to stay for the evening by sticking around and studying the pictures on the parlor walls. The one over the mantelpiece in particular stood out, Frank's wedding picture with his first wife. He looked real young and strong, not at all like the frail man who'd died last winter. His wife—Emily?—looked too frail for the rigors of ranch life. Edmund thought it curious that such a picture hadn't been put away eleven years ago when Frank married Lula May. With not a hint of dust coating the mahogany frame, the bowed-out glass shone bright and clear, Edmund could see she even took good care of it. Interesting.

He wandered over to the bookshelf and studied the two rows of books to see whether she had anything he hadn't added to his own library. Maybe they could exchange books from time to time once their agreement was over. Fortunately, when Lula May joined him in the parlor, she didn't chase him away, though her pretty face lacked the welcome offered the previous nights. Edmund harbored no fears that her change was due to him. Something wasn't right here, and he was determined to figure out what it was.

As on the previous nights, she took up her sewing basket, this time holding a frilly pink something or other no doubt intended for Pauline. Yet as she sat with those items on her lap, her fingers remained idle. Edmund settled in Frank's chair and tried to think of some way to start a conversation. Lula May usually had so much to say about, well, just about everything, yet tonight she was quieter than a mouse hiding from a cat and almost as skittish. Edmund supposed it was up to him to say something, but what did women like to talk about? Pretty dresses? Bonnets? He'd make a fool of himself if he brought up either of those.

"I've been wanting to ask you." She broke the silence, much to his relief.

"Yes, ma'am?" He couldn't stop a small grin, but she kept her eyes on her sewing and didn't seem to notice.

"Do you favor the gold or the silver standard?"

Edmund choked back a laugh. He sure didn't want to insult her, but he had no idea women thought about such things. But then, he'd already seen that Lula May wasn't like other women he'd met. Then again, he'd never known any woman very well, not even his sister-in-law.

"Well…" He drawled out the word to give himself time to think. "A man—" he stopped to clear his throat, his mind scrambling to find a way to include her "—or a woman who runs a ranch or a business has to think about which one can back the US dollar without failing. I'm convinced gold will be the best choice. It's always been considered the most valuable ore, even way back in Bible times."

"Hmm." Her eyes lit up with a hint of a challenge.

"That's true. But that doesn't mean silver lacks considerable value. We don't have any idea how long our US gold fields will continue to produce. Look what happened during the California Gold Rush. I don't think our silver mining has been tapped to its full potential. At least that's what I've read in Frank's business journals from New York. What with this bad economic depression the country's been in these past two years, it doesn't seem to me like gold has backed our dollar very well."

Was she just being contrary? Or did she have something there? In truth, Edmund really only knew cattle ranching. Beef generally sold well enough no matter how the economy fared in other parts of the country, and he hadn't suffered any significant losses during this current depression, except for those stolen cattle.

"I read that many businesses have failed back East—" She paused to bite off a thread, then rethreaded her needle. "There's high unemployment, especially in the larger cities. Of course that's led to violent strikes and such. I suppose these issues will affect next year's elections, especially the presidential election." She clicked her tongue like she was scolding somebody. "I don't know what those strikers think they can accomplish by destroying businesses that are trying to recover, that are trying to provide the very jobs those strikers want."

Edmund grunted his agreement. She'd changed the subject a couple of times while she was talking right then, a habit of hers he just realized he got a kick out of because she never ceased to surprise him. And nobody since Old Gad had ever been able to draw him out the way she could. After only three nights, it seemed only natural to add his own thoughts.

"It's pretty funny when some of those Easterners come out here trying to be cowboys."

"I'd imagine so." She rewarded him with her first real smile of the evening. "But you can't fault them for trying. Better than going on strike and destroying things and hurting people."

"That's true." Edmund chuckled. "Maybe after we get these Young Ranchers trained, we should open a school for tenderfoots wanting to be cowhands."

Her musical laugh, which seemed to come from way down deep inside, warmed Edmund's heart. He hadn't dug out the cause of her sadness, but at least he'd cheered her up. That would have to do for now. If the Lord wanted him to do more, He'd have to provide the opportunity.

As the children wandered into the parlor from their chores, Pauline and Daniel carried in apple pie with fresh cream for dessert. Calvin brought out the checkerboard, set it up on the coffee table and settled in a chair across from Edmund, a challenging glint in his eyes. Another warm feeling settled over Edmund. After tonight, he had only two more evenings with this family, these good people, and he was going to enjoy every minute.

All day long, determined to put Uncle out of her mind, Lula May had worked hard to come up with ideas to talk about with Edmund. She really had no idea whether the gold or the silver standard was best for the country. Nor did she concern herself too much with next year's elections since women couldn't even vote and she didn't have a husband to represent her opinions. What she did know was that she liked the way Edmund's bright green eyes lit up at her challenge to whatever he'd said. Talking with him was downright enjoyable. Oh, how she relished these evening talks. She'd noticed him perusing the bookshelves. Did he like to read? By tomorrow night, she'd come up with some ideas for conversation about her favorites. Right now, she enjoyed watching him interact with Calvin over checkers. She liked that he gave her stepson no advantages. And Calvin had no trouble holding his own because he'd learned the game from his father.

Only a smidgen of guilt pinched at her heart over enjoying another man's company so soon after Frank's death. After all, her husband had told her to marry again, the "last thing I'll ever order you to do," he'd said in a joking way only a week before he died. Yet Frank had always been too gentle to order her to do anything. Which had made her all the more eager to please him.

Still, *order* was just the right word to remind Lula May that she would never take orders from any man because of the way Uncle had been. It was all well and good to enjoy Edmund's company on these warm summer evenings, but that was as far as she could let him into her life. From the wily look in his eyes as he played checkers, she could see he had hidden depths, hidden strengths. He was a man who was used to being in charge, and all of her conversational challenges to him were intended to let him know she wouldn't be pushed around.

As for Uncle, she was already arming her emotions so he'd never get the chance to beat her down into submission with his cruel words, as he had all those long years ago when she'd arrived on his doorstep a helpless twelve-year-old orphan.

Thinking of him, she couldn't keep from glancing toward her office, where his vile letters lay in the top drawer hidden under some other papers so the children wouldn't happen to see them. But her stomach began to ache as it had off and on for the past twenty-four hours. Her respite from worry was over, and she heaved out a sigh that was far louder than she'd intended. Only Edmund looked her way, and one fine brown eyebrow lifted in a questioning manner. The temptation to confide everything to him nearly overwhelmed her. Then Calvin jumped three of his checkers and gave out a hoot of victory. Her momentary weakness dissolved, and she pasted on a smile.

"I do believe he's got you there, Edmund."

The next evening as Edmund and Jacob rode into the Barlow barnyard, Edmund felt as if he were coming home. That was a dangerous feeling, but he couldn't help himself. In spite of Lula May's random bouts of peevishness, nothing but good things had happened to him at this house over this past week, even losing that one game of checkers to Calvin last night. The meals were the best food he'd ever eaten in his thirty-three years, including those black-eyed peas. He couldn't wait to see what Lula May had cooked up for tonight. But the best part of the week had been exchanging thoughts and ideas with her. He got a kick out of the way she went off on tangents but always came back to the original discussion.

He could almost say that he'd grown more at ease with her. With *them*, he amended. Last evening, their discussion began to flow more naturally, and he didn't feel self-conscious when he spoke his mind. Nor did he feel embarrassed for talking so openly to her about his past. The woman was stubborn as a mule, but that was all right. He'd come to realize that running this horse ranch required a strong, assertive person, just as running a cattle ranch did. He'd even begun to enjoy the way she became so animated and engaged while they talked.

Tonight he would try to get her to talk about some of those books she had on her shelf. He'd seen a copy of Dickens's *A Tale of Two Cities*, which he'd wanted to read for a long time. Maybe she'd loan it to him. He also wanted to know more about what brought an Alabama plantation girl to Texas as a mail-order bride. Coming from North Texas, he didn't know much about other areas of the South and had always assumed all of the plantations had been destroyed during the War between the States. Of course, if she got to talking about something else, he'd go along with whatever it was.

Sure enough, she got busy talking as soon as they'd settled in the parlor after a fine supper of fried pork chops.

"Tell me more about yourself, Edmund." She started

to work mending a pair of trousers Jacob had torn the day before on some barbed wire. "You said you came from North Texas. Have you been out of the state at all?"

"Sure have." He would talk about the good things and keep the bad memories in the past where they belonged. "When I started out on my own, I decided to try something different from farmwork. I went down to New Orleans and worked on the docks for a while. Then I got this crazy idea to sign on to a ship hauling coffee to New York. We hadn't any more than left the dock when I knew I'd made a mistake. Got seasick real quick and jumped ship." He laughed at the memory *and* at her raised eyebrows. She sure was pretty when she looked surprised. "Well, I didn't quite jump ship. When we got out into the rough waters of the Gulf, the captain decided I was pretty much useless and sent me back to land on the first ship we passed headed that way."

"Oh, my." Lula May laughed in the musical way of hers. She'd not been as preoccupied this evening as she'd been last night and hadn't glanced toward her office once. "Then what happened?"

"I headed back to Texas."

"Walking?"

"Walking." His feet hurt at the memory of those many long miles over rutted, rocky roads in weather-beaten, thin-soled boots.

"Oh, my," she said again, and her pretty blue eyes got all round with wonder and a hint of sympathy. He didn't need any of that.

"Turned out it was the best thing that could've happened to me." He could hear the gruffness in his own voice, so he softened it real quick. "That old cowboy I told you about came along and took me under his wing. Taught me everything I know about cattle ranching, helped me get a job. Even staked me when I bought the ranch."

"What a blessing." Her eyes lit up in a different way now, like she understood what he meant.

Her kindly response and the interested light in those big blue eyes made him want to say more, so he went on to tell her a few stories about New Orleans, things he'd forgotten over the past seventeen or so years. "I found a little church with mostly poor folks, but they were mighty warmhearted. Got to do some carpentry work and painting on some fine houses in the Garden District. That kept body and soul together." He considered only telling her about the good things, but then found himself still talking. "Truth is, though, the city has some powerful temptations for a sixteen-year-old still not sure of his way in life, so after a while I high-tailed it out of there before I got caught in that net. Like I said, sea life didn't work out, so I headed back to Texas feeling like a failure. That's when Old Gad came along and told me different. He showed me how God had been directing me all the way."

As he talked, he realized how much he'd changed this past week, too. His heart felt lighter, and he rarely brooded. Life just seemed altogether better. He felt better. Almost mellow. And he had a feeling it had nothing to do with spending time with Jacob and the other boys teaching them about ranching. It was this pretty little lady and her warm, welcoming home. Not that he would set any store by it. He mustn't forget that she could turn peevish at any moment.

"Now it's your turn." He set up the checkerboard in anticipation of Calvin joining them once his chores were done. "Tell me about growing up on a plantation in Alabama."

Lula May's jaw dropped slightly, then she gripped her lower lip between her teeth for a moment and glanced toward her office. Edmund wanted to kick himself. Somehow he'd opened a wound, and he had no idea how to fix it. He started to apologize, but she spoke first.

"It wasn't a plantation, just a few acres." She shrugged. "Used to be part of a large cotton plantation, and a couple of the former slaves stayed on to work for my uncle for pay."

Edmund grasped that idea. "Like the old groom who taught you about horses."

She nodded but didn't say anything more.

The children chose that time to wander in, and the conversation drifted to other topics. Edmund felt a hitch of annoyance that Lula May wanted to know all about him but wouldn't tell him about her own life. Didn't she realize how hard it had been for him to open up? So much for their friendly chats. Maybe she hadn't asked him about his life because she was interested but just to pass the time. He'd spoken of deep things of his past while she only spoke of external matters. That wasn't very promising. So much for his earlier feelings of coming home. So much for his plans to talk about books.

Besides, he was content with his solitary life. It wouldn't make any sense to go from that to having a ready-made family with a noisy woman and five children. He wouldn't be able to abide for long that odd way she shut down from time to time. As much as she talked about everything else but wouldn't open up about her past, he decided she was just moody. He could do without that. And all the fried pork chops in the world wouldn't entice him back here once this week was over.

Chapter Five

Lula May had saved one of her best meals for Saturday night, and she went all out to make it exceptional: pan-fried steak with a mix of spicy seasonings she'd come up with several years ago, baked potatoes, corn and lima bean succotash, her special mixed garden pickles and a carrot cake topped with the thick, buttery icing she'd invented. The special ingredients for all of these dishes had put a dent in her food budget, and all took more time than she should spend in the kitchen, what with horses to train and endless chores to do. But Jacob's new self-confidence gave her plenty of reason to show her appreciation to the man who inspired it.

Further, she got a kick out of seeing Edmund's eyes light up as he sat down to supper each evening. Even before that, each time as he walked through the kitchen toward the dining room, he took in deep breaths like he enjoyed the aromas of her cooking. Had he been tempted to lift a pot lid to see what was cooking, as Frank used to do? As her stepsons still did? The thought of it gave her a laugh.

She'd also come up with a few topics of conversation not as personal as last night's to avoid having to share too much about herself. His story about Old Gad had touched her deeply. God truly had saved Edmund from many troubles and griefs in life. In return, oh, how she'd been tempted to tell him about Uncle. But to what end? That he might ride over here from his place and protect her from that evil man? Maybe Edmund would agree that she'd committed a crime by taking the necklace and, even worse, by selling it. No, she'd do best to manage Uncle on her own and work out whatever it took to protect herself and her children. She might be able to out-barter a cowboy when selling a horse, but she'd have to do some clever maneuvering to outwit Uncle Floyd Jones. Right now she had some people to feed.

Sure enough, after Edmund and Jacob washed up in the mudroom, Edmund paused at the kitchen door to draw in a deep breath. Eyes closed in apparent bliss, he grinned and shook his head.

"Miss Lula May Barlow, I have no idea how you manage to come up with so many fine-smelling meals, but I do believe you've outdone yourself this evening." Clearly feeling at home in her kitchen, he walked over to the stove and lifted the lid on the fry pan just long enough to see what was cooking. "Ouch!" The lid dropped back in place with a clatter, and he shook his singed fingers. Why didn't men ever think to use a pot holder? Fortunately, Edmund recovered quickly. "Steak. A cattleman's favorite meal. Thank you, ma'am, for keeping us in business." My, he was talkative this evening.

Just as Pauline and Daniel came back to the kitchen from setting the table, Edmund favored her with that crooked grin of his that made his face all the more good-looking. Against her will, Lula May felt her breath hitch slightly. The children took in the scene and shared a look and a giggle. She'd have to take them to task for it later. Right now she was having a hard time tamping down a silly little hiccup in her chest.

Did Edmund have any idea how attractive his grin was? She doubted it. Never once in her ten years of knowing him—although not well at all—had she ever seen him flirt with the unattached young ladies at church. Probably a confirmed bachelor. Which was fine with her. She was just as set in her newfound singleness.

"You're very welcome, Mr. Edmund McKay." She couldn't keep a playful tone from her voice, even as a hint of sadness struck her heart. This was his last night with them, and she was honest enough to admit, to herself anyway, that she'd miss him. She took a platter from the kitchen cabinet, forked the steaks onto it and held it out to him. "Now, make yourself useful and set this on the table. The children and I will bring the rest."

"Yes, ma'am." He took the platter, and their fingers brushed.

A shock shot up her arm, leaving behind a pleasant tingling feeling at the side of her neck. Lula May gasped softly. From Edmund's tiny jolt and wide-eyed look, she guessed he'd felt something, too. There was only one way out of this. Only one way to stamp out a plain old silly physical attraction that could get both of them nothing but trouble if they sought to encourage it.

She sniffed dramatically and gave his arm a little shove. "Get moving. Nobody likes cold steak."

He cleared his throat. "Yes, ma'am." From the way he strode toward the dining room, he appeared to have discovered new purpose in life. Or maybe he was in the same hurry to get away from unwelcomed feelings.

Lula May turned to dish up the succotash only to see her daughter and youngest son giving her those silly grins again. "All right, you two, get busy." She handed a bowl of food to each one, removed her apron and hung it on a peg by the kitchen door and followed them into the dining room.

What a good feeling their giggling gave her despite the mischief behind it. Carefree giggles had been few and far between in this house these past few years. They'd all grieved Frank's lengthy illness and death for a long time and, she supposed, they'd always miss their pa, as she still missed her own parents. Yet, in spite of losses, a person had to go on living; a mother had to see that her children had all they needed in life no matter how much work it took. Laughter lightened the load considerably.

As it turned out, she didn't need to bring up any of the topics of conversation she'd worked so hard to think of. At Edmund's urging and with Lula May's permission, Jacob spent most of the meal telling the story of the whole week.

After going on for several minutes, he said, "We even had a contest between ranch and town boys to see who could learn each job quickest." He gave his older brothers a smug, conspiratorial look. "O'course, we ranchers won." He shoveled in a bite of steak and chewed thoughtfully. "Those town boys weren't so bad after all."

Because he had the talking feather beside his plate, no one spoke as they waited for him to continue. This was Jacob's night, and Lula May had never seen him so outspoken or enthusiastic.

"That Elgin Arundel turned out to be pretty strong. He says he's been helping his folks carry stuff at the general store ever since he could walk. And that Georgie Henley, well, he's not a quitter." Jacob snorted out a derisive laugh. "He still struts like a dandy, just like his pa. I guess bankers need to put on airs so people will remember they're rich and important." No meanness colored his words, so Lula May let the comment pass.

While her other children laughed at his joke, her heart overflowed with happiness at these observations. She gave Edmund a grateful smile down the length of the table, but he was watching Jacob. Was that a hint of pride she saw in his eyes? Seemed like this week had been good for him, too.

"This afternoon, we went to town and visited the businesses, just like you said to do, Ma." Jacob gave her a nod. "Me and Adam… I mean, Adam and I can see that those folks work almost as hard as ranchers and cowboys. Almost." His blue eyes twinkled, reminding Lula May of Frank. "O'course, they're usually a lot cleaner than us."

Everyone laughed again. Calvin and Samuel started to speak at the same time, but Jacob held up the talking feather with surprising authority. "Hang on. I saved the best for last." He cast a quick, shy grin at Edmund, who returned a kindly nod. "Mr. McKay gave each of us a special Bible verse to take as our own."

Again, Lula May's heart skipped. She stared at Edmund. Was there no end to this man's surprises? "What's your verse, Jacob?"

Her son sat up straight in his chair and cleared his throat, just as Pastor Stillwater often did when he was about to speak from God's Word. "Psalm 135:4. 'For the Lord hath chosen Jacob unto Himself.'" He grinned just as if he'd received the finest gift of his life. "Mr. McKay said that verse was mainly about Israel, but it's all right to claim it for myself, too. God *chose* me for Himself."

A wondrous, joyous chill swept over Lula May, and tears sprang to her eyes. Edmund must have stayed up late at night searching for just the right verse for each boy. If all of them were as personal and life-changing as these beautiful words from the Psalms, those boys would no doubt walk with the Lord all the days of their lives. What a good man Edmund was to point them to God.

When she could speak without blubbering, she said, "That's mighty fine, son. I hope you never forget it." She'd heard about folks choosing a Bible verse to carry in their hearts, one with special meaning in their lives and which brought them closer to the Lord. Maybe she needed to do that herself. Without thinking, she said, "Edmund, what's your verse?" Oh, my. Why had she put him on the spot that way?

He didn't seem to mind because he answered without hesitation. "It's one Old Gad gave me shortly after we met. Ephesians 1:6. 'He hath made us accepted in the Beloved.'" The faraway look in his eyes and the soft smile on his handsome face indicated how deeply that verse still affected him.

"Ah, I do like that verse." From the story he told last night, Lula May guessed that was exactly what a lonely wandering orphan boy had needed to know: that God accepted him because of Jesus, the Beloved. What did she need to know? Maybe she should pray for a special verse, not only for herself, but for each of her other children beside Jacob.

The conversation around the table turned to other things while Lula May served a dessert of vanilla pudding and cookies, a treat too messy for the younger ones to eat in the parlor. When everyone finished and the children started clearing the table, Lula May waved a hand toward the other room. "Shall we?"

Edmund stood and shook his head. "Thank you, ma'am, but I'm afraid I'll have to decline tonight. I have some work to do before I can take off all day Sunday. I hope you'll excuse me."

For the briefest moment, Lula May could only stare at him while disappointment coursed through her. She managed to force a smile. "Of course. I have to be sure our church clothes are ready for tomorrow. That'll take a while." What a thing to say! She'd spent the morning washing and ironing shirts and dresses and making sure Daniel did a good job of polishing everyone's best shoes and boots.

"So you're glad to get rid of me?" His green eyes twinkled in a teasing way, something she'd never seen in the man before this week. He'd changed and for the better. She had, too. But she couldn't let him know it.

"Oh, my, yes. It's been a real burden having to entertain you all this week." She punctuated her words with a merry laugh.

"I thought so." His deep chuckle only added to her regret that he was leaving. He walked toward her, well, toward the door to the kitchen, which was behind her, and she felt her pulse race.

This is ridiculous. She was acting like a schoolgirl. Like the silly girls at church who clustered around Calvin.

Edmund stopped beside her and took her hand. "Lula May, this has been a pure pleasure. I'll miss your fine cooking." His eyes still wore that teasing expression.

"I'm so sorry you had to put up with our company just to get a decent meal."

Still holding her hand, he shook his head and clicked his tongue. "Well, now, sometimes a man has to suffer a bit to get the good things in life."

For longer than they should have, the two of them stared at each other. More than ever before in her life, Lula May felt the power of a man's presence, *this* man's presence. Yet she had no fear, no reservations. Just maybe a hint of longing that he wouldn't leave…ever. She shook herself inwardly. Edmund had done a wise thing to tease her. She'd done right to tease back.

Pulling her hand free, she touched his upper arm to give him a little shove toward the kitchen. "Don't let the door hit you on the way out."

Another of those warm chuckles emanated from deep within that broad chest. "Yes, ma'am." He ambled through the kitchen, saying goodbye to each of the children in a way to show he'd noticed them, another sign of his kindness.

He grabbed his hat from a peg by the back door, and the whole family followed him out into the yard where his stallion awaited him near the hitching rail but not tied there. As Edmund rode away, the children continued to wave and call goodbye until he was out of sight. Then they all stood staring in that direction until Lula May chased them back to their unfinished chores.

Yet as she made final preparations for tomorrow's church attendance, her mind remained focused on Edmund. He'd done so much good for her family. Was he as sorry for the week to be over as she was?

As he rode home, Edmund realized he hadn't felt this lonely in a long time, which was pretty foolish because he'd been alone most of his thirty-three years. Early this morning, he'd made the decision not to stay after supper, and he'd stuck to his guns. A wise move because he couldn't let himself get caught up any further with the Barlow family. Their joys, their sorrows, that kind of thing. Lula May had made it clear she wouldn't open up to him about whatever troubled her, while he could tell something unpleasant hung over her.

From watching Josiah and Betsy, he knew husbands and wives needed to talk about their deepest secrets so they could support one another. Not that he was looking to marry, of course, but…enough of that! He didn't know where those thoughts were headed. Best to cut them off right now. He'd done his duty by the Young Ranchers' Club, and he'd made friends with those boys and their families. Now he had to concentrate on the cattlemen's association and putting an end to the cattle rustling. Other than making sure Lula May got to next Tuesday's meeting, he'd back off from intruding into her life.

Even so, he did have to admit he'd enjoyed teasing with her this evening. She dished out as good as she took it. He liked that. And he looked forward to seeing the family tomorrow at church. Did he have a clean shirt? With managing the boys all week, he hadn't thought about washing clothes, his most hated chore after cooking. Usually he got by with wearing his one white shirt two Sundays in a row because he changed clothes right after going home from church. Now that somehow didn't seem good enough. He could just see Lula May's blue eyes get all big and round with horror if he looked *unkempt*, one of Old Gad's favorite words.

Now why all of a sudden did he worry about her approval? Must be the way she silently inspected her children all the time, probably making sure they'd washed up good and proper. He didn't need that sort of thing from her.

Still, he did have to admit he'd enjoyed teasing with her. Could enjoy more of it. But maybe she wouldn't want to. Maybe because he wouldn't be going back anymore, the connection that had begun to grow between them would be broken. The thought pained him.

He lifted his eyes toward the fading light over the prairie sky. Time for an earnest prayer about the matter. "Lord, why do I keep thinking about that pretty little lady?"

In answer to his heartfelt prayer, only one thing came to mind. He'd see her at church services in the morning. While that thought settled his mind, his emotions jumped just about as high as the bright evening star blinking in the darkening sky. Even Zephyr perked up and began to prance down the road at the thought of it.

To Lula May's consternation, after the children jumped down from the wagon in front of the church tent, they ran over to Edmund and greeted him like a long-lost relative instead of a neighbor they'd seen the evening before. All except Calvin. Hands stuck in his trouser pockets, he strolled toward Daisy Carson, his face all moon-eyed like a sick puppy. Oh, my. The last thing she needed was for her eldest stepson to get too involved with a girl. Lula May knew a local couple who'd married at sixteen and went on to live happily. But Calvin lacked the background to become the good husband every woman needed and deserved. His father's long illness had prevented Calvin from receiving the benefit of the wisdom Frank had garnered from two good marriages. Not only that, Calvin just plain needed to do a bit more growing up.

As Lula May's worries reared up to pester her, Daisy said something to Calvin and then stomped away toward her sister Molly, who stood with her new husband, CJ Thorn, and Nancy Bennett. Calvin's posture slumped. While Lula May's heart went out to him, she couldn't help but be relieved. He was young. He'd get over it.

The moment she began to feel smug about Daisy's behavior, Edmund stepped over to the wagon and held out his hand. "May I help you down, Lula May?"

The woodsy smell of his cologne reached her senses as he gave her that crooked grin of his. Her heart jumped into her throat, preventing her from answering...until she caught the speculative looks in Molly Thorn's and Nancy Bennett's eyes, not to mention CJ's raised eyebrows. In the distance, Constance Hickey, the town gossip, frowned in Lula May's direction. The last thing she needed was that woman gossiping about her.

"I can manage just fine, thank you very much." Her words came out more harshly than she'd intended, but nothing could be done about that. She clambered down, admittedly without a hint of gracefulness. As she descended, her skirt snagged on a splinter on the wagon, and she had to gently pull it free to avoid a larger tear.

"Humph." Edmund's pleasant expression faded into a frown. "Whatever you say." He strode away toward the church tent where Pastor Stillwater stood greeting folks.

Lula May's heart dropped. Her carefully honed

self-sufficiency…in truth, her *pride*…had caused her to be rude to a man who didn't deserve it just because she feared a nosy gossip. For the past three years, she'd built up a wall around herself and her family as protection against anyone who might take advantage of Frank's illness to somehow exploit the situation or gossip about the family. This past week with Edmund's nightly visits, she'd grown soft, but now, with Uncle's arrival imminent, she knew she must reinforce her wall. That didn't mean she had to rebuff the mannerly gesture of a man who'd only done good for her children.

She started to follow him, but he was already deep in conversation with the pastor, so she couldn't exactly go over and apologize. And she wasn't about to invite him to dinner after church just to make up for her bad manners. Nor would she offer to iron his Sunday shirt, which definitely needed a woman's touch. She'd noticed a small scorch mark on the white cotton fabric right next to the lapel of his black frock coat. Did he know how to remove scorches? Was he like Frank, who, before he married Lula May, had ironed only the fronts of his shirts when he was going to wear a jacket because the back of the shirt wouldn't be seen? She grinned to herself at the memory.

"What's so funny?" Molly Thorn approached, her face beaming with joy, no doubt a result of her recent marriage to CJ.

"Yes, you have to tell us." Nancy Bennett followed closely behind Molly. She glanced toward Edmund, smirked and leaned toward Lula May. "And why on earth didn't you let Mr. McKay help you down?"

The longing note in her voice caused Lula May a second wave of regret over her rudeness. She'd noticed Lucas didn't extend much in the way of husbandly courtesies toward his new wife. Of course she could never say such a thing.

"No reason. Just like to get down by myself. And why wouldn't a gal smile on a fine Sunday morning like this?" She waved a hand toward the bright blue sky, where only a few fluffy clouds drifted along in the wind.

"Uh-huh." Molly traded a look with Nancy, and they giggled, reminding Lula May of the way her children had giggled last evening before supper.

"Hush now." She clicked her tongue. "You'll embarrass Mr. McKay, and you know he's a very private man." Not to mention they shouldn't incite Mrs. Hickey's censure.

"Uh-huh," Molly repeated as the three of them joined other folks making their way toward the church tent.

To Lula May's relief, after her two friends greeted Pastor Stillwater and headed into the tent, they abandoned their teasing and took on more reverent demeanors as befitting a time of worship. Lula May did her best to do the same. But with Uncle's visit looming over her, she feared she would spend more time in pleading with the Lord than in honoring and praising Him. This coming week—tomorrow, in fact—she would be faced with a problem almost as overwhelming as Frank's illness and death because it also threatened all she held dear. She had no one to turn to but the Lord, and she prayed He would come through for her, and even more so for her children.

Pastor Stillwater's sermon on forgiveness helped Edmund get over his annoyance with Lula May, but he still felt troubled by her behavior. After last night's pleasant supper, he thought they'd continue their friendship, as good neighbors should. But her moodiness, her typical "just fine" remark seemed intended to keep him from extending even the simplest of courtesies toward her. He'd decided early on last week that her moodiness wasn't his fault. Something was bothering her, but since she wouldn't tell him what it was, what could he do?

After deciding he would forgive and forget her snappiness, in fact act like it hadn't even happened, he couldn't keep from glancing at her across the aisle between the two rows of benches that filled the church tent. Edmund didn't know squat about women, but the way she bent her slender brown eyebrows into a frown shouted "worry." He silently prayed that the Lord would help her out, whatever the problem was.

In that moment, a familiar sensation took root in Edmund's chest, a strong conviction of what the Lord wanted him to do. Despite his resolve not to intrude into Lula May's life, he was to look out for her whether she wanted him to or not, just as the Lord had been urging him to do. Of course if he was clever enough, she wouldn't even know he was doing it. Never having been a subtle person, Edmund had no idea how he'd accomplish such a feat. He supposed that, like everything else in his life, he'd need to rely on the Lord's leading step by step.

Chapter Six

As if Uncle's impending visit were not enough of a tempest about to slam into Lula May's life, Monday morning a full-blown Texas summer rainstorm began to pound the High Bar Ranch. Black thunderclouds churned out of the west and over the prairie toward the rolling hills of her pasturelands, while lightning streaked across the darkening sky. Her older horses would have the good sense to take refuge beneath the ridge on the east side of the hills, and foals would stay with their mamas, but her untrained yearlings might head farther down into the arroyo. At this time of year and with this kind of storm, a flash flood could sweep them away in an instant.

"Jacob, you take care of Pauline and Daniel." Lula May tugged on her oldest boots and hat and her leather work gloves. "And you two mind your brother. Daniel, no foolishness, you hear me?"

"Yes, ma'am," her youngest son's eyes were wide with fear. He hated storms, and her maternal instinct longed to hold him and rock him while the wind blew. Unfortunately, she didn't have the luxury of time for such nurturing.

"Jacob, you keep an eye out. If you see a tornado, head for the root cellar. Other than that, do not leave the house, no matter what happens."

"Yes, ma'am." Jacob stood up tall and straight. While she could see fear in his eyes, she also saw resolve. Last week had done a world of good for him. She owed Edmund more than a few good meals for making a man of her ten-year-old son.

With a quick prayer for their safety, Lula May saddled up with Calvin and Samuel and headed out into the blinding rain to round up the herd. As expected, led by the wise old lead mare, the horses had gathered under the ridge, all except for four yearlings that had made a dash for the lowest area, an ancient riverbed that saw water only during a rare flash flood. Lula May told Calvin to use the extra rope they'd brought to make a temporary corral among the scrub trees in case the herd became frightened and decided to stampede. She and Samuel rode after the four yearlings and managed to rope three of the frightened animals and get them back to the herd. But one rascally colt eluded them.

"You boys take care of these. I'm going back for that stray." Lula May heard Calvin call out for her not to go, but she would not be deterred. Every horse equaled money that would provide for the family, and the obstinate colt she went after gave every sign of being an excellent cow pony once she got him trained. Saving him was worth the effort.

Back at the lower ridge above the arroyo, she dismounted and tied Lady to a tree, then made her way down to the colt, rope in hand. He skittered away a few yards like he thought she meant to play a game, tossing his wet black mane and nickering.

"Come on, beauty." She raised her voice over the downpour. "Come to Mama. You'll be glad you did." She pulled a carrot from her trouser pocket and held it out.

Just as he took a step toward her, a thunderous roar from the north drowned out all other sounds. The terrified colt shot up the slope just as a wall of water appeared some fifty yards up the arroyo, moving fast. Lula May clambered up the slippery slope but tangled her feet in the rope she'd brought to lasso the colt. Clawing desperately at the rocks, she struggled out of the rope but couldn't gain a foothold.

"Lord, help me!" She couldn't even hear her own voice against the roar of the fast approaching flood.

Something grabbed her arm. A hand. Two hands. Had Samuel or Calvin come to rescue her? All she knew for certain was that she was being dragged up the side of the arroyo, over the ridge and out of danger only seconds before the water's furious onslaught swept by, carrying away trees and bushes as if they were twigs. Seated on the muddy bank, she even saw the floating remnants of an old wagon box left by long-ago pioneers, like many possessions discarded as people moved west.

Only when she stood up with the help of her rescuer did she realize her hat and one of her boots were gone.

"Oh, my." She shook off her shock, stood and brushed wet hair from her face, then turned to greet... Edmund? "Where did you come from?"

Even in the blinding rain as a torrent of water poured off the brim of his hat like a curtain, she could see his grin. "Just happened by. You see, I've got this ranch over the hill." Pointing west, he shouted into the wind, but she heard the humor in his voice. "Was out for a ride this fine day when I noticed you were about to go for a swim."

She tried to laugh, but only a sob came out. "I see." Her feet started to slip down the slope, and she grabbed his forearm to steady herself. He responded by grasping her upper arms and pulling her farther away from the churning arroyo. The strength of his grip sent a welcomed shock of warmth through her on this cold summer day.

"You okay?"

"I'm fine." She swept her stringy hair away from her face again. "Just fine. Gotta get back to my horses."

She marched past him toward her poor mare, who looked about as sad and bedraggled as any creature could. Only in that moment did Lula May realize she was crying. And she hadn't even thanked Edmund for saving her life. She swung back around just in time to see him mount his horse and ride after the pesky colt that had almost cost her her life.

Even with the rain beating down on him and his pulse still racing wildly, Edmund couldn't stop laughing at the picture in his mind: neat, tidy Lula May Barlow soaking wet, covered in reddish-gray mud, no hat, one boot missing. In spite of her condition, he had to admit she looked awful pretty. And he was getting used to her "just fine" claims. She seemed to say the words at the very moments when she was anything but just fine. If he hadn't come along, she'd be halfway to Mexico by now, swept away in that deadly flash flood.

His heart had nearly stopped when he saw the water headed her way as she tried to claw her way up that slickery ravine. Thank the Lord he'd been able to snatch her out of harm's way. Now what else could he do to help her that wouldn't be too obvious? Get that rascally colt, he supposed.

After two attempts and a bit of chasing, he lassoed the yearling. The feisty animal had almost got Lula May killed, but he could see why she'd made the effort to save him. Good conformation, a gleam in his eye, a spirited nature. After Lula May trained him, Edmund might consider buying this one for his remuda. He'd be a good reminder of today's adventure.

Earlier, when the storm rose up, Edmund and his hands had headed out to see to his cattle so they wouldn't stampede. The nine men working for him knew what to do in this kind of weather, so he hadn't needed to give any special orders. Then, right in the middle of rounding up some mavericks scared by lightning, Edmund had felt the urge to check on Lula May. He'd left orders with his foreman, Abel, and then rode over to her place. Jacob told him where to find her, and since the boy was doing a fine job of taking care of the younger ones, Edmund hurried after their ma.

He crossed the arroyo on Zephyr just in time to see her trying to scramble out of it, and he grabbed her hand, dug his boot heels into the rocky, soggy ground and held on for all he was worth as he pulled her up.

If she'd been a stray calf, he would have done the same thing. But his heart wouldn't still be pounding over the near tragedy. He thanked the Lord he'd got her to safety. Those young'uns had already lost their pa. They needed their ma something fierce. And to his consternation, Edmund was beginning to feel a strange sort of kinship to the woman himself.

Whoa! He had to stop that nonsense. She was a widow, a neighbor, someone the Lord wanted him to look after, like the Good Book said to do. But unless the Lord spoke out loud to him like He did to Moses at the burning bush, he had no intention of taking their friendship any further.

Once the storm passed and the horses were tended to, Lula May and the boys made their way back to the house. To her relief, the younger children were fine. In fact, they'd already fixed sandwiches for everyone. Even though the kitchen was a mess, they'd occupied themselves in a healthy way while she and their older brothers took care of business, just the way a family ought to operate. And one day soon, she'd make a cake for Edmund as a thank-you for saving her life.

She sat down to eat her late lunch, ignoring the dryness of the ham salad Jacob had concocted. She washed it down with the bitter coffee Pauline had boiled. They both needed a few more lessons in the kitchen, but at times like this, having anything to eat was cause for thanks.

She and the older boys hadn't sat at the table for five minutes when she looked up at the wall clock. "Four fifteen! How did it get so late?" If the storm hadn't held up the train, Uncle would be at the station by now, and he'd be furious over having to wait for her to pick him up.

She jumped to her feet and headed for the back door, remembering to grab a random boot to replace her lost one. This one must be Jacob's because it pinched her toes. "I'll be back in a while. Gotta run to town."

"Can't I go for you, Ma?" Calvin followed her outside.

"Just help me hitch up the wagon." Her stepson would find out soon enough about the trouble she was bringing home. She needed to be present when each one of her children met Uncle.

As she drove toward Little Horn, her pulse raced, and her heart filled with dread. If she'd been swept away in the flood this afternoon, Uncle might have come out to her ranch and taken over the children's lives, as he'd tried to do to hers years ago. Might still try to do. She would fight him all the way, but who knew what he'd throw at her. She'd decided not to mention the necklace to him. Would let him do all the talking, then figure out how to deal with whatever scheme he had up his sleeves.

Sure enough, he stood on the rain-soaked platform, frowning as he checked his pocket watch and tapping his foot impatiently. He was just as she remembered him, although with considerably more wrinkles on his pasty round face. As stout as he'd always been, he wore a rumpled tan suit, a white shirt and a black string tie. Straw-like gray hair stuck out from beneath the broad brim of his white hat. A red tapestry carpetbag sat at his feet, and, as always, his silver-headed ebony cane hung on his left arm. Lula May's back ached at the memory of the few times he'd used it on her. If he tried to use it on the children, she didn't know what she'd do, but she'd stop him one way or another.

"Well, there you are." He scowled at her and emitted a curse word she hadn't heard in eleven years. "Look at you, girlie. What a disgusting sight. But I didn't expect anything better of you. Don't you ever take a bath? Don't you even own a dress?"

For the briefest instant, Lula May couldn't figure out what he was talking about. Then she looked down at her muddy trousers and mismatched boots. Felt the tangled, mud-caked strings of her hair hanging over her shoulders. More memories of his past cruel remarks rose up to taunt her, accompanied by the bile rising up in her throat. For another brief instant, she started to answer in kind to this despicable man. Started to tell him to take the next train out of town and never try to come back into her life.

But what if he carried out his threats? What if he could have her arrested and put in jail? A quick glance down the street revealed Sheriff Fuller going door to door, probably checking up on everyone after the storm. If given the right evidence, even if it was a lie, would he arrest her?

Lula May swallowed hard and glared at Uncle. "Where's the rest of your baggage?" She might have to endure his presence, but she didn't have to be pleasant to him. At least not until they got to the ranch, where she'd need to set an example for the children.

"Hey, Miz Barlow." Amos Crenshaw, the middle-aged stationmaster, emerged from the depot and gave her his usual friendly smile that crinkled his deeply tanned complexion. "This fine gentleman tells me he's your uncle and he's come to live with you." His hazel eyes were lit with good humor, as always. "You're a lucky lady, being a widow and all, to have a close relative come out here to help you." He tipped his round black stationmaster's hat at Uncle and then placed the carpetbag into the back of the wagon. "Mr. Jones, I'll have that trunk loaded into Miz Barlow's wagon as soon as I find my helper." He hurried off.

Lula May snorted. Uncle was still the same *fine gentleman* who'd always put on airs and fooled people into believing he was good to the bone.

"Where did you learn such an unladylike sound?" Uncle climbed into the wagon, huffing out heavy breaths. "From the local cowboys?" In spite of his condemning tone, he opened his arms as if to embrace her.

Lula May instinctively pulled back. "Don't touch me."

Uncle's expression turned uglier than usual as he lowered his arms. "Had no plan to touch you, girlie, filthy as you are."

"Here you go." Mr. Crenshaw and his son, James, lugged the round-topped trunk along the platform and hefted it into the back of the wagon. "Y'all have a good day, y'hear?" He lifted that round hat in another salute.

"Much obliged, sir." Uncle's face grew jolly. "You have a good day, too. And may the good Lord bless you."

Lula May's churning stomach twisted even tighter. While waiting for her to arrive, Uncle must have learned that Mr. Crenshaw was a church deacon and now sought to impress the man with his own "saintly" ways. Knowing Mr. Crenshaw, by nightfall he'd have it all over town how fortunate she was to have a godly relative come to take care of her.

Pasting on a smile, she waved at the two men on the platform and then turned her team toward the road out of town.

"Girlie, you manage these horses just like a man, but don't you dare take that as a compliment. Ladies should never soil their hands with driving wagons."

As if a day hadn't passed since he'd seen her, Uncle launched into his old habit of criticizing everything and everyone. She'd brought a wagon instead of a proper buggy, and riding in a wagon was beneath the dignity of a man of his importance. From the looks of the town, he didn't think it was fit for decent people to live in. He was ashamed to be seen with her because she looked like a drowned cat.

She held back another snort. He had no idea how close that last insult came to reality. Rather than defending herself or explaining what had happened during the storm, Lula May clamped her mouth shut and prayed for grace to endure whatever Uncle planned to dish out for however long he planned to stay.

After Edmund learned from Abel, his foreman, that all the cattle had weathered the storm without injury, he washed the mud off his hair and clothes at the newly refilled water tank by the barn. Then he went inside, changed into a fresh outfit and headed into town. He was too tired to fix a meal, yet hungry as a bear from all of that activity during the storm. Lula May's cooking had spoiled him, so he'd made up his mind to eat at Mercy Green's café. At least this way he'd have something decent for supper. He couldn't do it every night, but it would give him a chance to check up on Mercy's son, Alec. For a boy raised in the city, Alec had done pretty well last week in spite of a twisted ankle on Saturday. To his credit, he hadn't cried as Edmund checked it for a possible break. With his father working for the railroad and gone most of the time, the boy had eaten up the attention Edmund and his hands had given him.

Up ahead of him on the road, a wagon lumbered into view coming from town. Even at a distance, it wasn't hard to make out Lula May driving the horses *or* that a man was seated beside her. Edmund's heart dipped a bit. Maybe she'd been so quiet about her life because she'd taken another mail-order husband. The thought was so unexpected and so depressing, Edmund turned his horse off into a side road and hid like a coward behind a stand of trees.

As soon as they'd passed by, he wanted to kick himself. From the way Lula May leaned away from the portly old man, she wasn't pleased to be in his company. Was she in danger? Should he ride after them?

No, that would be a mistake. Lula May didn't seem scared, just…well, *disgusted.* Maybe the man had brought bad news. Whatever the reason, Edmund still felt called of the Lord to watch out for her, at least from a distance. Except in this situation, he had no idea what to do. It wasn't like he could barge into her house and demand to know who the old coot was.

Whoa. No need to insult the man when he could very well be a fine, upstanding citizen. One would think Edmund was jealous. Well, he wasn't. No sir. Lula May could have company anytime she wanted to, and it was none of his business.

As he turned Zephyr back toward town, his appetite didn't seem quite so sharp. He gazed up into the evening sky and shook his head. "Lord, are You sure I'm still supposed to be watching out for Lula May? Or did You just want me to stick around until I needed to pull her out of that arroyo today?" For which she hadn't managed so much as a simple thank-you. Not that she'd had a chance, but still— "If You've sent a replacement protector, please let me know before I make a fool of myself."

In truth, from the way his heart had dropped just seeing her with another man, it was already too late. He was forced to admit that he cared about her. Cared about her a whole heap. But maybe this was best. He'd never planned to court her. Now there was probably no danger of that happening accidentally.

"Whew! See what I escaped?" He leaned down and patted Zephyr's neck. "No, sir. I have no plans to court Lula May or any other female." He thought about her stubbornness, her peevishness, for a moment. "Especially not Lula May."

The stallion responded with a toss of his head and a hearty whicker. If Edmund actually believed his horse understood him, he'd think he'd just been scolded.

As Lula May reined the horses toward the house, the children came out to greet her, just as she'd known they would. All the way home, she'd tried to think of how to protect them from Uncle's cruel words. She couldn't be with each one of them as they went about their various chores. Calvin and Samuel might be old enough to shrug off any criticism because they'd been around tough cowboys all their lives. But the younger ones, especially Jacob, could easily be hurt, maybe for life.

From the bewildered expressions on all of their faces, she could see the importance of taking charge before Uncle spoke. With a deep breath, she put on the most pleasant smile she could manage and jumped down from the driver's bench.

"Children, come say hello to Mr. Floyd Jones. He'll be staying with us for a few days."

Uncle clambered to the ground, chuckling like Clement Moore's jolly old elf in "'Twas the Night Before Christmas."

"Now, now, Lula May, you do not expect my niece and nephews to call me Mr. Jones, do you?" If she didn't know better, she'd think he was as wounded as his tone suggested. "Miss Barlow." He gave Pauline a courtly bow, and she gave him her sweetest, most accepting smile. "Gentlemen." He honored each of her four sons with a nod. "I am your mama's uncle Floyd, and that is what you must call me."

The children turned confused, questioning gazes on Lula May.

"That's right. This is my uncle Floyd. Calvin and Samuel, will you please unload his trunk and then see to the horses and wagon?" How would she manage the other three? Fully aware of the mud caked all over her, at least what the rain hadn't washed off after her near drowning, she could only think of one solution. She gave them a playful grin and beckoned to them. "Come with me to the horse trough and help me get rid of all this mud." She waved a hand toward the house. "Uncle, go sit a spell in the kitchen." He'd have plenty to complain about when he saw that messy room. "We'll have you some supper shortly."

Not waiting for a reply, she marched off toward the barn with her children in tow. She didn't trust Uncle alone in the house, but she trusted him even less with the children if she wasn't there to deflect any cruel thing he might say to them.

Once at the side of the barn, she gave each child a bucket, then took off her boots and stepped into the horse trough. "I want you to pour water over me until this mud's all gone."

Giggling with delight, the children took turns dousing her with bucket after bucketful of the cold rainwater until she was once again soaked to the skin and her clothes were moderately free of mud. It would have to do.

When Calvin and Samuel joined her, her oldest stepson took charge of the questioning. "Who's that man, Ma? You never told us you had a living relative."

She gazed around at the sweet, innocent looks in all of their eyes. Other than the cattle rustling, which hadn't touched their family yet and probably never would, they'd never seen true evil up close. How could she explain Uncle without making them scared to be in the same house with him? The Lord knew *she* was scared to be with the old man, so she lifted a silent prayer for wisdom.

"We didn't have the best parting when I came out here to marry your pa eleven years ago." She took a reluctant step toward the house. The longer Uncle was alone, the more chances he had to sneak around her house. Two days ago in anticipation of his coming, she'd hidden all of her important papers in the secret place Frank had devised in the office. She hadn't had a chance to lock the office, but a locked door had never stopped Uncle.

"Maybe he came out to make amends." Ever the optimist, Samuel spoke with a hopeful tone.

Lula May held on to a bitter laugh trying to burst out of her. "We'll see. You all treat him with respect, but..." She clamped down on a warning to ignore anything he might say that was hurtful.

Stopping at the back door, she made eye contact with each of her precious children. Her two stepsons traded a look and gave her a nod. Understanding seemed to fill their eyes. Her own children stared at her, their eyes round.

To her surprise, Calvin took over where she'd left off. "Treat him with respect and good manners, just like you taught us, eh, Ma?"

"That's right, son." Lula May felt a bit of the weight shift off her chest. "Pauline, honey, run get me a towel so I don't track water all the way to my room."

Her daughter dashed indoors to obey. Lula May prayed Uncle wouldn't waylay her.

"Jacob and Daniel, you go set the table. Samuel, are the cows milked?" If she spread them out with chores, she'd have a chance to change clothes before gathering them all to help with supper.

"It's all done, Ma." Calvin gave her his cute grin that all the girls at church liked so much.

"We didn't know where or how long you'd be gone," Samuel said, "but we figured we'd all have to eat."

"You gotta forgive Calvin for the tough biscuits." Jacob snickered as he talked, and Calvin responded by ruffling Jacob's hair. Teasing his older brother was something new for Jacob, something she needed to thank Edmund for, along with saving her life.

As if hearing her thoughts about the man, Daniel said, "Sure do wish Mr. McKay was coming to supper tonight." He poked his thumb into his mouth, a sign that her anxiety about Uncle was rubbing off on him. For his sake, she needed to hide her emotions better.

His brothers voiced their agreement with Daniel, which sent an odd prickle down Lula May's spine. If

Edmund were here, it would certainly make things…
interesting.

As she stepped into the mudroom, she caught the
aroma of must-go stew, the children's favorite concoction of leftovers because it never tasted the same. Whatever they had in the icebox was dumped into the pot
and generously flavored with onions and a few sprigs
of cilantro and served over biscuits. What clever children she had. Her stomach rumbled, but fortunately not
loud enough for Uncle to hear through the doorway.
According to what he'd always said, real ladies never
let on they were hungry. She'd never been able to figure
out how a person could keep a growling stomach quiet.

Once Pauline brought the towel and Lula May
had patted herself as dry as possible, she entered the
kitchen, expecting to see the mess she'd left in a hurry
two hours ago. Instead, the room was as nearly spotless
as a kitchen could be while meal preparations were in
progress. The floor was swept. Counters were wiped
down. Cooking utensils washed and put away. Only her
cast-iron pot bubbled on the stove, and a pan of biscuits
sat on the counter covered with a tea towel. Tears stung
Lula May's eyes, and for the first time since she'd received Uncle's first letter, she felt sure that she and the
children would make it through this trial.

The feeling lasted for about three seconds. Then
she looked at Uncle's oily, ingratiating smile, and her
stomach turned.

Chapter Seven

Edmund spooned another bite of stew into his mouth and chewed on the tough meat. Lula May's stew had been tastier, the gravy thicker and the meat more tender. Her biscuits were lighter, her coffee tastier and her family better company than the empty chair across from him in Mercy Green's café.

He heaved out a sigh. Lula May had spoiled him, that was certain. How she could manage everything from cooking to keeping house to raising five children to breeding and training prime cow ponies, and do it all very well, was beyond him. No wonder she was so independent. She didn't need a man to take care of her like his sister-in-law Betsy needed his brother Josiah. Not that Edmund thought he should take care of Lula May any further than the Lord directed from one day to the next. No, sir. He had enough to do what with running his own place and participating in the cattlemen's association. Those rustlers had to be stopped, so Edmund didn't have time to involve himself with a woman. Besides, there was still the matter of his preference for peace and quiet in the evening.

Against his better judgment, he ordered a slice of apple pie topped with cream. He didn't expect it to live up to Lula May's, and he was right. Maybe Mercy used a different kind of apple because this pie was tart as all get out.

"'Evening, McKay." Hank Snowden entered the café and hung his hat on a peg by the door. "Mind if I join you?"

"Have a seat." Edmund waved him to the empty chair.

Before he could whisper a warning, Snowden ordered a bowl of stew. Mercy brought it right out, and he dug in. "Boy, this is good. Best I've tasted in a long while."

Edmund considered contradicting his friend, but decided against it. No need to tempt another bachelor, a good-looking one at that, to ride out and sample Lula May's cooking. *Oh, no.* There he went again, thinking about that pretty, blue-eyed widow lady when he should be asking Lucas Bennett's representative at the cattlemen's meetings about work.

"How'd your herd make out today during the storm?"

"Not too bad." Snowden chewed into a biscuit that looked about as tough as the hardtack Edmund had eaten during his few seafaring days. "We didn't get hit by the storm as bad as you folks over there on the west side of the county. How about you?"

"We had a few mavericks get spooked, but no injuries to man or beast." Edmund felt the urge to tell him about Lula May's near disaster, but couldn't figure out a way to say it without bragging. Or sounding crazy by saying he knew for sure the Lord had sent him to the arroyo.

He should talk about tomorrow night's meeting of the ranchers. He remembered that Lula May would be coming with him, and his spirits lifted considerably. Maybe he could wrangle an invitation to supper beforehand. *Whoa.* Why couldn't he stop thinking about her? Best to think of a different, safer person to discuss. "You think Bennett will be at the meeting tomorrow night?"

"Nope." Snowden shook his head, and confusion crossed his face. "You'd think he'd want to know what's happening firsthand. In fact, last week after I returned from our meeting, he wanted to know all the details." He frowned. "He got a bit riled when I said we voted to let Lula May Barlow join us. Said it was no place for a woman."

"Humph." Edmund tried not to let his indignation show. If Lucas Bennett refused to attend, he hardly had any right to say Lula May couldn't. Besides, it had been Edmund's idea for her to come, and he wasn't about to turn around and tell her she had to stay home. "So, have you all lost any cattle to the rustlers?"

"Nope." Snowden took a swig of coffee. "The boys and I take turns keeping watch every night, so rustlers would have a hard time getting past us. How about you?"

"None since that first time." Edmund shook his head

at the memory. "They got about twenty head. Since then, like you and Lucas, I've kept a half dozen cowhands out every night. Rustlers would be fools to come against that many guns."

They chatted about the price of feed and a few other mundane matters. Just to be sociable, Edmund stayed while Snowden finished his supper. After he had dessert, they parted company and went their separate ways with a "See you tomorrow night."

With no sense of urgency to get home, Edmund gave Zephyr his head and cantered most of the way. When they neared the arched entryway into his property, he expected Zephyr to slow, but the stallion kept up his pace, passing the drive and continuing eastward toward the High Bar Ranch.

"Whoa, boy. Whoa." Edmund reined the animal to a stop. "What's the matter with you? One week of going over there and you think that's where we live now?" He nudged Zephyr with his knees and reined him around toward home. "Stupid horse."

In response, the stallion whickered and tossed his head. As he had on the way into town, Edmund got the strangest impression that Zephyr was scolding him.

But of course that was just his imagination.

"A very fine meal, children." In spite of her words of praise, Lula May had to force herself to eat the concoction they'd made for supper. Even though the leftover ham, steak, potatoes and black-eyed peas tasted surprisingly good all mixed together, she no longer had an appetite. Having to stare down the length of her dinner table at Uncle, who'd sat himself in Frank's chair as if he owned it, was much different from seeing Edmund seated there. Downright turned her stomach.

The children seemed to understand they wouldn't use the talking feather tonight because the adults would lead the conversation. Eating quietly and with good manners, they didn't tease each other, but maintained a proper interest in what was being said, just as they'd been taught. Uncle would find no cause to criticize them, at least at mealtime. At least not a valid cause.

"You must tell us about your trip." Lula May took care to speak in a well-modulated tone to avoid Uncle's censure. According to what he'd always said, ladies never raised their voices.

"I thought you'd never ask." He broke a biscuit into his second bowl of stew and spooned some gravy over it from the tureen. From the gleam in his eyes, she could see he was still hungry and that he liked the stew. If he criticized it, she'd point that out to him.

He launched into a spirited, lengthy account of his travels from Alabama to Texas. Lula May had to give him credit for being able to tell a story in an interesting way, something she'd never realized before this night. The children all listened wide-eyed at his description of his train crossing the Mississippi River on tracks built on a high trellis over the deep, flowing waters. Lula May barely remembered her own journey to Texas because she'd been so scared he'd be right behind her trying to drag her back to Alabama to marry his horrid old friend.

As he spoke, however, she began to wonder whether he'd changed. Maybe he hadn't come to destroy their lives. Then halfway into his disparaging descriptions of some of his fellow passengers, she saw glimpses of his old wiliness and realized he was doing just what he'd done with Amos Crenshaw at the train station. Charm them, win them, then take power over them. But with all of her insights, she had no idea how to keep her children from falling into his trap. Her only defense was to take charge before he did, so she stopped him at the end of a sentence as he paused to breathe.

"We'll have to hear the rest of your story another time." She stood, and the children did likewise. "Chore time, then an early bedtime."

Unspoken questions hung in the air as the children cast bewildered glances her way. Even before Edmund started coming over, they'd always enjoyed their evenings in the parlor at the end of each day. But Lula May was not about to let Uncle get that cozy with her family, at least not on his first night here. Never, in fact, if she had anything to do with it. She gave the younger children a gentle flick of her hand, and they set about clearing the table.

While Uncle had talked about his trip, she'd considered where to put him for the night. She'd thought about putting him in the room Frank had built in the barn for the occasional wandering cowboys needing a resting spot for a night or two. But she wouldn't be able to keep an eye on Uncle if he was out there. Only one solution presented itself.

"Calvin, Samuel, would you please move your things out to the barn? Uncle Floyd can use your room for the short time he's here."

Before Uncle could contradict her words, her step-sons chorused their eagerness to go along with the plan.

"We've been wanting to sleep out there," Calvin said, "ever since the cattle rustling started."

"Yep." Samuel have a decisive nod. "It'd be just like those snakes to steal our few head of cattle because they think we can't defend ourselves."

Lula May's heart twisted in two directions. She was proud of them for wanting to protect their property, but thinking of them in a shoot-out with rustlers sent a jolt of fear through her. "Never mind about that. Just get a move on so Uncle Floyd can settle in for the night. I'm sure he's tired from his travels."

The boys hurried away like they were going to a picnic.

"What's this about cattle rustling?" Uncle Floyd gave her a long, narrow-eyed look, like he thought it was her fault.

"Nothing to worry about." Lula May gave an indifferent sniff. "The ranchers have formed a cattlemen's association to put an end to it. They'll be meeting tomorrow night." Too much information! She needed to be more careful about what she said to him.

Uncle puffed up like a bantam rooster. "Well, now, seems like I have arrived just in time to represent this paltry piece of property at that meeting." He pulled a cigar from his jacket pocket. "Where did that husband of yours put his humidor? I need a light."

Lula May glared at him, something she'd refrained from when the children were present. "You'll not be smoking that stinky cigar in my house."

He returned the glare, but put away the horrid brown roll. "Now, where is this meeting? I shall require your buggy to get there."

Lula May ground her teeth for a moment. "Not a good idea, Floyd. This meeting is by invitation only, and you're not invited." She wouldn't mention that she almost hadn't been included, either. "Something you need to know about these Texans is that they don't like it when people push themselves in where they're not welcomed."

"Humph. Seems like Southern hospitality does not extend to this wilderness, even if Texas did fight for the Confederacy." He found his way into the parlor where he made himself at home in Frank's chair and picked up a cattlemen's journal. No doubt he'd try to pick up some local jargon so he could impress any ranchers he might meet.

When the boys brought in his trunk, he didn't make a move to help, just as Lula May expected. She left him in the parlor where he couldn't get into any trouble… or do any snooping. Getting the sleeping arrangements organized and putting the younger children to bed took most of the evening. She sat at each of their bedsides to hear their prayers, ending with Pauline, who had slept with her since Frank's death. Lula May made sure Uncle was fast asleep before she checked the safe and locked the office door.

She lay awake for some time recounting the day's happenings. A moment of delayed but quiet hysteria set in when she recalled almost being swept away in the flash flood. Not only had she forgotten to thank Edmund, she'd also forgotten to thank the Lord. Kneeling beside her bed, she wiped away tears of gratitude as she whispered her prayer. She climbed back into bed with three firm resolutions for tomorrow. She would somehow manage Uncle and keep him from harming her family. She would impress the men at the cattlemen's meeting. And she would bake Edmund a lemon cake that he'd never forget.

The next morning, Lula May wasn't the least bit surprised when Uncle slept in, which pleased her no end because the family could return to its normal routine now that Jacob's week at Edmund's ranch had ended. The children seemed eager to finish their chores, and they kept returning to the kitchen where she had begun her baking and supper preparations. Maybe they hoped to see Uncle. She still hadn't figured out a way to let them know he wasn't to be trusted. Nor did she wish for them to be alone with him.

With horses needing to be trained today, she decided to take the younger ones out to the pasture with her, but that would be later this morning. Maybe this evening they all could go to town and she could leave them with Mercy Green while she attended the cattlemen's meeting. Anything to keep them away from Uncle when she couldn't be present.

After a trip to the garden to pull onions for tonight's chicken supper, Lula May found all five children whispering and giggling in the kitchen.

"What mischief are you all up to?" She hid a smile at their sudden silence.

They traded looks and grins.

"Nothing." Samuel blinked his blue eyes, looking decidedly guilty.

"Nothing," chorused the others.

"Uh-huh." Lula May gave them each a stern look. "Looks like I need to put you all to work. Calvin, don't you have some fencing to mend? That new barbed wire is in the barn."

"Yes, ma'am." He winked at the others and headed out the door.

"The rest of you…" Lula May thought for a moment. "There's a garden to weed, dogs and chickens to feed and horses to tend. Get busy."

They dashed away to obey just as Uncle wandered into the kitchen and looked expectantly at the stove.

"Breakfast ready?" He coughed and wheezed and cleared his throat noisily.

"That covered plate on the back of the stove is for you. Help yourself to coffee."

He frowned and grumbled something about having to serve himself, but Lula May continued mixing Edmund's cake. A stray thought shot across her mind. Wouldn't it be nice if Edmund were the man sitting down at her kitchen table instead of Uncle? Just as quick, she rejected the thought. No need to complicate her life by thinking of her handsome neighbor.

After eating his eggs, bacon and biscuits, complaining all the time about how cold they were, Uncle sat back to sip his coffee. And to pester Lula May.

"That bedroom is a might drafty. You need to get a man out here to fix it before the weather turns cold.

I have rheumatism and cannot stand the cold like I used to."

"You won't be here for the cold." Lula May beat the cake batter with extra vigor.

"That is what you think, girlie." He spoke matter-of-factly, as though she had no say in his decision. "I sold my place back home and packed my meager belongings in that one trunk so I could be near my only living kin. 'Course those older boys are not my kin, but they will likely desert you when they are old enough to go it alone. And I have already seen how your real offspring need a man's hand to guide them. No, missy, don't be expecting me to run out on my duty to family like you did."

Lula May cringed. Should she throw him out now or let him finish his threats? After all these years, all of Frank's kindnesses, all the respect Edmund had shown her, why did she have to struggle not to fall back into her old acquiescing ways?

"I'm ashamed of you for not wearing widow's weeds." Uncle pulled out his cigar. "How long has that husband of yours been dead? Not even a year. You could at least wear a dress, as fitting a lady. I'm ashamed of you for dressing like a man." He went to the stove and bent to light the cigar.

Lula May stopped whipping her batter. "I told you don't light that nasty thing in here." If he did, she'd consider dumping the whole bowlful over his head.

Grunting with disgust, he put it away and sat back down.

"How did you find me, Floyd?" The question had

nagged at her since his first letter arrived. "How did you know my husband died?"

"I will never tell you that." He chuckled in his unpleasant way. "Just know that some of your neighbors were glad to tell me all they knew about you…for a price."

An icy chill swept down Lula May's back. Who would sell information about her? Who would hate her that much? Yet, as she rejected everyone she knew as the culprit, another thought took precedence. This was Uncle's way of manipulating her: keep her from trusting her neighbors, make her fearful and alone and then take control of her life with the pretext of taking care of her.

"Now about my mama's necklace." He took a long drink of his coffee. "I want to see it as soon as you get that cake in the oven. I am assuming it is a welcome cake for me."

"No and no." Gulping down her fears and trepidation, Lula May poured the batter into two round tin pans she'd greased and floured. She set the bowl and spoon aside for the children to lick when they came back inside. "The cake is for a neighbor who did me a favor." More than a favor. He'd saved her life!

Another grunt of disgust. "Well, go get that necklace, then. I want to see how you have taken care of it after stealing it from me. Where on earth would you wear it around here anyway? While I waited so long for you at the train station, I did not even see a hotel where a ball could be held. And these ranch houses are nothing like the plantation house where I grew up. Do you wear it to church to show it off? To pretend to be some fine lady, which you are not?"

Holding her temper as best she could, Lula May gently set the cake pans in the oven, closed the door and checked the fire.

"Well, go get it." Uncle poured himself another cup of coffee and then slammed the pot back down on the stove. If he did that again once her cake rose and made it fall, she wouldn't be responsible for her actions. "What are you waiting for?"

She fisted her hands at her waist. Might as well get this over with. "I don't have *my* mother's necklace."

"What?" Uncle took a menacing step toward her.

In the corner of her eye, she saw her rolling pin on the cabinet counter. If he hit her...

"I don't have my mother's necklace. When Frank got sick, I sold it to pay bills." She'd paid off the ranch and had managed to keep it going since then, with a little left over in the bank for a rainy day. But she wouldn't tell him that.

"Sold it?" He slumped back down onto the chair, and his pasty face grew paler. "Sold it!"

His pale blue eyes blazed, and he sputtered as if unable to think of words strong enough to condemn her. Finally, he sat back and a slow, evil grin spread across his face. "Well, well, now, how are you going to pay me back so I will not have to call the law on you? Hmm?" As though he'd planned it all along, he grunted with satisfaction in answer to his own question. "Why, I will just take this puny little farm off your hands. 'Course, those older boys will have to go, but if you are real good to me, you and those three brats of yours, I may just let you stay here and work it for me."

Seated in his sparsely equipped kitchen, Edmund picked up the stale beef sandwich Mushy had sent over from the bunkhouse and bit into it. It was dry, as usual, but he might as well get used to it. The days of looking forward to Lula May's fine cooking had come to an end.

In spite of yesterday's excitement during the storm, the ranch had seemed awful quiet these past few days. He missed those young'uns being here. Missed having supper at the Barlow ranch each evening. He'd tried to convince himself he was glad to go back to his silent, solitary meals, but it was no use. Not that he could do anything about it. Might as well finish his noon meal and get back out to the barn to mend those weakened stalls.

Just as he set his plate and coffee cup into the sink, a knock sounded on the back door. Expecting to see one of his cowhands, he opened it.

"Pauline!" He couldn't keep the surprise and gladness from his voice. Behind the sweet little gal, who looked like a miniature version of her mama except for the child's red hair, stood Jacob and Daniel. "What are you young'uns doing here?" He glanced out into the barnyard with the vague hope that Lula May would be with them…and tried not to show his disappointment that she wasn't. All he saw was Jacob's horse tied to the hitching rail. The three of them must have ridden over here together.

"Mama thinks you need to work on your imagination." Pauline held out a book. "This will help you."

Edmund laughed out loud. One of their disagreements had been about an idea of hers that he said was impractical, the one about the cattlemen's association gathering food for the less fortunate in the community. He'd countered that the project was more suited to the ladies' quilting bee. To his surprise, she'd agreed. It was the first debate with her that he'd won. And yet here she'd sent him a book to stir up his imagination.

"Why, thank you, young lady."

Edmund took the volume in hand and read the title: *Robinson Crusoe.* Had Lula May noticed the time he'd looked at her library and thought he'd focused on this one? His hopes of discussing books with her hadn't been realized or she would know he already owned a copy of it, along with a substantial collection of other titles, some of which she didn't appear to own. What he really wanted to borrow was her *A Tale of Two Cities.*

Before he returned the book to Pauline, he had an idea. Maybe this was Lula May's way of inviting him back over to her place. In response to her challenge to his imagination, he would dig out his copy of the pamphlet *Common Sense*, tuck it inside the book, and take it over to her this afternoon, then ask if he could borrow the Dickens book. Maybe she'd invite him to stay for supper and they could go to the cattlemen's association meeting together. He'd feel better knowing she wasn't traveling back home alone after dark.

No, that might not work. He recalled the man who'd been in the wagon with Lula May last evening. He didn't want to seem nosy, and he sure didn't want her or these children to know he'd hidden from view as they passed by. He still felt awful foolish for that. If he hadn't ducked behind that stand of trees, he'd already know who the man was.

"How's your ma?" Had she told them about the flash flood? Had she recovered from the near tragedy?

"She's fine." Jacob stepped up beside his sister, followed by little Daniel. "You need anything done around here?" He inspected the front of the barn like he felt responsible for it.

Edmund coughed to hide a laugh. These young'uns sure did keep on surprising him. "No, thank you, son. My cowhands pretty much have it under control." He glanced back into the kitchen where a plate of Mushy's molasses cookies sat on the table. They were among the few tasty things his cook made.

"You all want some cookies?" He'd gladly sacrifice the treat to find out what he wanted to know, despite feeling sneaky for doing it.

"Sure."

"Yessir."

"Uh-huh." They spoke at the same time, and their faces lit up in anticipation.

Edmund had them sit on the back stoop while he fetched the plate, then let them dig in while he went back for a pitcher of milk from his icebox and some tin cups. Nothing in his house resembled the pretty china Lula May had, but the children didn't seem to mind.

While they enjoyed their treat, he tried again to find out about that stranger. "What are your mama and brothers doing today?" He sat down beside them with his long legs stuck out uncomfortably in front of him.

"Ma and Samuel are working with some of the cow ponies," Jacob said. "We were gonna help her, but she said we were more trouble than help so—"

For some odd reason, Pauline punched her brother's arm. "So this was a good time for us to bring you the book."

Daniel clearly didn't want to be left out of the conversation. "Calvin's out working on that broken fence between our property and yours."

"Hmm." Was it only a week and a day ago when Lula May had been insulted by his comments about that fence? No matter. He still wasn't finding out what he wanted to know. Being a loner all his life, a very private person who shielded himself from anyone who tried to pry into his life, he hadn't figured out the subtleties of drawing from other people information that bordered on being downright nosy.

"We have company." Daniel, whose lips had cookie crumbs and milk all over them, blinked innocently. "He's our uncle."

Relief swept through Edmund like yesterday's flash flood had swept down that arroyo. Confusion followed right behind. He had no claim on Lula May. She could entertain whomever she pleased, and it was none of his business. Still—

"Uncle, huh?" Edmund munched one of the cookies to keep from grinning. Then he sobered. Lula May had been reluctant to talk about her past. She'd leaned away from her uncle in the wagon. Was this visit good for her or nothing but trouble? Edmund sure wouldn't want his unpleasant cousin to show up at the ranch after all these years.

"I don't like him." Daniel, finished with his treats, stuck his thumb in his mouth and frowned.

"Daniel!" Pauline nudged her younger brother. She sure did keep watch on what her brothers said.

Edmund had to hide another laugh. He'd only spent six evenings with these children, yet he felt like he'd known them all their young lives. Then an odd little prickle crept up his neck, reminding him of some suspicions he'd had last week. Were these little rascals matchmaking? Had Lula May really sent the book over, or was this a scheme the children had come up with to get them together? Surely not.

Daniel lifted his chin and glared at his sister. "Well, I don't like him. He makes Mama unhappy."

Pauline bit her lower lip and looked down at her hands. Jacob stared out toward the corral.

"We'd better be going." Jacob stood and brushed his hands across his trousers. "Thank you for the cookies." Like the man he was becoming, he reached out to shake Edmund's hand.

Edmund responded in kind. "Tell your ma thanks for the book."

He wouldn't let on that he planned to go over to their place later. Whether they were matchmaking or not, Daniel's innocent confession about not liking their uncle reminded him that the Lord still wanted him to keep watch on Lula May and her children. Whether she invited him to supper or not, he'd invite her to travel with him to the cattlemen's meeting tonight and on the way try to find out more about the uncle. In fact, maybe her sending the book to him was a silent cry for help. Or not.

Just like Old Gad had always told him, women were hard to figure out, and Lula May Barlow was one of the most confusing of all. If she said everything was "just fine," he'd know she was in trouble. And whether she liked it or not, he'd find a way to help her.

An hour later, after giving orders to Abel for the afternoon, Edmund headed toward the Barlow place. If Zephyr's prancing gait was any indication, the stallion seemed as happy as he was. Edmund came up with an idea for what was pulling his mount in that direction: Lula May's fine brown mare. Not that the two Barlow stallions would approve of his horning in on their herd, but at least Zephyr's behavior now made sense.

Halfway between their two properties, he spied Calvin out in the pasture working on the fence, just as Daniel said. A quick glance made it clear the boy was having trouble pulling the new barbed wire between two fence posts. Zephyr didn't like it much when Edmund reined him in that direction, but Calvin's face lit up in a Texas-sized smile.

"Hey, Mr. McKay." He let go of the wire and wiped his sleeve over his sweat-drenched forehead. "How you doing today?"

"Fair to middlin'." Edmund glanced around the scene. "Need some help?" As soon as the words were out of his mouth, he wanted to take them back. Even a man as young as Calvin had his pride. "Looks like you're doing a fine job, but I could help you get it done faster so we can both get out of this heat."

"I'd be much obliged, Mr. McKay." Calvin huffed out a breath. "This is the first time I've done this without either Pa or Ma."

"Your ma works on the fences?" Edmund dismounted and retrieved his leather gloves from his saddlebags.

"Sure. Ain't any man's work she ain't done these past three years." Calvin winced slightly. "Shouldn't have said that. Don't tell her I told you."

"All right. I won't tell her you said 'ain't.'" Edmund chuckled as he grabbed the line of wire Calvin had dropped and pulled it to the nearest fence post.

Grinning his appreciation, Calvin hammered a nail into place and bent it around the wire to secure it. "Thank you, sir. It's sure easier when two men do it."

"You've done a fine job of setting these new fence posts." Edmund gripped the nearest post and tried to jiggle it. It didn't budge. "Now let's get the rest of this wire strung."

They quickly fell into a rhythm as they attached three rows of wire down the line of posts. No words were needed, and neither one seemed inclined to break the silence. For Edmund's part, he had a lot to think on after Calvin's comment about Lula May.

All the time Frank was sick, they'd never asked for a lick of help, so he'd assumed they were getting along all right. To his shame, he'd never come over to ask. So much for his pride over being a loner, because by protecting his own privacy, he'd let his neighbors down in a big way. And all that time, Lula May had to work like a man. Yet look how well she'd done. Even with losing Frank, she'd made that ranch work. Edmund's respect and appreciation for her shot up about a mile. What a woman!

When they reached the first of the older posts that didn't need to be replaced, they used pliers to twist the old and new wire together.

"That ought to do it." Despite his words, Calvin studied his work, checking a few places to be sure they were secure.

Edmund clapped him on the shoulder. "Good job."

"You thirsty?" Calvin waved toward the wagon. "I got a crock of fresh-pumped water over there. It's probably warm, but it's wet."

They sank to the ground in the shade of the wagon to rest a bit and take a refreshing drink. Calvin stared off into the afternoon sky, where the few white clouds seemed to indicate there'd be no storm today.

"Mr. McKay, can I ask you something?"

Edmund felt a moment of nostalgia. He used to start every question to Old Gad, "Can I ask you something?" Old Gad would say...

"You *may* ask. Don't know if I *can* help you, but I'll try." Edmund lifted the dipper to his lips for another sip of water.

Calvin grinned, then got serious. "Do you know much about women?"

Edmund spewed the water all over his trousers. "Women?" An ache grew in his chest. The Barlow boys could learn everything about ranching from their ma, but they wouldn't have a man to teach them about courting or how to be good husbands. Not that he knew how to do either, of course. Old Gad hadn't taught him those skills. "Why would you ask a confirmed bachelor about women?"

Calvin stared at him for a moment, then gave him a sheepish look. "I see what you mean."

Edmund laughed. "Go ahead, son. Ask the question. Maybe we can figure it out together."

"I've got this girl...well, she isn't *my* girl, but I'd like for her to be."

"Daisy Carson." Edmund had seen them at church several Sundays. Daisy was a pretty little thing, but she appeared to have a temper.

"Yessir." Calvin stared off like a moon-eyed calf. "She's just about the sweetest, kindest, most beautiful woman I've ever seen." His expression grew sorrowful. "We were friends growing up, and I thought we still were, but lately she gets mad at everything I do or say." He settled a sober look on Edmund. "What's a man supposed to do if he wants to court a woman? What would *you* do? That is, if you weren't a confirmed bachelor?"

"Huh. Can't really say." Edmund took another drink of water to give himself time to think. Daisy sounded an awful lot like Lula May, getting mad at any random thing Edmund said. "I expect if the time came...that is...if I *un*confirmed my bachelor status—" he grinned at Calvin, who chuckled "—I'd figure something out."

Now Calvin laughed out loud. "Thanks. You're a real help." He stood and brushed dust from his trousers. "And if I figure out what to do, I'll tell you so you can follow my lead. Agreed?" He held out his hand.

Edmund gripped it and let the boy pull him to his feet. "Agreed." Then, for a brief moment, he suspected…feared…that Calvin was in on the apparent matchmaking scheme of his sister and brothers. If the older boys were in on it, that meant real trouble. Well, Edmund wasn't having any of it. He'd take that book back to Lula May and then make himself scarce.

Yet he had to confess he felt a kinship with Calvin, just as earlier he'd felt like he'd known the little ones all their short lives. And he couldn't forget the enjoyable discussions and arguments he'd had with their ma. A man could get used to that.

Oh, no. He was in trouble, and he had no idea how to get himself out of it.

Chapter Eight

Hearing the rumble of heavy wheels, Lula May looked up from thinning carrots in her kitchen garden and saw Edmund trailing behind the wagon as Calvin drove it into the barnyard. Her heart jumped. What on earth could he want? It was too early to go to the ranchers' meeting, so he couldn't be here to ask if she'd like to travel to town with him. Not that he'd promised to… Not that she didn't want him to…

Calvin waved as he drove past her toward the barn.

"Howdy." Edmund also lifted his hand in greeting.

"Hello." She stood and rested her hands against her aching back. Training those cow ponies this afternoon had worn her out. "What brings you this way?"

"Just wanted to return your book."

Book?

Edmund dismounted and tied his horse to the hitching rail—odd, since he usually ground-tied the stallion. He pulled a familiar-looking book from his saddlebag and held it out to her. "I appreciate your sending it over, but as it turns out, I have *Robinson Crusoe* myself." He gave her that attractive crooked grin of his, and her heart tumbled in the most annoying way. "So I thought I'd stop by your lending library and trade it for *A Tale of Two Cities.*"

"Sending it over?" In the corner of her eye, Lula May saw her younger children slinking out of the barn. She gave them a quick study.

Daniel had dark crumbs next to his lips, and all three wore slightly guilty looks on their faces. So that's why they'd made such nuisances of themselves out at the pasture. They wanted her to send them off to play so they could take the book to Edmund. And she knew exactly why. Those little rascals were full-out matchmaking! She'd take them to task later. Right now, she had to head off any misunderstanding between Edmund and her without letting on that they planned this bit of mischief. "You're welcome to borrow any of my books. I didn't know you were a reader."

He gave her an odd look, then shrugged. "Yep. I have a number of books myself. We'll have to compare our libraries. Maybe trade ones we haven't read."

"Maybe." Lula May bent down and gathered the baby carrots she'd thinned out and plopped them into her wicker basket. "Pauline, Daniel, get these washed and cut for supper." She gave them a meaningful look to let them know she'd figured out what they'd done.

"Yes, ma'am," they chorused as each one grabbed a basket handle and hurried toward the house…giggling.

She wouldn't worry about them running into Uncle because he was down for a nap after a hard day of doing nothing. Casting a look at Edmund, she faced the inevitable, which wasn't really all that bad. "Will you come in for coffee?"

He tilted his hat back to reveal his broad forehead, where dark blond curls clustered and made him look younger than his thirty-three years. "Coffee would be good."

"Jacob, you have stalls to muck out."

"But—"

She cut him off with a wave of her hand and a sharp command. "Go help your brothers in the barn."

"Yessum." Grinning, he scampered off to obey.

Lula May shook her head. Just over a week ago, he would have cringed if she'd used that tone of voice. While his actions had been pure mischief, she couldn't help but be pleased with his newfound spirit and gumption. All thanks to this man who stood in front of her looking bemused.

She shook her head again. "Sometimes I don't know what to do with them."

He laughed in that chest-deep way of his, and her heart did another bothersome somersault.

After a quick handwashing at the outdoor pump, Lula May led him in through the back door. To her horror, Uncle sat at the kitchen table hungrily eyeing the cake she'd made for Edmund...and almost forgot about. Now she'd have no excuse for not introducing them before she figured out how to get rid of Floyd.

"Edmund, this is Floyd Jones." She forced herself to add, "My uncle. Floyd, this is my neighbor, Edmund McKay." She knew very well that manners dictated presenting the younger person to the older one, but she just couldn't bring herself to do it because it gave Uncle a place of honor he didn't deserve. He'd no doubt scold her later, but she didn't care.

Uncle also lacked proper manners in that he didn't stand to greet Edmund. Still, Edmund reached out to shake his hand. Uncle managed to respond in kind to that.

"Have a seat." Lula May waved Edmund to a chair across from Uncle. So much for a nice chat about books with her neighbor. "Would you like some cake?"

"Sounds good."

"I've been waiting for you to offer me some." Uncle made it sound like she'd somehow neglected him. Or made the cake for him. At least he hadn't helped himself. Probably because he wanted to be served.

Over at the sink, Pauline pumped water into a pan while she and Daniel kept an eye on the grown-ups and giggled.

"Children." She gave them her best scolding look, and they puckered away their grins.

"Well, Mr. McKay," Uncle said. "What brings you over to our house today?"

Edmund gave Lula May a quick look. To his credit, he wasn't thrown by Uncle's proprietary claims. "I came to return a book, to borrow another and to ask Lula May if she'd ride with me to the cattlemen's meeting tonight." He gave her another look and the tiniest nod. Did he see through Uncle already?

"Oh, well, I wasn't sure I could go—"

"Nonsense, girlie. Of course we'll go. It's our responsibility." Uncle pulled out two cigars and offered one to Edmund.

"No, thanks." Edmund's nose twitched. "Never could stand the smell of those things."

"Humph. I wouldn't suppose so. The elegant fragrance of a fine *imported* Cuban cigar requires the refined instincts of a gentleman." Uncle laughed in what should have been a pleasant way. From him it sounded like pure evil. "Not a cowboy's."

Again, to his credit, Edmund didn't appear offended. "About our meeting tonight, I'm sorry, sir, but our cattlemen's association is for members only. We'll have to find out if the other *cowboys* mind if you attend sometime."

Lula May bit back a laugh and turned away to the cupboard to get plates, cups and silverware. She turned back to see Uncle scowling at Edmund and Edmund smiling blandly at Uncle.

"You'll have to stay for supper, Edmund." The words came out without her thinking them through, but she plowed ahead anyway. "I have a beef roast in the oven, and there's no sense in you going home and coming back."

"I knew I smelled some of your delicious cooking. I'd be pleased to stay. Thank you."

Her plans quickly formed for the rest of the evening. She would take the younger children to town and have them stay with Mercy Green above the café. But what to do with Calvin and Samuel? And did she really want to leave Uncle here at the house to snoop while she was gone? Not an easy decision.

As the children had noted last week when Edmund first stepped into her kitchen, he took up a good portion of the room. Even Uncle seemed a bit unsettled by his presence. While the men chatted about the weather, however, Lula May could see the old wiliness and false charm creeping into Uncle's words and facial expressions. She recognized the old man's attempt to figure Edmund out so he could control him.

Pauline and Daniel continued to work at the sink, their heads close together and urgent whispers going back and forth. Why had they become so bold in their matchmaking? Was it possible they sensed the danger of Uncle's presence and wanted to lure Edmund over here to protect her? She wouldn't have any of that. She'd find a solution without any help from anybody, especially not her neighbor. Her only regret was that she hadn't been able to protect the children from realizing Uncle wasn't a good man. If she could have found a way to be nicer to him... No, that wasn't possible. Not when he'd come here for the distinct purpose of seizing everything she owned.

The men enjoyed their coffee and cake, after which Edmund suggested they take a walk around the property to build up an appetite for supper.

"No, no. Walking's not for me, and Lula May has yet to give me a horse of my own." Uncle cast a scolding look her way. He'd been here less than twenty-four hours. When would she have had time to choose a horse for him? "I'll just entertain these children—" He waved a hand at Pauline and Daniel as if they were pesky flies. "I'll see if they're bright enough to learn to play checkers."

"We'd like to go for a walk with you, Mr. McKay." Pauline dried her hands and presented Lula May with a bowl for freshly washed baby carrots. "May we, Mama?"

Lula May hesitated. Let them continue their matchmaking or make them spend time with Uncle? Neither option pleased her. When had she lost control of her household? About a week before Uncle arrived, that's when, the day when Edmund walked into her kitchen and invited himself into her...or rather, Jacob's life.

"I'd welcome their company." Edmund's open smile encouraged her. He truly did like her children. Maybe this wouldn't be so bad after all. "We can go see if the other boys need any help with their chores." How like Edmund to offer to help.

"You may go, but don't pester Mr. McKay." She gave the children a narrow-eyed look of warning.

Their innocent blinks did nothing to reassure her.

While the children skipped happily ahead, Edmund strolled after them. The three older boys had their chores well in hand, so Daniel and Pauline offered to show Edmund their special place down by Kettle Creek. He rarely had leisure time. Probably should have ridden home for supper with his cowhands and then come back to escort Lula May to the meeting. But Abel, his foreman, could tend to the work for one evening, and the lure of her pot roast proved too tempting to decline.

"Here we are." Pauline stopped under a weeping willow by the creek, where flat rocks provided seating and a wide pond hinted at good fishing. The blue-green depths of the water reflected the few white clouds floating by in the rich blue sky. "Before Papa got sick, he taught us how to fish and swim down here."

"Not me." Daniel's thumb lingered near his lips. "I was too little."

"Oh." Pauline's blue eyes got a little red around the edges. "I forgot."

A strange lump formed in Edmund's throat. He couldn't even remember his parents, but Josiah claimed they'd been good folks and loving in their ways. These young'uns had known Frank, a kind father who'd tried to show them how to get on in life. What a shame no one could fill that place.

Oh, no. There went those crazy thoughts again. Edmund decided he needed to change the subject. He studied the area. Yesterday's storm had swollen Kettle Creek for several hours. Now that the flood had subsided, the mud residue lining the banks had baked hard in today's blazing summer sun. While Daniel scuffed through it like a puppy in a pile of leaves, Pauline picked her way along the bank in a dainty, girlish way. As before, Edmund saw in her a miniature of her mother. He wouldn't dare bring these young'uns home wet or covered with dirt.

"I don't think we should get into the water, and we didn't bring our poles, but I know something else to do at a fine glassy pond like this one. What do you think?"

The eager lights in their eyes was answer enough.

He bent down and scratched through some rocks littering the area, searching for the right palm-sized triangular shapes. He found a half dozen.

"Now, here's what you do." He stood straight, took the proper stance and flung one stone over the surface, watching with disappointment as it skipped only four times before disappearing into the depths below. He sure was out of practice. The children didn't seem to think his performance was a failure, though.

"Wow." Daniel's eyes got round as saucers.

"Will you teach us how to do that?" Pauline hopped up and down a few times like she was going to a party.

"Sure thing."

Over the next half hour or so, he showed them how to select their rocks, stand at the proper angle to the water, throw faster instead of harder and put a spin on the stone, all the things Old Gad had taught him. After numerous failures and plenty of giggles, Pauline managed to skip one rock three times and Daniel skipped his once. From their triumphant cheers, Edmund could see it was best he hadn't demonstrated with his usual eight to ten skips. No need to set the bar too high and discourage them.

Just hearing their carefree laughter stirred something deep inside of Edmund. He could get used to that sound. Maybe he should take all the young'uns fishing or rock-skipping from time to time. With them not having a pa, they needed a man's influence, even sweet little Pauline. The wary looks she'd given Lula May's uncle seemed to indicate a dislike, maybe even a distrust of the man, so he sure couldn't fill that role.

For his part, Edmund had taken the man's measure real quick. Something wasn't quite right about him or the situation when Lula May had obviously been reluctant to introduce them. Once again, he wondered if she was asking for help, first by sending over the book and then by inviting him to stay for supper. Just as he'd suspected last week, the little lady needed somebody to look out for her. Edmund was pleased that the Lord had chosen him. He might have to put up with these matchmaking children, but better for him to help out than a married man, which could cast aspersions on Lula May's character. The challenge would be to obey the Lord while dodging the children's schemes. Edmund might even make a secret game of it. He chuckled at the thought.

Lula May didn't have a chance to offer Edmund the seat at the head of the table. Uncle plopped himself down in Frank's chair, just as he had the night before. He didn't even seem to notice the boys standing at their places waiting for her to sit or Edmund holding her chair for her as he'd done last week. The children noticed, though, and those mischievous glances shot around the table like a ricocheting bullet.

She served up supper and passed the plates, all the while wondering how to guide a pleasant table conversation, the duty of a good hostess. Should they pass the talking feather and risk Uncle's ridicule? As soon as Calvin had offered the prayer, however, Jacob piped up and put an end to her concerns.

"Mr. McKay, we sure did have a good time last

week." He cut a bite of beef and swirled it in the gravy on his plate but didn't lift it to his lips. "Me and the boys..." He glanced at Lula May and apologized with a grin and a shrug. "*The boys and I* were wondering if we could have some more ranching lessons. It's all we could talk about Sunday afternoon. After all, it's summer, and we don't have school, so we have extra time to learn more stuff."

Straightening as high as his modest stature permitted, he continued before anyone could interrupt. "We think, the boys and I, that we're gaining a solid ranching education that will help us be a part of the community both now and when we grow up." He gave Edmund a mischievous smirk. "Even the Gillen brothers."

My, how grown-up he already sounded. And speaking up this way was so uncharacteristic of him. Lula May couldn't answer him due to the emotion rising in her throat. Besides, he'd addressed Edmund, not her.

Edmund's green eyes twinkled, and he seemed to be fighting a smile as he glanced at Lula May. "We'll have to talk to your parents, Jacob. Not sure they'll be able to spare you from your chores for another week."

Uncle, whose graying eyebrows were bent into a frown, opened his mouth as if to speak, but Pauline spoke first.

"Some of us girls want to learn, too." Looking small seated next to Edmund, Pauline gazed up at him with an adoring smile. "After all, Mama runs this ranch, so women need to know that stuff, too."

"Lula May?" Edmund questioned her with arched eyebrows and a half grin that sent her heart skipping.

Somehow she managed to find her voice. "I don't see why not." Anything to get the children away from Uncle. "What do you think, Edmund?"

"I don't see why not, either. We'll ask the folks this evening at the meeting. If they agree, we can start next Monday."

Apparently satisfied, Jacob and Pauline happily dug into their supper.

All this time, Uncle had been huffing and clearing his throat importantly, as though he wished to speak. Now that silence came over the table, Lula May scrambled to think of another topic to prevent him from dominating the conversation.

"I made chocolate macaroon cookies for the meeting tonight." She directed her comment to Edmund. "Do you think the men will like them?"

"If they're as good as the oatmeal cookies you made last week, they will."

"Harrumph!" Uncle slammed his knife and fork down on the table and leaned toward Edmund with a menacing scowl. "Am I to understand you have been taking your meals here at my niece's house for some time?"

Edmund slowly chewed the bite he'd taken, swallowed and took a sip of coffee. Lula May prayed that his answer wouldn't set Uncle off, not only now but later this evening after she returned home from the meeting.

"I appreciate your concern, sir. Let me set your mind at ease." Edmund took another bite and gave it the same slow treatment. "You see, we had a bargain. I would teach Jacob some cattle ranching skills, and she would feed me supper." He gave Uncle a bland smile. "I'll take tonight's supper as a thank-you for helping Calvin with the fencing." He paused a second or two. "Although now that I see you're here, I feel bad for taking over when I'm sure you meant to help out with that fencing."

Lula May almost snorted her mouthful of coffee. Somehow she managed to swallow it.

"Why, I—I…" Uncle sputtered and coughed and pretended to choke on his string beans, a ploy she'd seen before.

"Children," she said, "time to clean up. I've decided we'll all go to town. Uncle, you don't mind staying home and resting, do you? I know you've had a tiring day."

While the three younger children scrambled to obey, Calvin gave Samuel a look. "Ma, we'd like to stay home, if you don't mind."

"That's right." Samuel gave her an innocent grin, the one he saved for his rare times of mischief…or secret surprises.

Maybe her stepsons were more mature than she gave them credit for. Then again, Uncle might try to root out any weaknesses to find hurtful things to say to them. On the other hand, if they stayed home, stayed in the house, Uncle wouldn't dare snoop around. She studied the boys and saw their eagerness to stay written all over their faces.

"Fine. You can play checkers with Uncle Floyd."

From the scowl on Uncle's face, Lula May knew she'd made the right decision.

* * *

The meeting tent was in an uproar when Edmund drove Lula May's wagon onto the church property. Even so, when the two of them entered the room and the ranchers noticed Lula May, their language improved right away. Not their anger, though. Clustered around Sheriff Fuller, the men all talked at once, shouting over one another.

Edmund sidled up to Hank Snowden. "What's going on?"

Snowden shook his head in disgust. "Sawyer lost eighteen head of cattle to the rustlers before dawn today. Yesterday, Magnuson lost close to thirty."

Edmund grunted. At these meetings, he usually stayed at the edge of the turmoil and listened to each man's complaint so he could work on a solution. Tonight was no different, although it was hard to sort out fifteen different voices barking at Sheriff Fuller.

A movement beside him reminded him of his guest. He started to offer her a chair, but as always, she had a mind of her own. Strutting up to the front of the room, she plopped her bag of cookies on the preacher's lectern.

"Cookies, anyone?" Only one or two noticed her, so she raised her voice considerably. "I said, chocolate macaroon cookies, anyone?"

For a moment, all the men went silent, to Edmund's amusement. Beside him, Snowden chuckled softly.

"Not now, Lula May." Magnuson waved in her direction like she was a pesky fly. "We got important business to take care of."

"And I see you're solving all your problems very well." She gave the man a scolding look. "You all sound like a bunch of children in the school yard all fighting over a ball."

Sheriff Fuller took that opportunity to break from the crowd. "I'd like one of those cookies, Mrs. Barlow. I've been tracking rustlers all day and haven't had a chance to eat."

"Good. You all sit down, and I'll pass them out." She gave a smug smile, and Edmund felt an odd sense of pride in her commanding attitude. Maybe sometimes that bossiness came in handy. "This might be a tent, but it's also a church. *Our* church." She gave Edmund a stare that he interpreted to mean "our church *for now*."

Despite exchanging a bunch of different looks among themselves—some offended, others confused, the ranchers did as they were told. My, this little lady would make a fine schoolteacher. Must come from rearing five young'uns. He could only pray she didn't bring up the subject of raising money for building the church. At least not tonight when they needed to solve the problem of the cattle rustlers.

As she started passing out the cookies, she stared at Edmund and arched one eyebrow. He questioned her with an arched eyebrow of his own. She rolled her eyes and mouthed, "the coffee."

"Oh. Right."

He hurried back to the wagon and retrieved the jugs of cold coffee she'd brought. They served it in the tin cups someone had donated to the church. Then Lula May returned to the lectern. Edmund could see she wanted to speak, so he gave her an encouraging nod. Her pretty smile was more reward than he'd expected, and his heart took a leap...to his annoyance.

"Gentlemen, while you're busy with your refreshments, I'd like to say a few words." She bit her lip, again questioning Edmund with a look. Again he nodded. "First of all, thank you for inviting me to join you."

Several men grumbled that they hadn't invited her, but others shushed them. "Don't discourage her. She brings refreshments," Gabe Dooley said.

Several others laughed and added their agreement.

"With this cattle rustling going on, it may not seem that I have much to lose because I only have five head." She surveyed the group like she was used to talking to a crowd.

Edmund felt a pinch of envy. He had a real hard time talking in front of other people.

"But when people set about to do wrong, they don't care a whit whom they hurt." Lula May rested a forearm on the lectern, just like the preacher often did. "Some of you have small places like mine, but don't think being small makes us safe. Besides, who's to say the rustlers won't start stealing my horses, too? A thief's a thief."

"That's true." Zeke, the cowboy who'd bought one of her horses last week, piped up from the back of the room, giving Lula May an admiring perusal as he had the other day. If Edmund had been standing near the man, he'd have punched him in the shoulder. "You keep an eye out, Miz Barlow. Those are the best cow ponies around."

A hum of agreement swept through the room. Even in the dim lamplight of the church tent, Edmund could see a pleased blush fill her smooth, tanned cheeks. Again, pride filled him, this time for her ranching skills. But why? She wasn't his wife. And never would be, he reminded himself. Speaking of pesky flies, that's what such bothersome thoughts were!

"Thank you, Zeke." Lula May straightened a bit taller. So that's where Jacob learned to do that when he sensed approval. Edmund knew all the men respected Lula May for her horses. That meant a whole heap out here. "And thank you all for listening to me." She glanced around and gave them a pretty smile. "Well, I suppose I'd best turn this meeting over to your…our chairman." She arched those fine brown eyebrows. "Who is…?"

The men muttered among themselves.

"We don't have a chairman, Mrs. Barlow," Sheriff Fuller said. "But it seems like you're doing a fine job of corralling these here mustangs."

"Must be your experience raising those fine cow ponies," someone else called out.

"Or five chilluns," someone else chimed in.

The room erupted in laughter. Even Edmund broke out in a laugh he felt clear down to his belly.

"Oh, but—" Her big blue eyes got rounder than usual. "I just—"

"I vote we elect Miz Barlow as our chairman," Abe Sawyer called out.

"I second that." Edmund said the words without

thinking, and drew a dozen stares of surprise. Not to mention some speculative looks.

The usual grumbling objections filled the room, while others shouted their agreement.

"Wouldn't that be chairlady?" Sheriff Fuller moved up to stand beside Lula May. Tall and lean, the blond fella lent an air of authority to everything he said and did.

Edmund wasn't jealous of the newly married younger man, but he did wish he'd been the one to step up beside Lula May.

"I never heard such nonsense." Magnuson stood up and waved a fist in the air. "What kind of man ties himself to a woman's apron strings? Is she gonna ride out with us after the rustlers?" He pinned several men with a harsh stare. "Bake 'em cookies to get 'em to stop stealing our livelihoods?"

Lula May stiffened. "I can shoot as well as any man, and I have land and family to protect, just like you do. If need be, I can ride out with you. But it seems what you need more than anything is some organization. Have you all formed groups to keep watch on the herds? Instead of each rancher protecting only his own herd, you could take turns and protect a different herd each night. The rustlers won't know which herd you're watching, so they'll think twice about coming up on the wrong place for fear they'll get outgunned."

"Good idea," several men said.

Edmund could see more men now listening to Lula May's ideas with obvious respect. Once again, pride filled his chest. Bringing her had been the best idea he'd had in a long time.

"All right, then." Lula May paced across the front of the room. "Let's name a captain for each group and then make up a schedule."

After much debate, Edmund, CJ Thorn and Abe Sawyer were named, and they chose their teams.

"My team will take this first night," Sawyer said. "Since my place was hit last night, they probably won't come back, at least for a while. Let's go out to Smitty's place."

A verbal list soon met with everyone's approval, with the agreement that no one would talk about the schedule to anyone outside of the association.

"Just one more thing." Lula May raised her voice and rapped her knuckles on the lectern to get their attention. "An organization needs a name, and I want to propose the Lone Star Cowboy League. What do you gentlemen think?"

Once again, her idea met with approval. Seemed to Edmund that everyone was pleased to have someone else take charge, even if that someone was a woman.

Later, as the men filed out of the church tent, Abe Sawyer made his way over to Edmund and patted him on the back. "That's quite a woman you got there, McKay."

"Um. Well. No." Edmund searched desperately for a way to deflect such an idea, which could quickly become a rumor that could hurt them both. "Just wanted to include my rancher neighbor in our association."

"Oh, sure." Sawyer's guffaw trailed him out the door.

* * *

"That went well." Lula May sat beside Edmund on the wagon bench. She'd never had quite so much fun in her life. Most of those men respected her and had listened to her ideas. So much for needing Edmund to voice them for her. On the way out of the church tent, the two of them had even managed to speak to the appropriate fathers about resuming the Young Ranchers' Club. Next week, she would come by herself. And she would bring up the church building.

"Yep." He guided the horses down the darkened main street past the bank and toward Mercy Green's café.

A thread of doubt wove into her. "Is that all you have to say?" She bit her lip. "Did I overstep any boundaries? Embarrass you? Are you sorry you invited me?"

"Yes, no, no and no."

Even in the dark, she could see a twinkle in his eyes. She had the urge to smack his shoulder playfully, but managed to keep her hands to herself. Instead, she gazed up at the three-quarter moon and countless stars sprinkled across the inky sky. "We forgot to talk about Thursday's celebration."

"I thought the townsfolk were responsible for the Fourth of July events. I'm pretty sure they have everything all planned."

"Oh, yes. Of course." She tried to think of another topic to fill the time on the way home. Funny how she could be so talkative in front of the ranchers, and yet now her mind refused to produce a sensible thought.

At the café, they climbed the back steps to Mercy's

living quarters. After many thanks to her friend for keeping the children, Lula May herded them down the steps and into the wagon. Daniel was sleepwalking most of the way, but Pauline and Jacob were full of chatter. Mercy's son Alec and Jacob had made friends last week during their ranching lessons, so they'd entertained each other while Pauline had helped Mercy make bread for tomorrow's breakfast customers at the café. But even those two grew sleepy on the ride home and curled up on the blankets Lula May had brought.

For all the success of the evening, the closer they came to her ranch, the more Lula May felt her trepidation grow. What if Uncle told Calvin and Samuel that he planned to take over the ranch and send them packing? What if—

"For a lady who's had a successful evening, you're mighty quiet." Hands firmly holding the reins, Edmund nudged her with his elbow.

Before she could stop herself, instinct had her nudging him back, as she would one of her children. Which sent a wave of heat over and through her that had nothing to do with the warm July evening. How mortifying to be so familiar with this man. She really needed to stop it. If the wrong person saw such behavior, her reputation could be ruined.

While Jacob managed to make it to his room on his own, both of the younger children were fast asleep. Lula May carried Daniel inside, and Edmund carried Pauline, who had grown too heavy for Lula May. There was something inexplicably sweet about this large man's tenderness toward the children as he helped her put them to bed. Then he seemed to come to himself.

"Well, I'd best get home. Got a full day ahead of me tomorrow."

"Yes, of course." Hearing Uncle snoring in her step-sons' room, she walked Edmund down the hallway toward the parlor, where he paused.

"Say, I'd like to get started on *A Tale of Two Cities*. You still willing to let me borrow it?"

"Yes, indeed." She retrieved the book for him, pleased to provide something he would enjoy in addition to her cooking.

They made their way outside in the dim moonlight, where Calvin had already taken care of the horses and wagon. Samuel brought Edmund's stallion from the barn to the hitching rail and returned to the barn to help Calvin.

"You haven't told me about your uncle." Edmund stuck the book into his saddlebag.

"Nothing much to tell." Lula May glanced away, afraid of those probing green eyes. If ever there was an honorable man, it was Edmund McKay. The kind regard he'd shown her and the children this evening, the whole past week, would disappear if Uncle found a way to prove she'd stolen the necklace.

"Hmm." His skeptical look made it clear he didn't believe her. "You sure everything's all right?"

"Everything's fine. Just fine. See you Thursday." She backed up so he could mount Zephyr. "I'll be entering the cake-baking contest. Are you doing anything special?"

"I think I'll try to get on as a judge of the cake-baking contest." His twinkle had returned.

They shared a laugh that seemed all too companionable. And yet Lula May had to force herself to stop watching him as he rode away into the darkness. She turned toward the house just as Calvin and Samuel joined her.

"Aren't you boys tired? Don't you want to turn in?" She nodded toward the barn.

"We'd like a word with you in the parlor, Ma." For a change, Samuel took the lead in the conversation.

As tired as she was, her pulse began to race. Did something happen with Uncle? "All right."

With Uncle still sawing logs in the bedroom, he wasn't likely to hear their conversation.

Calvin brought a kerosene lamp from the kitchen, and both boys stood in the center of the room.

"What's this all about?" She looked from one to the other.

"Ma, we think it's time to move that picture." Samuel pointed to the mahogany-framed wedding portrait of his parents that had hung over the mantelpiece for nearly twenty years.

Lula May's eyes suddenly burned. "What makes you say that?" She had no doubt Uncle had said something cruel to her stepsons. "Those are your parents. I don't want you ever to forget them."

"I'll never forget Pa." Samuel gently gripped her shoulders and stared deep into her eyes. "But I can't forget what I never knew. What I mean is, I don't remember my ma at all. I'm grateful to her for birthing me, but you're the only ma I've ever known. You nursed me though sickness, taught me to read and ride a horse…everything."

"But—"

"Mama was a good, sweet lady, and I loved her," Calvin said. "It would have been nice if she and Pa could have raised us here in this house. But God had a different plan. He meant for you to come out and marry Pa and give us two bothersome little brothers and one perfect little sister."

The brothers chuckled. Lula May hoped they wouldn't notice her desperate attempt not to cry.

"Even when Pa was dying," said Calvin, "he said it was God's plan, so he didn't want us to grieve overmuch."

Samuel reclaimed her gaze. "God also brought you out here to give you a better life than you had in Alabama."

So they knew about her wretched years with Floyd! But what did they know? Somehow she managed to hold on to a sob, even when Samuel pulled her into a strong embrace.

"What happened while I was gone?" She looked up at him, surprised at how tall he'd grown lately.

They traded a sly look.

After a long pause, Calvin said, "He cheats at checkers." As if that explained it all. From the way they clammed up, though, it was all she would get out of them.

"What a shame. I'm glad the younger ones didn't see his bad example." And look at how these boys… young *men* had seen the truth about Uncle's character.

Samuel released her and went to the wall, where he gently lifted down the picture frame. "We'll wrap this up real good and put it in storage. Maybe later when the folks of Little Horn build a town hall, we can hang it there to remind everyone of one of the founding pioneer couples of the county, two people we're proud to be descended from." He glanced at Lula May. "That is, if it's all right with you, Ma."

The gentleness in his voice almost broke her hold on her tears. "That would be fine."

A sudden realization swept over her and sent a chill down her spine. How wrong she'd been all these years to call Calvin and Samuel her stepsons. All that time, in the back of her mind...and her heart...she'd thought of them as different from the children she'd given birth to, somehow not as good, somehow not as dear. But that wasn't true. They might not have come from her body, but in every way that mattered, they were her sons, her children just as Pauline, Jacob and Daniel were. And she loved them more dearly now than she ever had. Not only that, but these two had just shown her much more spiritual and emotional maturity than their years warranted. They never ceased to surprise her.

"That's a fine idea, Sammy." She drew in a deep, shuddering breath. "Now you boys get to bed. It'll be a short night for you as it is."

"Of course you realize we'll have to put another picture in that spot." Calvin tilted his head toward the pale oval spot on the floral wallpaper revealing where the picture had been. "Maybe another wedding picture." He sent her an innocent look.

"Are you referring to you and Daisy Carson? Because that's not going to happen anytime soon."

Calvin gave her a rueful shrug. "No, ma'am. I know that." A smile brightened his face. "I was thinking of you and…"

"Shh!" She waved him toward the door. "Get out of here. You're not too big for me to whip."

The boys ducked out, laughing softly as they carried away the reminder of their parents…and leaving behind a stepmother, no, a much-blessed *mother* who had to protect them and their inheritance, no matter what it cost her.

Chapter Nine

Edmund took his time returning home. Since buying his ranch, he hadn't spent much time out on the road by himself, so this was his chance to do some thinking without having to be busy with some chore, like cleaning his guns or oiling harnesses. Besides, he liked to linger beneath the stars and enjoy the moonlight over the Texas prairie. It reminded him of his days alone after he'd left his cousin's home when he spent many a night sleeping outside, those stars his only companions.

Because "home" had never been a happy or even a safe place for him, he'd learned long ago to treasure his solitary life. Not only was it all he'd ever known, but it was pointless for a man to grieve for what he never could have. Even during his years with Old Gad, they'd respected each other's times of solitude. Trouble was, after hanging around Lula May and her children, Edmund felt an odd hankering for a loving family of his own. Putting those sleepy young'uns to bed, seeing their absolute trust in their ma...in *him*...had melted some of the self-protective shell he'd built around his heart since before he could remember. They made him want to be a better man. A family man. It was getting harder to shove away those feelings.

Speaking of protection, after today, he was even more certain the Lord wanted him to keep watch over the Barlows. Something wasn't quite right about Floyd Jones. Something peculiar was going on at the horse ranch. Edmund just wasn't sure how he could dig out the truth, especially since Lula May insisted that everything was "just fine." Stubborn woman. No matter. She could reject his attempts to help her all she wanted to. He would keep checking up on her for her own good. A man had to obey the Lord, not some bossy female.

Good thing Jacob had the idea to continue the Young Ranchers' Club. That would make it easy to visit Lula May every day, assuming she'd want to continue feeding him in gratitude for his spending time with her son. While none of the other parents felt the same obligation, nor did they need to, her insistence on repaying him would make it easier for him to obey the Lord.

Edmund chuckled, and Zephyr perked up his ears. Edmund leaned down and patted his neck. "Yep, old boy. I'm going to enjoy some of that nice cooking again. Don't worry. I'll try not to eat too much. Wouldn't want to get too heavy for you."

Zephyr snorted and pranced along the dusty roadway, probably trying to prove himself stronger than Edmund gave him credit for.

But just how strong was Edmund? Would he be

able to protect Lula May and her young'uns without letting go of his solitude? His privacy? And most of all, his heart?

In spite of her older sons' grand, heart-melting gesture, in spite of being bone weary, Lula May lay awake for some time pondering her long day and trying to sort things out.

What on earth had prompted her to behave as she had at the ranchers' meeting? What did those men really think of her? More important, what would their wives, her friends in the quilting bee, think when they learned about her brazen ways. It was one thing to take over her own ranch when Frank became sick, another entirely to take over the ranchers' meeting. Maybe in the back of her mind, she'd just been trying to compensate for her helplessness in the face of Uncle's threats. To prove to herself that she might not be able to control Uncle, but she could control the other important parts of her life. She'd always been so careful to do what was right. Didn't seem like it had done her any good at all.

There was one thing she could set straight. Her children and their shenanigans about that book Edmund brought back. First thing in the morning over breakfast, she took them to task.

"Why on earth did you take a book over to Mr. McKay yesterday and say I sent it?" As she and the three younger children sat around the kitchen table, she kept her voice soft so as not to wake up Uncle. Calvin and Samuel had eaten early and were out in the pasture working the horses.

The children got busy with their bacon and eggs as though she hadn't said a word. Time to go for the weakest link in their chain of silence. "Daniel?" She gave him a warm smile so he wouldn't think he was in trouble. Not that being in trouble ever really bothered him, the little rascal.

He blinked his big blue eyes at her. "Ma'am?" Oh, my. He could become a real lady's man one day.

"The book?"

"Mama, it's my fault." Pauline, ever the protector of her brothers, spoke up. Funny how she didn't really look all that guilty, either. "We didn't tell a lie. We said you said Mr. McKay needed to work on his imagination. We just repeated what we heard you say one night last week." She glanced at each of her brothers. "And we wanted him to come back."

"We've missed him," Daniel said.

"It was nice having him here last night," Jacob added.

"That's real sweet, my little honeys." Their innocence touched a deep chord in Lula May's heart, just as Calvin and Samuel had last night. They wouldn't understand that it could look bad for her reputation if Edmund spent too much time here when everybody knew they weren't courting. "But I'm afraid you can't keep bothering the man. He has a ranch to run. Now he's going to have all of you to watch out for next week when you go over there, so he probably has a lot of preparation for it." She'd already decided to send Daniel along with Pauline and Jacob to keep him away from Uncle. If nothing else, Pauline could mind him as she did at home.

"But he likes being here." Jacob buttered a biscuit and spooned on some peach preserves.

The other two nodded.

"We'd like him to be here all the time," said Pauline.

Lula May gasped and then laughed. "He can't be here all the time…"

"He could if you two got married." Jacob waggled his eyebrows at her.

"What?" Lula May shook her head. "Why you little matchmakers. What am I going to do with you?" At least their mischief was out in the open now.

They looked at each other and giggled.

"Matchmakers. Is that what you call somebody who's trying to get two stubborn people who like each other to get hitched?" Jacob giggled high and loud at his own joke, and the other two joined in noisily.

"That's not funny." Lula May gave them each her darkest scolding scowl. "And you have to stop it. Mr. McKay is…"

"But, Ma." Now Pauline spoke in her serious grown-up tone, the one she used when trying to teach Daniel something. "You're different since he started coming over. Happier. Not so…burdened."

Too stunned to reply, Lula May huffed out a breath. Did she appear "burdened" to her children? Was she truly happier when Edmund was here?

"Yeah," Daniel said. "So we want him to be around all the time." He rubbed his thumb just below his lower lip as if tempted to put it in his mouth. Lula May's heart dropped. He only sucked his thumb when he was troubled. "Especially since that old man showed up."

"Shh!" Pauline scolded. "He'll hear you."

"I don't care."

Lula May forced herself to speak, choosing her words carefully. "I know it's hard having Uncle Floyd here. But you must behave with good manners around him, just as you do with Mr. McKay or any guest. Don't ever let another person's words or actions determine how you behave." She thought for a moment. "And leave poor Mr. McKay alone. He likes living by himself. Otherwise he would have found a wife long ago." Edmund didn't act in the least interested in marriage. Not that she wanted him to. Not at all. So why did that simple truth send her heart plummeting? "Understand?"

All three nodded solemnly. They finished breakfast in silence and then set about doing their chores. Lula May gathered the ingredients for the squash cake she was making for tomorrow's Fourth of July celebration. Remembering Edmund's comment about signing up to judge the cakes, her heart warmed. Of course he wouldn't know which cake was hers because he hadn't tasted this particular recipe. And she wasn't about to cheat and tell him it was hers. But just maybe, he'd really like it. Oh, bother. Why did she keep thinking about pleasing that man?

As she grated the fresh green squash from her garden into a bowl, she couldn't help but be touched by the sweet concern of her children. Annoyed, too. In their innocence and their ignorance of the whole truth, they just wanted her to be happy. If Uncle proved his claims about the necklace and had her arrested, her children would be devastated.

"Breakfast ready?" Uncle appeared in the doorway, his slicked-back hair and clean-shaven cheeks giving evidence that he'd used the pitcher of hot water she'd put in his room an hour ago.

"Get yourself a cup of coffee, and I'll fry you an egg." Lula May couldn't bring herself to smile, but she did manage a decent tone of voice to set an example for the children.

"Aren't you going to bring me coffee?" His voice was laced with sarcasm. "I have no doubt you would bring coffee to that cowboy if he was here."

"You—" Pauline stood at the sink with a wet dish-rag in hand and fire in her eyes.

"Pauline, take Daniel out to gather eggs. Jacob, go muck out the barn."

"Yes, ma'am." All three hastened to obey while Lula May let out a quiet breath of relief. What had gotten into her daughter? Too much of her mother, that's what. They'd have a talk about it later, no mistake.

The moment the children were out the door, Uncle grabbed Lula May's arm. "I never thought a niece of mine would show such a lack of moral character by taking up with a cowboy less than a year after your husband died. No wonder you don't wear proper widow's weeds. For shame."

"Let go of me." Lula May jerked away. She still hadn't figured out how he knew so much about her. Who among her friends would have informed him of when Frank died? She had no doubt he'd waited to come to Texas until then. Even at his sickest or with his last breath, Frank would have set this man straight.

"You had better treat me right, girlie." Uncle poured a cup of coffee and plopped down at the table. "You had better teach those brats to treat me right, too." After a noisy slurp from his cup, he peered at the stove. "Make that four eggs. And heat up that bacon. I cannot abide congealed meat."

Lula May shook as she did his bidding, both from rage and fear. He could do as he wished to her, but the moment he set a hand on one of her children, she wouldn't be responsible for her actions in retaliation.

"Now, it is time you quit shilly-shallying around. I want to see the deed to this farm, and I want to see it today. My lawyer is coming out next week to witness you signing this place over to me."

Lula May counted to ten. "It's a ranch, Floyd."

"What?" His eyes blazed.

"A ranch, not a farm. If you want your neighbors to respect you, to invite you to their ranchers' meeting, you have to use the right words." Before she could stop herself, she added, "And Mr. McKay is a rancher, not a cowboy." She clenched her teeth to keep from adding that Edmund was one of the most successful ranchers in the area. No sense in Floyd knowing her neighbor was getting right close to what folks would call wealthy, at least in these parts. All the more reason for her children to quit their matchmaking. She'd rather die than have Edmund think she was after his money. However, Uncle would have no such compunctions.

"Rancher, cowboy. What is the difference?" He wasn't asking a question. "Now, girlie, I mean what I say. You sign this place over to me, or I will have you arrested for stealing my mama's valuable necklace."

Lula May set his breakfast in front of him. "Four eggs over easy and hot bacon. Biscuits are in the basket." She waved toward them. "Butter and jam right there." She turned back toward the sink. With so much to do today, she needed to get that cake made. She took a step toward the cupboard to get out her crockery mixing bowl.

Uncle stood, grabbed her wrist and pulled her back. "I mean what I say."

"Don't you always, Floyd?" She resisted the urge to twist away from him. That would only bruise her wrist, which would worry the children. She couldn't let Uncle get to her. Had to find a way out of this somehow.

"By the by." He thrust her hand away and took on a milder tone, as if he hadn't just threatened all she held dear. "Last night I looked all over this place and could not find anything decent to drink. Where did that husband of yours keep the good stuff?"

So that explained why her secret sign was broken. Before she left for the ranchers' meeting, she used flour glue to paste a tiny strip of dark paper to her office door, down close to the floor where it wouldn't be noticed. Last night Calvin and Samuel must have been out doing chores when Uncle broke into the office. Picking the lock was the only way he could have achieved that, but she'd known him to pick a lock before. She'd have to check later to see what mischief he got up to. If he still wanted for her to show him the deed to the ranch, that meant he hadn't found it in her secret hiding place.

"My husband didn't imbibe in spirits." She lifted the mixing bowl down and took a wooden spoon from a drawer.

"Not a real man, eh? Just like that cowboy neighbor of yours. Well, girlie, you sure know how to pick 'em, don't you?"

His words slammed into her, and for a moment, Lula May was thrust back into her childhood. Back then, according to Uncle, she'd never measured up to his vague and ever-changing standards about what a Southern girl, a Southern belle, should be. Nor had she ever owned anything he didn't claim belonged to him. Even with Frank, she'd been second-rate, never measuring up to Emily's perfection, although Frank had never said so.

Trying hard to swallow her fear and self-doubt, she set the mixing bowl and bowl of grated squash toward the back of the counter. The cake would have to wait. Without a word, she retreated to her room and shut and locked the door. There, she knelt at her bedside. Or, rather, fell to her knees with emotional exhaustion.

"Lord, I don't know what to do. No matter how hard I've tried to keep things together, I'm about to lose everything I've worked for, including my children's futures." She'd managed everything while Frank was ill, even for all these many months since he died. Now Uncle was threatening, her children were taking matters into their own hands and she felt crushed. The final straw was Uncle making cruel remarks to her children, just as he used to do to her. How could she stop him? If he got angry enough, he'd simply cast her out, along with the children. "Please help me. Please help us all."

"Ma?" Calvin's muted voice came through the door. "Mr. Bennett came to buy that horse. You want me to handle it?"

Furiously brushing away her tears, Lula May got to her feet. "No. No. I'll be right out." A quick check in the mirror revealed her reddened complexion, always a bothersome reaction to her emotions. She splashed cool water from her pitcher onto her cheeks and eyes, dried them and hurried out the door.

To her chagrin, Uncle followed her out to the barnyard. Would she never get rid of his intrusions into her life?

"Hello, Mr. Bennett." Lula May tilted her head toward Uncle. "This is Floyd Jones, my uncle."

"How do, Mr. Bennett." Uncle reached out and gladhanded Lucas like a politician, even clapping him on the shoulder. Oddly, Lucas didn't seem to mind. Usually, he held himself apart from other people even more than Edmund did. "Good to meet you."

"Good to meet you, too, Mr. Jones." Lucas turned his attention to Lula May, and she could see his eyes were bloodshot. Poor man. He didn't have many cowhands, and he probably stayed up all night watching his herd to keep away the cattle rustlers. He needed to attend the meetings and get help from his neighbors. "Mrs. Barlow, my old mare is about done for." He nodded in the direction of his horse. Sure enough, the poor old girl obviously needed to be cooled down and put out to a shady pasture. "I'm ready to take that paint gelding."

Now she was in a quandary. Of course she wanted Lucas to take the horse, but when he paid her, Uncle might claim the money, which she needed badly for supplies and feed.

"I'm sorry to say," Lucas went on, "I don't have the cash today, but I expect to have some by next week. Would that be all right?" He leaned one arm heavily on the corral railing.

Strange relief filled Lula May. She needed that money, but it appeared she wouldn't get it today either way. Maybe she could arrange to meet Lucas over at his house next week so she could be sure to hide the money from Uncle. Indecision briefly plagued her. That poor old brown mare looked like she'd been "rode hard and put away wet," as the cowboys always said of an over-worked horse. Lucas usually treated his animals better than that, but she could see the man was exhausted. Pity for both man and beast was the deciding factor.

"Sure. No rush." Lula May stuck out her hand. "It's a deal."

Lucas's hand felt like a limp fish in hers, another sign of his exhaustion. "Much obliged."

"You can leave your mare here for a rest over the weekend, if you like. I'll bring her by your place on Monday and have a visit with Nancy." Of course she'd see Nancy tomorrow and on Sunday, but taking the mare on Monday would give her an excuse to go to his ranch to get paid, not something she'd say in Uncle's hearing. "Don't forget to keep an eye on the paint's nose. Don't want him to get sunburned." The pink nose was a characteristic of these horses, but a little care kept them from getting too much sun.

"That'll be fine."

While Calvin led the gelding out of the corral and gave it a quick brushing, Lucas removed his saddle from the mare to put on his new horse. Lucas turned to Uncle. "Good to meet you, Mr. Jones. Have a good day."

"You have a good day, too, Lucas." Uncle waved as Lucas mounted up and rode away.

In spite of the morning heat rolling over her, a violent shiver swept down Lula May's back. She hadn't said Lucas's first name, had she? Yet Uncle addressed him that way. Had Calvin mentioned it to Uncle on his way to her room a while ago? Had anyone said his Christian name within Uncle's hearing? Her breakfast threatened to come back up, but she swallowed hard and stiffened her spine.

"That how you always do business, girlie? Letting a man ride away without paying?" Uncle gave her his usual sneer of disgust. "No wonder your little farm is in such trouble. Once it is mine, that will change."

"Calvin, pour some water over the mare to cool her down. I have cooking to do." She marched away, praying her sneaky uncle hadn't searched out all of her friends to somehow cause them injury. Nancy Bennett didn't need any trouble, feeling poorly as she was these days. Yet if Lula May tried to investigate the matter, she might bring suspicion on herself. Although she was innocent of any wrongdoing, Uncle had a way of convincing people of anything he wanted them to believe.

Lucas Bennett's visit may have interrupted her prayer, but she'd start right now to pray without ceasing, as the Bible said. She should have been doing that all along.

Chapter Ten

"What do you mean this town has no saloon?" Lula May's uncle sat on the bench in her wagon at the edge of the city park, an ugly scowl decorating his pasty round face.

From Lula May's curved shoulders as she took baskets from the back of the wagon, Edmund figured the old man had been browbeating her for some time. Time to step in and do the job the Lord gave him. He ambled over to them.

"Howdy, Lula May, Floyd, young'uns." He greeted each one with a nod, then gave Floyd Jones a lazy grin. "No need for a saloon in Little Horn. Folks around here know how to have a good time without that sort of thing." He waved a hand toward the park, where the community had gathered to celebrate the Fourth of July. Banners decorated makeshift stalls, and the Stars and Stripes hung from every corner. "Horse races, three-legged races, cake walks, that sort of thing."

"Humph." The old man climbed down, pulled out

one of those foul cigars, clipped one end and lit up. The smell quickly filled the air like the stink of rancid meat. "I could show them a thing or two about having a good time."

No telling what Floyd considered a good time, and Edmund wasn't about to ask him. From the look in Lula May's eyes, he figured she'd prefer his distracting Floyd instead of helping her. Besides, he didn't want to accidentally see the cake she'd baked for the contest.

"While Lula May and the children take care of their responsibilities, let me introduce you to some folks." He hadn't had a chance to warn anyone about Floyd, but his friends would take the man's measure pretty quick.

"Thank you." Lula May gave him a tight smile before marching off with the children, each of them carrying a basket or box.

Edmund did catch sight of yellow icing on a cake in one basket, which was half covered by a tea towel. He looked away and tried to forget the image. And hoped the cake would be mixed in with other yellow ones so he wouldn't recognize it and favor Lula May in the judging.

His mouth watered at the thought of that particular duty. How far he'd come from his days of eating leftovers and only rare desserts in his cousin's kitchen. Now he had more than enough and to spare. *And no one to share it with.* Now where had that thought come from? Without thinking, he glanced toward Lula May and the young'uns traipsing across the park. No, his job wasn't to share his life with them. It was to protect them. And that was that.

"Come on, Floyd. I'll introduce you to my brother."

"And just who is this brother of yours that I should want to meet him?" Floyd huffed a cloud of white smoke into Edmund's face.

Not many things riled Edmund, but the gesture was clearly meant to punctuate the insult about his brother. Only remembering his job to protect Lula May kept him from…well, he didn't know what. But this little man sure did get Edmund's dander up.

He fanned away the smoke with his hand and caught a welcomed whiff of the side of beef roasting over an open pit across the park. "Josiah runs the lumber mill. He's on Little Horn's town committee." Mischief nudged him to add, "I'll go see if he has time to make your acquaintance." He walked away from Floyd. Would the little man follow?

"Lumber mill, eh?" Floyd hurried to catch up, huffing all the way. "He must be doing pretty well with all the new buildings going up in town." He sounded impressed, which gave Edmund another insight into his character. He considered himself too important to meet just anyone. Like the "cowboy" who lived on the ranch next to his niece's.

"Mmm." Edmund wouldn't agree or disagree with Floyd's comment, but the truth was Josiah was doing very well. Not only that, but since growing closer to his brother, Edmund had been inspired by Josiah's generosity to those less fortunate. He was a good, decent man, a credit to the relatives who'd reared him and to their own parents, some of whose teachings Josiah remembered.

They found Josiah with his sleeves rolled up and helping an Indian lady build her booth.

"Hey, Edmund, you're just in time. Hand me that short board over there." Holding a piece of lumber in place, Josiah pointed with the hammer in his other hand toward his stack of wood.

Edmund did as he asked. "Mrs. Longfeather, I see you're bringing your fine jewelry to sell."

Although wearing a calico dress like the other local ladies, the middle-aged woman wore leather moccasins. Her thick black hair was held up on her head with a fancy jeweled comb, and around her waist hung a shiny silver and turquoise belt. Her dark piercing eyes and high cheekbones further marked her as an attractive woman despite her years. "Yes, Mr. McKay. You need something? If I don't have it, I'll make it for you."

Lula May might like one of those fancy combs. *Whoa.* He couldn't buy presents for her. "Thank you, ma'am. Once you get your wares all set out, I'll take a look." Maybe he should buy himself a new belt buckle to help the lady's business. "Josiah, this here's Floyd Jones, Lula May's uncle." He urged Floyd forward with a little wave.

Josiah finished nailing the board into place before brushing his hands on his trousers. He reached out to Floyd, whose reluctance to accept the gesture was obvious by the sneer on his face.

"Surely you have hired men who can do such

things." Floyd gave Josiah a brief handshake, after which he drew out a linen cloth and wiped his hand.

Edmund couldn't help but wonder if his brother thought the same thing he had about Floyd's soft, smooth hands. If he'd ever done a lick of work in his life, it didn't show. Edmund opened his mouth to introduce Mrs. Longfeather to Floyd, but Floyd had already turned his back on her. Another measure of the man. Edmund's patience was running thin. He recalled Lula May saying she grew up on her uncle's plantation. From the frayed edges of Floyd's well-made suit jacket, Edmund could see he was no longer a wealthy man. Probably lost everything in the war and hadn't been able to recoup the losses in the thirty years since Appomattox. Yet he still carried an attitude of superiority, not to mention a streak of mean, if the way the young'uns shied away from him was any indication.

Since Founders' Day had been held just a few weeks ago, not as many folks came to town to celebrate July Fourth as had attended that event. Some couldn't afford another day off from working their land in the middle of summer. Edmund had also heard some folks, the older Southerners, say they still didn't feel like celebrating the birth of the United States of America. That was a shame, since the War between the States had made the North and the South one country again. Edmund wished they could all live in peace, but he supposed bitterness and resentment was a way of life for some. Old Gad had taught him that bitterness only hurt the man who held it close, like coddling a rattlesnake. Edmund was glad to remember that, because he could very easily resent a man like Floyd Jones who, sure as the sun came out hot in July, treated his flesh and blood awful poorly.

Lula May had more important things to worry about than winning ribbons for her cake. Still she was pleased with the red ribbon attached to her china plate at the end of the competition. She'd watched Edmund arguing in a friendly fashion in favor of her cake with the other two judges, banker George Henley and a gruff older rancher named Clyde Parker, both of whom had voted for a chocolate cake. At last he relented, and ribbons were passed out. Turned out Mrs. Carson made the chocolate. After her family's devastating fire, the older woman needed some cheering up, so Lula May was glad to see the blue ribbon go to her.

Calvin made a good showing in the horse race, but he was beaten by a weathered old cowboy who rode much too dangerously in Lula May's way of thinking. A five-dollar gold piece wasn't worth a lifetime of suffering from an injury. She was glad to see Daisy Carson congratulate Calvin. And just as glad to see Daisy not linger around Calvin with the other girls, all giggling and making eyes at him while he shuffled his feet and stared after Daisy.

The family stayed until after dark and enjoyed the fireworks display. The younger children seemed to have enjoyed their day, probably ate too much and gladly fell asleep on the blankets in the back of the wagon. Calvin and Samuel rode on ahead to milk and feed the cows. As Lula May drove home, she could smell Uncle's awful cigars on his breath and clothes, as well as another unpleasant smell recalled from her years in his home. She hadn't tried to keep up with whatever he was doing today, but apparently he'd found someone to supply a harder beverage than the lemonade and strawberry punch others were drinking.

Several other families took the same southbound road out of town, each one giving friendly waves as they turned their wagons onto the long drives leading to their own ranches. Finally, Lula May and her family were alone on the road, with the bright almost-full moon lighting their way.

"Ho, the wagon." Edmund galloped up beside her on Zephyr and tipped his hat. "Did you all have a good time?" Gentleman that he was, he included Uncle in his question.

"Yes, indeed. It's always nice to break away from the routine and have a celebration and see my friends. Winning that red ribbon just added to the fun." She wouldn't try to guess whether he knew the squash cake was hers before tasting and judging it. He'd liked it enough to stick up for it, and that was all that mattered.

"Humph. You call that a celebration?" Uncle wobbled on the bench, and for a moment, Lula May feared he would fall over. He huffed out a rank-smelling breath and nearly knocked her off *her* seat.

"Yep." Edmund lingered near her side of the wagon as they traveled. "Nice clean fun, and no regrets the next day."

"Humph." Uncle repeated his favorite word. "I never regret anything." He then fell into a sort of stupor.

"I was pleased to see that was your cake I voted for."

The moon hung low and cast a light on his handsome face because his hat was tipped back just a bit. She saw no guile there, so she felt an extra measure of happiness that he'd liked the cake. But why would she look for guile in him? He was nothing like her wily uncle, whose every word must be parsed for underlying meanings. She really must not become suspicious of other people just because Uncle wore insincerity like a badge.

"Thank you. I'm glad, too."

For some reason, Edmund kept riding beside her, even passing the arched entrance to his ranch without turning in.

"You don't need to see us home."

"Thought maybe I could help you put those young'uns to bed."

She laughed softly. "You mean you want to be sure the cattle rustlers didn't take advantage of our day in town to steal my few head of cattle."

He grinned. "That, too."

"I do appreciate at it, but you don't need to watch over us." She had a strange longing for that exact thing, but with Uncle's threats hanging over her, she didn't dare lean on Edmund.

"Me?" He put a hand on his chest and gave her a mock-wounded look. "Watch over you? The independent, capable Mrs. Lula May Barlow?"

Hmm. Maybe he wasn't so guileless after all. But at least she knew he meant her no harm. She rewarded his little performance with another light laugh and the skeptical arching of one eyebrow.

And was rewarded with that chest-deep chuckle she'd come to like far too much.

It turned out Uncle needed more help getting to bed than the children. Lula May gratefully surrendered that chore to Edmund. Once they had everyone settled, Lula May walked Edmund out to the hitching rail where Zephyr awaited his master.

"Why have you started tying him up?" She patted the stallion's neck, admiring his conformation, and he nickered his appreciation. "First day you showed up here, you ground-tied him."

"Well," Edmund cleared his throat. "I think he's developed an attraction to your pretty little mare." He looked across the barnyard toward the corral, where Lady's shiny brown coat gleamed in the lowering moonlight. Now Edmund gazed down at Lula May. Unlike out on the road, she couldn't make out his expression due to the shadow cast by his Stetson. But his tone was gentle. Kind. Even questioning. "Sometimes I have a hard time getting him to go home."

"Oh. I see." Heat flooded her face. Was he talking about their horses or about his own feelings? No, she must not attribute such sentiments to him. Even if she wanted to deepen their friendship, she didn't dare, not until she solved her problems with Uncle.

"See you at church on Sunday?" He gripped the pommel.

"Yes. We're looking forward to it." She stepped back so he could swing up into the saddle. As much as she wanted to watch him ride away, she forced herself back inside the house. No sense in fostering feelings she couldn't follow up on.

She retreated to her office with the intention of making sure her property deed was still safely tucked in its hiding place. When she opened the door, a wave of stale cigar smoke struck her. Despite her orders and no doubt to spite her, Uncle had deliberately smoked in her private office to show her who was in charge. Her heart sank.

She sat at the desk and bowed her head against her crossed forearms, not daring to pray out loud, even with the door closed. *Lord, what am I going to do? I want to trust You, but how can I know what You want me to do?*

Pulling off her boots, she slid one sock-covered foot over the well-worn floor and up the right inside wall of the desk. Not a single bump or splinter gave evidence of the safe hidden within a complex system of sliding boards that eventually opened behind the false back of the inside of the desk. Using both feet, she dusted the whole area so it would look as though she'd simply removed her boots after a tiring day and sat down to work. To further throw off suspicion, she lit a kerosene lamp, pulled out a piece of scrap paper and started a grocery list. She'd leave it here on the desk half-finished. Was there anything else she could do to throw Uncle off? When his lawyer showed up next week, would he bring Sheriff Fuller out to demand that she surrender the deed? Only time would tell.

Later, as she lay in bed, she continued her prayer, yet

all she could manage was, *Help me, Lord. Please help me*, over and over again. Instead of an answer, what she saw in her dreams was Edmund's kind, handsome face with a gentle smile aimed directly at her, reminding her that she still hadn't thanked him for saving her life.

Uncle slept late again the next day, giving Lula May time to devise some diversions. She chose one of her older, gentler horses for him and cleaned up Frank's long-unused saddle. How she hated to think of Floyd in that saddle, which had long served a far nobler man.

Once up and dressed, however, he wasn't in a mood for riding. Or much of anything else. He lingered long enough over breakfast, coffee and an old newspaper that the children came in for dinner before he finished. To prevent him from unleashing the abuse threatening on his brow, Lula May told the children to pack sandwiches. "You can take dinner to Calvin and Samuel." Her older sons had told her they would spend the day in the pasture working the particular cow ponies they hoped to sell. "Then you can go picnic by the creek."

"Goody." Daniel shot a superior glance at Jacob. "We can practice what Mr. McKay taught us." Just like the little rascal to lord it over his older brother that he'd had a bit of fun Jacob had missed out on.

Jacob opened his mouth as if to speak, but a quick glance at Uncle changed his mind.

Lula May winced inside. All the confidence he'd gained last week was slowly draining away under Uncle's scowls. "And just what did he teach you?" She'd been too busy to ask Edmund or the children about how they'd spent Tuesday afternoon.

"Rock skipping." Pauline looped an arm in Jacob's like a wise little mama wanting to include all of her children. "We'll show you, Jacob. It's fun."

After instructing them not to go swimming or to fall in the creek "accidentally," Lula May sent them off for the afternoon of fun before turning back to Uncle.

Who was nowhere to be found. Not at the kitchen table, not in the parlor. Not even in her office, which she'd carefully locked last night before turning in. At last the unmistakable sound of Uncle's snoring wafted down the hallway. Yesterday must have been harder on him than she'd thought.

She couldn't get it out of her mind that he must have connected with his spy at the celebration. Not only had he imbibed in spirits, which none of her neighbors would have provided, but he'd been out of sight most of the day. Although after the horse race, she did see him accepting some cash from someone standing in the shadows. Why would anyone be giving him money? Was it about the horse race? She should have marched over to find out who that person was and exactly what was going on.

With a ranch to run, she didn't have time to solve that mystery. Her twice-a-month laundry day was coming up tomorrow, and she needed to be sure the children's clothes were mended before she washed them. As she gathered and sorted the garments, a random thought crossed her mind. Had Edmund been able to get that scorch mark out of his shirtfront? Maybe she'd find out at church on Sunday. If the scorch was still there, she might even offer to remove it for him. Or

not. That would bring more condemnation from Uncle
or Constance Hickey, the last thing she needed. Which
reminded her that she'd need to wash Uncle's clothes,
including his linen suit. And iron all of it, too.

As if she didn't already have enough to do.

When Edmund dismounted in front of the church
tent on Sunday, about twenty young'uns gathered
around him, both boys and girls.

"Are we really going to start the Young Ranchers'
Club again, Uncle Edmund?" Adam looped an arm
around his in a proprietary way.

"Do we girls really get to come?" A little girl,
whose face was familiar but whose name he didn't
know, gripped his other hand and gazed up at him.
Her adoring trust touched that tender spot in his heart
he tried to keep hidden.

Before he could answer, Josiah and Betsy approached him. Betsy looked a mite peaked, and Edmund prayed his sweet sister-in-law wasn't coming
down with something.

"You really think you can corral all of these little
cowboys?" Josiah held his two-year-old son, Eddie,
in his arms.

Blessed every time he saw his tiny namesake, Edmund reached out to the babe, who gripped his hand
with baby fingers and grinned. "Guess I'll have to. A
promise is a promise." In truth, he was mighty pleased
to renew the lessons, even though the girls would add a
complication. Maybe Lula May could help out. Maybe
that would be just the thing to get her away from her

uncle. That was, if she could spare the time from her own ranch work.

Right then, she drove her wagon into the church yard, with Calvin and Samuel following behind on their horses. The three young'uns piled out of the back, Bibles in hand. Only Floyd was missing.

Edmund disengaged from his brother and the group of children as politely as he could and strode over to the wagon. "I hope Floyd hasn't taken sick." This time, without asking if she wanted help, he reached up. As natural as if they'd done this often, she let him grab her waist and lift her down.

"Thank you." She straightened her frilly blue dress and adjusted her matching bonnet. The color reflected in her eyes, making them as blue as the Texas sky above them. "Floyd decided to stay home." To her credit, not a hint of dislike or disapproval shaded her tone. Not even relief.

"Too bad. He'll be missing a fine sermon."

Again, it seemed natural to accompany her and her brood into the tent and take a seat with them on one of the long benches halfway to the pulpit. If folks wanted to keep on staring, they could do so. The Lord had given Edmund a job to do, and he had no intention of letting others' opinions and nosiness deter him from the task. Besides, they'd all come here to worship and learn about the Lord, so people would do well to pay attention to the preacher instead of Edmund and Lula May. Who were not courting, no matter what it looked like.

As if to deny his thoughts, Mrs. Constance Hickey,

town gossip and troublemaker who'd caused his good friend CJ Thorn a heap of grief by spreading rumors about his brother Ned, peered at them from her perch on the wagon carrying the piano. The instrument had to be carted over from the schoolhouse every Sunday, and Constance Hickey played it with a fervor that far exceeded her talent. Right now, from her interest in Edmund and Lula May, she seemed to be forgetting her duty was to play that piano, not make judgments about people in the congregation.

With everyone watching their every move, Lula May didn't have the nerve to tell Edmund she'd be happy to get that scorch mark out of his shirt. In fact, after Pastor Stillwater said his final "amen," she made a beeline to where several ladies from the quilting bee had gathered to serve coffee for the monthly after-church social hour. A couple of her friends gave her knowing looks. Unfortunately, Constance Hickey also joined the group but didn't lift a hand to help serve the beverages.

"Edmund McKay is a handsome man." Mrs. Hickey's pursed lips and clipped tone made it sound like Edmund's looks were a moral failure of some sort. "Everybody's wondered for years why he hasn't married. Now we know why."

Lula May's face felt like it had caught on fire.

"Shh!" Molly Thorn hissed. "Don't say such things."

"That does sound a little odd." Nancy gently squeezed Lula May's hand. "Being a widow must be so hard. People can get the wrong idea if a man even speaks to you." She shot a cross look at Mrs. Hickey.

"Well, I never!" Mrs. Hickey's narrowed eyes and flaring nostrils held a threat. Crossing this woman could prove disastrous. Church pianist though she was, the woman seemed not to hold an ounce of Christian charity.

"No, you didn't." Molly put an arm around Lula May's waist. "You never thought at all how terrible that sounded."

"Coffee?" Nancy held out a cup to the woman, who spun on her heels and strode away.

In seconds she had found another like-minded gossip and was voicing her opinion in a none-too-quiet tone.

"Oh, that woman." Molly glared at Mrs. Hickey. "Why doesn't she mind her own business?"

"Don't let her bother you," added Nancy.

"Thank you." Lula May didn't mean to, but she glanced toward Edmund, who was standing across the churchyard with Molly's new husband, CJ, and the pastor.

Edmund lifted his coffee cup in a salute and gave her that lopsided grin. Surely he knew that giving her such notice in public as he had today would only incite Mrs. Hickey's wrath. The woman had said some very cruel things during Frank's illness, making it sound like it was Lula May's fault he was sick. If Edmund actually were courting her—which he wasn't— no telling what Mrs. Hickey would say. Good thing Uncle hadn't come to church today. He would make friends with that busybody lickety-split just to see how much of her gossip he could use for his nefarious purposes.

Now Lula May wouldn't dare invite Edmund to dinner, no matter how much he liked her fried chicken. She needn't have worried. Betsy and Josiah claimed him as a dinner guest, and they departed for their home across town.

"I wish we'd asked Mr. McKay to dinner first," Pauline said as she climbed into the back of the wagon.

"Yeah, me, too." Daniel's wistful expression held none of his usual mischief.

"Now, children." Lula May took her place on the driver's bench beside Jacob, who was thoroughly enjoying his momentary elevated status above his sister and younger brother. "Let's not be selfish. He has a family he enjoys spending time with."

"Wish we could be his family." Daniel hung his arms over the back of the driver's bench.

"Daniel, don't say such things!" Lula May cast a worried glance around the area to see if anyone had heard him. Fortunately, Mrs. Hickey was busy giving orders to the men who were carting the piano back to the schoolhouse.

Jacob reached back and tousled his younger brother's hair. "Hey." He used his quiet voice, maybe knowing instinctively not to broadcast Daniel's longings. "He'll be coming to supper tomorrow night. Right, Ma?"

Much to her annoyance, her heart skipped at the thought. "Yes." Then her heart plummeted. Of course Uncle would be there, too.

* * *

"Just who is rearing those brats, Lula May?" Uncle sat at the breakfast table eating his second round of eggs, ham and grits. "You or that cowboy?"

"Now, Floyd." With the children already out of the house, Lula May didn't worry about setting an example in the way she responded, but she also didn't want to set Uncle off any worse than he already was. "Mr. McKay's teaching *all* of the local children about cattle ranching, things they *all* need to know."

"Humph." He shuffled Saturday's well-read newspaper as though looking for something he hadn't read yet. "By the by, my lawyer should be here tomorrow. You gonna get that deed out for me, or do I have to tear this house apart?"

"No, I'm not going to give it to you." Her chest felt as though a boulder were sitting on it, and she could hardly catch her breath. Tomorrow. She had to solve her problem by tomorrow. Sipping from her coffee cup, she swallowed hard. "What makes you think I have it here? What makes you think I don't owe money on this place, and the deed's with the bank?"

He snorted. "What makes you think I am fool enough to believe that hogwash?" He pulled out a half-smoked cigar and lit up, defying her with a scowl to forbid him. "Last week at that puny Fourth of July shindig, I spoke with Henley from the bank. He says you are one of the few local ranchers who owns your land outright." He emitted an evil laugh. "I had a hard time not telling him that I am the rightful owner of this place." Another chuckle. "That news will come soon enough."

Because Uncle was her relative, Lula May couldn't fault Mr. Henley for telling him she owned the ranch. Besides, it was common knowledge that she owned it.

Tomorrow. Again the imminent threat of his lawyer's arrival filled her mind and heart. Suddenly a fear such as she'd never known overcame Lula May, and her knees threatened to give way. Even when she'd surrendered to the certainty that Frank would die, she hadn't felt this hopeless and afraid. Frank was with the Lord, and she and the children would see him again one day. But in the here and now, how would she take care of those children if Uncle's threats became reality?

"I have to take Lucas's mare back." She took off her apron, laid it over a chair back and retreated to her bedroom to change into riding garb. Once there, she knelt at her bedside. *Lord, please, please help me? What am I going to do? What if he destroys my house, my children's home, while I'm away?*

Reason managed to break through her anguished thoughts. Uncle would be more than foolish if he tore the house apart to look for the deed. That was, if he planned to live here. It wasn't a fancy home, but it was well built and nicely furnished, if a bit tattered around the edges. Not that she thought for a minute he could run a horse ranch. He'd raised Tennessee Walkers in Alabama and had never seen a profit, even though Tobias had been an excellent groom. Lula May had only suspicions about what Uncle did with his money. Would he run this place into the ground, too?

After she forced herself to offer the courtesy of saying goodbye to Floyd, she saddled Lady and put a lead halter on Lucas's mare. Once she had the money in hand from the sale of the gelding, she would stop at the general store, settle her account and purchase what supplies she could carry home in her saddlebags. Maybe she'd put the rest in the bank. No, that would mean running into Mr. Henley. No telling what he'd say to her about his conversation with Uncle.

She didn't trust herself to speak to anyone. If it weren't for having to get the money from Lucas, she would hide in her room until the children came home. Only trouble was, Edmund would be with them. Lula May hadn't the slightest doubt Uncle would do everything in his evil power to discredit her to Edmund. And she had no way to defend herself.

Chapter Eleven

"I'm so sorry." Nancy Bennett wrung her hands and bit her lip. "I don't know what else to say. Lucas… he…he…"

With her friend in such a state, Lula May couldn't be angry. Devastated, yes, but she wouldn't let Nancy know that. Instead she put her arms around her and held on for a moment. "It's all right. We'll get along just fine until he can pay me."

Tears clogged Nancy's voice. "I know it's not much help, but he said you can keep his mare as a down payment on the gelding."

Still holding Nancy close, Lula May was glad her friend couldn't see the disappointment in her face. Now what would she do? She wasn't entirely broke, but she also didn't dare withdraw money from the bank, or Uncle might find out about it. As for that poor old mare, she might not make it back to Lula May's ranch. Still, she couldn't refuse Lucas's gesture of goodwill.

"Tell him thank you for me." She gave Nancy another squeeze and stepped back. "Well, I have to stop by the general store—" Without being able to settle her bill! "—so you take care." She touched Nancy's pale cheek. "Are you feeling all right?"

"Oh, I'll be fine." Sorrow flooded her face. "Have a safe ride home."

"Why do you say that?" Lula May laughed. "What do you know that I don't?"

Now Nancy managed a smile. "Oh, nothing. It's just with those cattle rustlers around... Lucas told me they struck Ogdens' place last night and stole at least fourteen steers."

Lula May shook her head. "How did they know— never mind." No one outside of the cattlemen's association was supposed to know the posse's schedule for watching the various ranches. They'd all vowed to keep it a secret. Had someone blabbed the information and the rustlers overheard it? She would have to bring it up at the meeting on Tuesday night. That was, if she was able to attend. If Uncle's lawyer arrived tomorrow, she might not be going anyplace but to jail. That thought caused her heart to drop even lower than not being paid for the gelding. With no other option, she headed home, knowing it would be hours before the children returned.

"Lord, I don't know what you have in mind, but these burdens are getting awfully heavy to carry. Please show me what to do. Please?" It felt good to pray aloud, as she always had at home until Uncle showed up. But with no answer forthcoming from the Lord, her heart soon sank back down to her stomach, where it had been residing for weeks now. Her only hope was to get home without encountering anybody who wanted to chat.

When she reached Little Horn, she saw Edmund in the distance tying up his stallion in front of the general store. What was he doing in town when he should be watching over her children? Maternal instincts overruled her desire not to see anyone right now. Good sense had her tie Lady and the old mare to a hitching post in front of Mercy Green's café before approaching Edmund so no one would think they were together.

Inside the general store, she found him in front of the glass candy case, where a large variety of sweets were displayed to tempt customers.

"Lula May, you're just in time." He gave her that appealing grin of his, as though nothing were out of order here.

She clamped down on her anger. It wasn't his fault her life was falling apart, so she mustn't take it out on him. She did, however, intend to get an explanation. Before she could speak, he beckoned her closer and waved a hand over the display case.

"The young'uns wanted to have a competition between the boys and the girls, with sweets going to the winner. What do you think? Should I get lemon drops, taffy or peppermint sticks?"

"Is that what you're doing in town? Getting candy?" She couldn't keep the annoyance from her voice.

He gave her a long look. "Something bothering you?" Then he blinked those green eyes as understanding seemed to dawn on him. "Abel, my foreman, is riding herd on the young'uns. He's got five cowhands helping him, good men, and not one of 'em will let anything go amiss."

Heat filled her cheeks. After all of his kindness to the children, she'd come close to accusing him of neglect. Candy, of all things! Such a rare treat. Lula May's eyes burned, and she cleared her throat.

"Licorice." She stepped closer, catching the pleasant fragrance of his leathery soap. She had to give him credit for being mighty clean for a rancher who worked so hard on his own spread. She pointed to the curled black strings in the case, Jacob's favorite sweet. "And for anyone who doesn't like that, lemon drops."

"Much obliged." He ordered the candy and paid the clerk two dimes, then turned to her. "Coffee?"

It was her turn to blink. Did she dare risk being seen by gossips who could help Uncle by casting aspersions on her character?

"Come on." Chuckling, he took her arm and guided her out of the store and back down the street to Mercy's café.

While Lula May looked up and down the road to see who might see *them*, Edmund focused on the café as if he didn't have a care in the world. Which he probably didn't. Once inside the café, he did have the good sense to settle them at a back table where few people would notice them. He pulled out the chair in the corner for her and, once she was seated, took the seat facing her, where his large frame easily shielded her from view. Had he done that on purpose? If so, it was a kind gesture that made her feel protected for the first

time since Frank fell ill. In light of her current storm
of difficulties, it felt good, felt right. Maybe for just a
few minutes, as long as it took to drink a cup of coffee,
she could hide behind Edmund and let herself enjoy
the sentiment.

After bringing coffee and sweet rolls, Mercy gave
Lula May a wink. So much for hiding. At least Mercy
wasn't a gossip, as proved by the fact that no one at
church seemed to know about Edmund helping Lula
May home with the children after last week's cattlemen's meeting. If Constance Hickey or any of her
friends heard that bit of news, they surely would have
confronted Lula May and scolded her, just as Uncle
had done, for "taking up" with Edmund so soon after
Frank's death.

She studied her steaming cup for a few moments,
then looked up. Edmund stared at her like he had something on his mind.

"How's your visit with your uncle going?"

The shock of his perfectly polite question, spoken in
the hushed voice he used when talking to Zephyr, along
with the kind intensity in his green eyes, touched something deep inside her. Suddenly her own eyes burned
and her throat tightened in a vain attempt to hold on
to her emotions.

"Fine. Just fine." The words came out strangled and
shaky.

Edmund huffed out an impatient sigh. "Now, Lula
May—" his eyebrows bent into a scolding frown "—I
know better than that. Floyd Jones is a shyster, if ever

I saw one. Why don't you show him the door before he pulls some mean trick on you and your young'uns?"

No matter how desperately she tried to rein in her emotions, tears slid down her cheeks, and her throat ached from unleashed sobs. *Lord, help me not to fall apart. Please, please help me...* Smack in the middle of her prayer, she sensed the Lord's answer. Almost heard it, in fact. *Help is here. Look across the table.*

She gasped softly. *Edmund?* As clearly as if the Lord had spoken aloud, she heard in her mind, *Yes, Edmund.*

How long had she been ignoring the answer He had already provided? Edmund was the only one who had seen through Uncle's tricks. And even if Lula May had to lose Edmund's respect, he might be willing to help her for the sake of the children.

Trembling, stammering, and swallowing sobs between her disjointed sentences, she began to pour out her sorry tale. *Lord, please don't let this good man despise me.* She didn't dare pray for more than that.

Edmund did his best not to shift in his chair, no matter how uncomfortable Lula May's tears made him feel. He had no idea how to console her, but the Lord wanted him here and he'd do his best. He decided the best thing was to reach across the table and pat her hand, as he'd seen Josiah do for Betsy when she got emotional. In return, Lula May gave him a watery smile.

"I've told you my parents died when I was twelve years old. Floyd Jones was my mother's only brother, my only living relative, so I was sent to live with him. He wasn't any happier about it than I was, and he pretty much kept me isolated from other people except to attend church." She sniffed and swallowed like she was trying to get a hold on her tears. "Even though he never had a kind word for me, when I was about to turn eighteen, he announced his plans to marry me off to a wealthy friend of his so the man would pay off Floyd's debts." She shuddered involuntarily as though trying to shake off the memory.

"I take it you didn't think much of that friend."

"No." She dabbed at her tears with the red-checkered napkin Mercy had provided with their rolls and coffee. "He was old and not at all pleasant. When he looked at me, I felt…uncomfortable."

Edmund took a bite of his sweet roll so she wouldn't see the anger building up inside of him. The bread was so sweet, it set his teeth on edge, reminding him that Lula May's desserts always tasted just right. He dunked a corner of the roll into his cup of bitter coffee and took another small bite, then a sip. Neither was improved by the gesture. "How'd you persuade Floyd not to force you into the marriage?"

"Oh, he had every intention of forcing me once I turned eighteen. One day I realized the only safe place for me was in another marriage, one of my own choosing." She laughed at the obvious irony. "I prayed desperately for the Lord's guidance. Tobias…you remember my talking about him?" At Edmund's nod, she continued.

"I wasn't allowed to read anything but the Bible, but Tobias found a newspaper advertisement for a mail-order bride and told me he'd help me get away, if that was what I wanted. I couldn't have done it without him and his sweet wife, Annie. Knowing Floyd would intercept any letters with my name on them at our local Theodore post office, I asked Tobias and Annie to mail my letters from Mobile. Once Frank and I agreed to meet to see if we were compatible, he sent money for my travel expenses through Tobias."

"Well, good for you and Tobias and Annie." Edmund relaxed a bit. No doubt this solved her problem. What could Floyd do to her now? He sure couldn't force her into another marriage.

"That's not all." Guilt covered her face, and she chewed her lower lip.

To his horror, Edmund had the oddest urge to plant a kiss on that lip. That made him no better than the old man who'd tried to marry her against her wishes. He studied the wall behind Lula May until he could get over the feeling. The last thing she needed was that sort of intrusion when he was supposed to be helping her. In truth, he had no idea how to kiss a woman. He cleared his throat. "Go on."

"My mother left me a pearl-and-diamond necklace, one her mother had given to her. When I went to live with Floyd, he laid claim to it. He said his mother never would have given it to a daughter who married a Yankee, as my mother did. But Grandma gave it to her for her sixteenth birthday, four years before she married my father."

Edmund had a hunch he knew what was coming. He gave her another nod of encouragement and picked up his coffee cup to occupy his hands so he wouldn't clench them into fists.

"When I left, I—I took the necklace. I mean, it truly was mine, but I have no proof."

A vague tickle crept up the back of Edmund's neck. "What do you mean *was* yours?"

"When Frank got sick, I sold it to pay off the ranch."

"Whew." Edmund blew out a long breath. "Must have been a mighty nice necklace." *And expensive.* He shrugged. "Sounds like the Lord provided it for a good purpose." Too bad she couldn't have that fancy gewgaw back to remember her ma by.

"You don't understand. Floyd has threatened to have me arrested for stealing it."

"What?" Edmund set down his cup with a bit too much force, clattering it into the saucer and sloshing some of the contents onto the tablecloth. "Why, that no account—" He bit back his temper. No use in getting riled when he just needed to hear her out and see what he could do to help.

"But he did have another solution." Lula May laughed bitterly. "He said he would take ownership of the ranch. All I have to do is turn the deed over to him."

"That's no surprise." Maybe no surprise, but just as crooked as a dog's hind leg. "Where's the deed now?"

"Hidden where he's not likely to find it."

"That's good." Edmund wouldn't ask where she'd hidden it. "So now we just have to prove the necklace belonged to you."

Lula May got a funny look on her face. "So you don't think I'm a thief?"

"A thief?" Edmund sat back and stared at her. "Not a bit. If the necklace was yours, you had the right to sell it. As for Floyd Jones, any man with any sense can see he's a crook and a shyster. Anybody would believe you over him any day."

She slumped back in her chair, her mouth hanging open like she didn't believe him, but still looking pretty as a daisy. "Honest?"

He had to laugh. She sounded like one of the young'uns. Sounded surprised that he believed her. "Honest. And I think the first thing we need to do is to talk to Sheriff Fuller."

"Oh, no!" She grasped his hand across the table, and her eyes widened with fear. "Please. You mustn't. Floyd's lawyer is arriving tomorrow, and Floyd says he has evidence to prove I stole the necklace."

"What kind of evidence?"

"I don't know. Probably Grandma's will. Floyd claims she disowned Mama and never would have given her a leftover biscuit, much less a valuable necklace. I don't have anything to prove otherwise." She released his hand. "Promise me you won't speak to the sheriff."

Edmund thought for a bit. This situation could get serious real soon with some city lawyer causing Lula May trouble. They should tell the sheriff, but her desperation held him back. "Against my better judgment, I promise."

"Thank you." She sighed real deep and sank back into her chair. "The last thing I need is more trouble. I'd rather solve my problems myself. Though I would appreciate your prayers. Sometimes I feel like the Lord is so far away, He can't hear me."

"I'm already praying." She had no idea how much he prayed for her and her family. "Sure do hate to see you suffer under your uncle's thumb."

He pondered the situation for a moment before risking another thought. "You remember a few weeks ago when Pastor Stillwater gave a sermon about suffering?" She nodded. "Not that I mean to preach or anything, but like the pastor pointed out, our suffering doesn't mean the Lord has abandoned us. He's never closer than when we're in need." He took a deep breath before continuing. The last thing he wanted to do was make Lula May think he was questioning her faith. "Have you talked to the Lord about your uncle?"

"Oh, yes." She nodded again, this time giving him a sweet smile he felt deep down inside. "The Lord finally answered. Or maybe I should say, I finally heard the answer He sent two weeks ago. That's why I'm sitting here with you."

Warm satisfaction filled his chest. This was further confirmation that he was supposed to watch over her. "I'm honored that you think so." Even so, that didn't solve her problem. Outwitting Floyd would take some mighty clever maneuvering.

They sat quietly for another minute or two. More customers entered the café and took seats far enough away not to hear Edmund and Lula May's conversation. Probably had their own private matters to talk about.

"You want something to eat?" He glanced over the table where a menu hung on the wall.

"No. This was enough." She poked her sweet roll and gave a little grimace.

Edmund forced away a grin. Most other folks seemed to enjoy Mercy's cooking, but he'd found someone else who didn't.

Lula May leaned toward him and spoke softly. "I never dreamed Floyd would follow me out here. How did he even know where I live? Or when Frank died?" She huffed in frustration. "Why, he even knew Lucas Bennett's first name, even though I didn't say it when I introduced them. Makes me wonder what else he knows about our friends."

Another prickle teased at the back of Edmund's neck. "Huh. That is mighty strange." He pondered the mystery for a moment. Mostly he wanted to figure out how they could prove Floyd's claim to the necklace was false. But what about his knowing Lucas's first name? In the back of his mind, Edmund wanted to give the old man a good thrashing for being so mean to Lula May. 'Course, that wouldn't solve anything and probably would land Edmund in jail.

Watching helplessly at the despair in Lula May's face and posture, he sent up a prayer for the Lord's help to calm down. Just as when they'd spent those relaxing evenings in her parlor with all of the young'uns around, he sensed a growing measure of peace fill him. Along with it came an unexpected realization. He cared about Lula May. Cared a whole heap. He wouldn't call it love because he had no idea what love was. Mainly he felt like somebody had lassoed something deep inside him and tugged him toward her, causing him to want to do whatever it took to make her safe from her uncle and any other trouble that came her way, like when he'd pulled her out of that arroyo before the flash flood could carry her off to Mexico. He couldn't stand to think of anything bad happening to her. Or the young'uns, either.

Something scratched at his mind. Something he'd just read the other day in *A Tale of Two Cities*. A dissolute lawyer, Sydney Carton, loved Lucie Manette and promised to "embrace any sacrifice for you and those dear to you." Little did Sydney know that promise meant one day he would take her husband's place and die on the guillotine, a "far, far better thing to do than I have ever done," all for the sake of his love for Lucie.

Edmund had never been spontaneous. He'd learned at a young age to think things through before taking action. But in this case, just like at the arroyo last week, he knew in an instant what he needed to do, knew the sacrifice he must make, and he needed to do it before he lost his courage. He reached across the table, reclaimed her hand and spoke to her in a hushed, hurried tone.

"Lula May, let's get married."

Chapter Twelve

Lula May didn't know whether to laugh or cry or get up and walk out on Edmund McKay. Marry him? The very idea!

But as she looked up into that broad, handsome, *sincere* face, she knew she could do none of those things. His shadowed green eyes exuded a deep, kind earnestness, and laughing might deeply wound him. She'd already done enough crying, so more tears would be pointless. And walking out on one of the most decent, selfless men she'd ever met beside Papa and Frank? She would never insult him that way. But neither could she agree to marry him, as dear as he'd become to her over these past two weeks, something she hadn't realized until this moment.

"If we were married, Floyd Jones wouldn't dare tangle with me."

Edmund gave her that winsome crooked grin, but his eyes held a hint of sorrow, not the joy Lula May had seen in CJ's eyes when he married Molly. Edmund might like her, might believe in her, but he sure didn't love her. Instead, his proposal was intended as a protection for her at the sacrifice of the solitude he held so dearly. Lula May truly was moved.

Frank had told her to marry again because he knew the children would need a father. She'd promised to obey him, mostly to please him and give him peace as he died. Yet in the back of her mind, she had already decided she would never marry again unless the man loved her for herself and believed in her. Frank might have believed in Lula May, but he had never stopped loving Emily. And Lula May wouldn't mind being in love herself, if she could be as happy as her good friend Molly was with CJ. Over these past two weeks, Lula may had come to like Edmund a great deal, but...

"What do you say?" Edmund gave her hand another squeeze.

"I say thank you." She gently slid her hand from his grasp. "That's a mighty fine and generous offer, but I can't accept. I'll have to work this out some other way if I want to get Floyd out of my life for good."

She expected to see relief in his eyes, but he seemed more surprised than pleased. Still, he took her response with a brisk nod.

"All right, then, *we'll* have to figure out something else."

Hope sprang up inside her, shoving aside the desperation she'd increasingly felt since Uncle's first letter arrived weeks ago. Edmund truly was an answer to her prayers for help. She no longer had to go it alone. As hard as it was to receive his help, she must, for the children's sakes. In fact, it would feel good to have a friend beside her. "That's an offer I will accept."

"Good." He thumped his fist on the table like a judge bringing down a gavel. The heavy china plates and cups clattered like a round of applause. "Now, let's head on back home. I got some young'uns to ride herd on, and you have an uncle to outwit."

Laughing more freely than she had in a long time, she gave her cheeks one last swipe with her napkin, then stood. "You go on ahead. I have Lucas's old mare, and I don't want to hold you back."

"What?" Edmund rose, too. "What are you doing with his mare?"

Suddenly reminded of his impressive masculine height, she spoke a bit breathlessly as she explained the deal she'd made with Lucas.

"And he still didn't have the money to pay you today?" Anger rekindled in his eyes. "Lula May, I don't think—"

"Don't worry." She couldn't let him fight all of her battles. "He's good for it. I'm sure he's good for it."

A low growl was his only answer as he took her elbow and accompanied her out of the café.

As he rode home at a canter, Edmund wasn't entirely sure what had happened back there at the café. He'd plunged into the marriage proposal feeling like he was headed for the guillotine. And yet her refusal left a gaping hole in his chest. Hardly the reaction of a man who'd been saved from certain death, at least death to his life of comfortable solitude. Was that love? He had no idea. All he knew was that he wanted to spend the rest of his years on this earth taking care of Lula May. In spite of her independent spirit, not only was her uncle about to steal her home, but Lucas had cheated her out of one of her finest cow ponies. She needed protection, and those young'uns need a pa. How could he convince her he was the man for both of those jobs? When had he decided he even wanted them? Probably the moment when she finally broke down and admitted things were *not* "fine, just fine." Instead, she'd opened up to him, sharing the deepest pain in her heart. That kind of trust meant the world to Edmund.

Still, from Lula May's rejection, he could tell he hadn't done something right. What was it? He could tell she liked him, respected him. Maybe even depended on him more than she realized. What could he have done different? What more could he have said? Did he need to change some habit? Something about his appearance? Not that Lula May had asked him to change. She'd simply turned him down flat. Yet he must lack some quality she thought was important. Whatever it was, she was worth the trouble of figuring it out.

Maybe that was love. In fact, he was sure of it. That being the case, he'd have to prove to Lula May that he loved her enough to try to win her love in return. An unfamiliar excitement filled his chest. This was a bigger, more important challenge than any he'd ever undertaken. He had no doubt at all that he was up to it.

Funny how just two weeks ago he'd thought Lula May was like his cousin Judith. Nothing could be further from the truth. Or could it be? As a boy growing up in a home where he wasn't wanted, he'd never considered anything beyond Judith's constant anger at him. But he also recalled hearing her crying from time to time. Hard, bitter tears not entirely different from those Lula May shed not an hour ago because of the helplessness she felt against the onslaught of troubles in her life.

Judith had been widowed early in the war and left with four young'uns. She'd taken in sewing to survive and later received a small pension from the Union army for her husband's service as an enlisted man, not enough to feed and clothe her young'uns. That couldn't have been easy for her. Then another hungry boy was placed in her care and her burden got heavier. No wonder she was angry all the time and never had a kind word for Edmund. He'd seen that same kind of anger and snappishness in Lula May that morning when he went to invite Jacob to the Young Ranchers' Club. The Lord had sent Edmund to help Lula May with her troubles. Who had been there to help Judith? No one other than an elderly cook with rheumatiz who'd stuck around because she had no other place to go.

For the second time in the space of a half hour, Edmund was struck with an important realization. Judith and Lula May were alike after all. He'd seen pretty quick why Lula May wore that chip on her shoulder. Now he finally understood Judith. Words from Pastor Stillwater's sermon on forgiveness came back to mind. And in the blink of an eye, Edmund forgave Judith, truly and completely forgave her, just like Old Gad had encouraged him to do years ago. The burden of bitterness Edmund had carried for most of his thirty-three years rolled off his chest just like a stone rolling down a mountainside.

And he felt a jubilant freedom much akin to the joy he'd felt when the Lord Jesus came into his life. He shouldn't have waited so long to put the matter to rest.

Edmund arrived at his ranch to find the Young Ranchers, both boys and girls, engaged in a treasure hunt overseen by Abel, his foreman, whose name was specially fitting today. As Abel explained it, instead of the girls against the boys, he'd formed several teams, partnering older young'uns with the littler ones to find "treasures." Those treasures were tools, tack and other essentials used on the ranch. The teams had to find each one and then write down where it was kept and what it was used for. The team to finish first and have all the right answers got twice as many of Mushy's molasses cookies as the other team, not to mention bragging rights. And of course the candy Edmund had promised to bring.

"Good idea." He clapped Abel on the shoulder and headed toward the barn.

Pauline broke away from her brothers and ran to greet him, throwing her arms around him like he was a long-lost friend. At least that's what it felt like to Edmund, and he'd fight any man who claimed otherwise. He couldn't help giving her a squeeze in return.

"Mr. McKay," the little redhead chirped like a robin in springtime. "You're coming to supper tonight, right?"

Right behind her, Daniel and Jacob and, now that he

saw them, just about all of the children had gathered, their treasure hunt forgotten. Every single one of them grinned up at him like they shared a secret. Matchmaking, that's what they were doing. Only thing was, this time Edmund didn't mind in the least.

"I'd planned on it."

His answer brought a chorus of giggles and nudges among the group. He shook his head. "Don't you think you'd better get back to your hunt? Don't want to miss out on the cookies and candy."

They quickly scattered, almost falling all over themselves to resume their game. All except Jacob Barlow.

"May I take care of Zephyr for you, Mr. McKay?" The boy stared at Edmund's stallion with admiration. Not tall enough yet to reach the horse's back to remove the heavy saddle, he still appeared confident he could manage the job.

"Let's see how you do." Edmund handed the reins over to him and followed boy and horse into the barn. Zephyr turned his large head and gave him a look that could be called quizzical. Edmund returned a nod and a pat on the animal's rump.

Speaking in a soothing voice, Jacob urged Zephyr into the stall and secured the reins to the board. Keeping an eye on the horse's hooves, he lifted the left stirrup over the saddle, released the girth, moved around to the other side, reached under and grabbed the girth and secured it to the saddle with the cinch. He lifted the saddle, grunting at the weight, and it slid to the stall floor. The saddle pad also fell into the dirt. Jacob gave Edmund an apologetic smile.

"Could use a little help."

Edmund swallowed a chuckle. Old Gad never laughed at him, and Edmund wouldn't laugh at Jacob. "Sure thing." He lifted the saddle, giving a little grunt of his own for Jacob's sake, and carried it outside the stall to air on the saddle rack. By the time he returned, Jacob had brushed off the saddle pad and hung it upside down on the side of the stall. Now he was brushing Zephyr, who contentedly munched oats in his feed box.

"Looks like you have this under control."

"Yessir." Jacob beamed at the compliment.

The boy had changed a good deal in the past two weeks. Had gained a lot of confidence. Edmund would make sure Floyd Jones never had a chance to take that away from him.

All this time, noisy children had been running around inside and outside of the barn, busy with their treasure hunt. At the other end of the building, Pauline, so like her mama except in hair color, held Daniel's hand and showed him some of the sharper tools on Edmund's workbench.

"We don't need to touch those, just write down what they do." She dictated the purpose of each one and waited while her younger brother wrote the words. "That's an awl. It's for poking holes in leather. That's a curry brush for brushing horses."

Being only six, he took a while to write what she said, but she didn't seem in a hurry to win the game. Edmund liked that.

Maybe these young'uns were on their best behavior to impress him, but he couldn't fault them for that. It

just meant they approved of him enough to play matchmakers. Now if he could only get their mama to feel
the same way. What could he do? Maybe help her outwit Floyd?

So how do we do that, Lord? He left the young'uns
to their game and walked toward the house. Some of
the others were a heap more competitive, racing here
and there to hunt for tools and such and making sure
their lists were right. Edmund could identify with their
enthusiasm because he enjoyed an occasional competition. Enjoyed hunting for...

Hunting? Searching? That was it. He knew just how
to start beating Floyd at his own game. Tonight after
supper, he'd tell Lula May and see what she thought
of his idea.

Lula May hadn't even reached the edge of Little
Horn before she realized she still hadn't thanked Edmund for saving her life at the arroyo. What must he
think of her? Plodding along the dusty road toward
home, she sighed. Too bad she couldn't catch up to him
right now, but Lucas's poor old mare had been wheez-
ing all morning and might not survive a run.

These darker horses suffered in the hot summer sun,
so Lula May would wash her down and put her in the
shade. But if she had colic, Lula May would have to
put her down. She'd only had to do that once. It was a
horrific experience. The only solution was for a horse
to walk it out and try to eliminate the cause. If the old
gal survived heat and belly troubles and her health improved, she might be useful for something. At barely

fourteen years, she deserved a chance. Lula May didn't have the heart to deny her that.

A surprising conviction struck her. If only she could feel as kindly toward Uncle Floyd as she did toward this mare. Mama once told Lula May she'd grown up in a home full of love, so Floyd would have, too. What on earth had turned him so stinky mean? She supposed it was the war, when he'd lost almost all his property to debt and his wife and child to illness. But why couldn't he have done what the wiser Southerners did, take what was left and move on with their lives? Despite losing the larger plantation to taxes, he'd been able to keep the house and that horse farm, but wasted all the profits. Now he wanted to take Lula May's livelihood. It made no sense, and try though she might, she couldn't put herself in his place.

However, if the Lord had allowed these trials in her life, as Edmund claimed, she could trust Him to show her the way to solve them. One thing she knew for sure was that the Lord wanted His children to forgive those who offended them. Lula May sure did want her children to do the same, so she had to set an example. No matter what turned Uncle into such a mean man, she'd pray to have a forgiving heart toward him.

Yet forgiving wasn't the same as letting Floyd destroy their lives. She had the right and responsibility to protect them all from his rudeness and especially from his schemes. Now that she had Edmund on her side, her feelings of helplessness had disappeared, but she still had to figure out how to prove Uncle's claims about Mama's necklace to be false. In the meantime, she must treat him with the respect due an elder.

She snorted to herself. Even when she treated him with respect, he sneered at her and claimed she was being nice so she could cheat him out of what he was owed. Well, she'd tried to teach the children not to let another person's actions control theirs. Maybe it was time to stiffen her spine and do the same. *Lord, I'm depending on You for strength and wisdom.*

An hour later, she'd finished brushing and washing down Lady and the old mare and turned them out, where they headed straight for the small stand of trees at the far side of the pasture. The long walk had the desired effect on the mare and one of her problems had been eliminated. She'd perked up and now pranced around with Lady like she was feeling better. Lula May sent up a prayer of thanks for that recovery. She felt better herself. Along with her prayer and resolution to treat Uncle kindly, she now possessed the emotional energy required to deal with him.

At the outdoor pump, she splashed water on her face to wash off any remaining appearance of tears. She wouldn't give Uncle the satisfaction of knowing he'd made her cry. Nor would she tell him about Lucas not paying her. Besides, after unloading all of her troubles onto Edmund's broad shoulders, she felt lighthearted, almost giddy over whatever came next. It would be exciting to see how the Lord was going to work everything out.

She walked into the house and found Uncle search-

ing through every book and ledger in her office. He
hadn't even bothered to return them to the shelves.
Hadn't even closed them. Instead, they lay around the
floor, the chairs and her desk, pages fluttering in the
hot breeze blowing in through the western window.
How would he feel if she went through his belongings
this way and left them strewn about?

"May I help you find something?" She kept her
voice cheerfully curious, praying for strength and wisdom with each word.

Barely glancing at her, he spat out his favorite curse
word. "You know very well what I am looking for,
girlie. You had better get that deed for me before my
lawyer arrives tomorrow."

She refused to be dismayed by the mess he'd made.
Partly because she was determined to treat him at least
as well as she did Lucas's mare and partly because he
was nowhere near the secret safe under her desk. Hmm.
That was a new thought. *Her* desk, not Frank's. Her
good, dear husband didn't need it any longer and had
left it in her safekeeping. That sweet notion warmed
her heart.

She leaned against the doorjamb, trying not to be
amused by the spectacle he made, all dressed up in his
tan suit, long-sleeved shirt and black tie...and sweating profusely. Maybe she should explain that, unlike
in his genteel Alabama society, in Texas, a man could
go about in his shirtsleeves and still be considered a
gentleman.

"What would you like for dinner?"

He perked up and gave her his full attention. But then, any mention of food brought the same reaction. "I did not think much of that supper last night, but it was filling. You have any of it left?"

"It's in the icebox. I'll heat it up for you." She left him to his search and did as she'd said. Even sat down at the kitchen table and ate with him.

Naturally, he criticized her manners and how much she ate. "You never did have much of a figure, but if you keep on eating that much food, you will resemble those cows out in your pasture. A real lady never eats—"

"Steers." She reminded herself not to let his insults hurt. In truth, she always ate plenty so she'd have the much-needed energy to do all of her work, and she always worked it off. She'd never carried any extra weight even when she was expecting. If anything, her muscular frame could use a few more just-right feminine curves like her friend Nancy's. Not to mention Uncle was hardly a model of self-control or perfection.

"What?"

"Steers. Not cows. I keep telling you that you need to pay attention to the terms people use out here, or you'll never fit in." She stood and picked up her plate. "I'm headed out to the pasture to take dinner to Calvin and Samuel. Want to come?"

"Certainly not." He huffed out his indignation.

She left him to his own devices, knowing full well he would keep looking for the deed. If he got more creative in his search, he might crawl under the desk and…no, she wouldn't worry. God was in control, and

He had sent Edmund to help her. Together they would figure something out to keep Uncle from stealing her land and robbing her children of their futures.

Edmund caught the aroma of chicken the second he rode into Lula May's barnyard, and his mouth began to water. Instead of waiting while the three young'uns tended Buster, he tied up Zephyr and headed straight for the house. If he could talk to Lula May alone before supper, that would be all the better.

He entered the mudroom feeling as if he belonged there, then hesitated, watching her through the inside door as she worked on biscuit dough on the counter facing him. She'd freshened up and put on the pretty blue dress that brightened the color of her eyes. Their rich sky blue intensity always gave him a kick in the chest, and especially so after their heartfelt discussion today. He could see coming home to her every night. For the first time in his life, that sounded like a better idea than going home to an empty house and an evening that sometimes stretched out before him all endless and quiet. At last he could admit, at least to himself, that he'd always claimed to prefer his solitude because he'd had no other option. But now he did, if Lula May would just see it that way.

"Come on in." She brushed a strand of that strawberry blond hair off of her forehead with the back of one floured hand, a useless gesture, because the strand fell right back in front of her left eye.

Without thinking, he stepped across the room and pushed the hair back, tucking it behind her ear.

"There." Then he realized what he'd done, the familiarity with which he'd acted without her permission. "Um… I…uh…"

She stared up at him, those big blue eyes all round and her lips parted in shock. His knees almost buckled. Had he ruined everything? Lost his chance to win her by moving too fast? It wasn't as if he'd meant to take liberties.

A sound from the other room made them both take a step back.

"Thank you." All businesslike now, Lula May returned to her biscuit making. "Should have pinned that back before I got started."

Floyd Jones entered the kitchen and shot accusing looks at the two of them. "What are you doing here?"

Edmund gave him a bland smile. "Came to supper."

"Again?"

"Again."

Floyd sat himself down at the kitchen table. "Lula May, bring me some coffee."

Edmund opened his mouth to say, "Get it yourself," but Lula May beat him to it.

"Floyd, you know where the cups are. Coffee's hot. While you're helping yourself, pour a cup for Edmund."

Edmund gave her a sly wink, which she returned. Maybe he hadn't lost his chance with her after all.

Throughout supper, Lula May tried to figure out how to get time alone with Edmund. She could see in those piercing green eyes that he wanted to speak with her. But how could she talk privately when Uncle inserted himself into everything that happened in the house.

Edmund solved the problem for her. After supper, he invited Uncle to play checkers, let him win, then turned his chair over to Calvin. He must have told her son that he wanted to talk to her, because Calvin took his place despite his aversion to Uncle's cheating.

"All right, Uncle Floyd." Calvin rubbed his hands together eagerly. "Last time you beat me three out of three, so I demand a rematch."

"Humph. Will not do you any good, boy." Seated in Frank's chair like a king holding court, Uncle lifted one corner of his lips into a sneer. "I am on my game tonight."

"Since you all are entertaining each other, I'll go check on Lucas's mare." Lula May did her part to arrange her private talk with Edmund. "Anyone want to go with me?"

"Nope. No, ma'am." Her other children spoke all together, and for once, she was glad for their matchmaking. All four of them looked directly at Edmund.

"Well…" Edmund drawled out the word, sighed, and then rolled his shoulders as if he was too weary to take on yet another task at the end of a hard day. "It's getting dark, so I guess I'd better go with you in case those cattle rustlers head this way."

"Why, thank you, sir." Lula May spoke like the Southern belles Uncle had always wanted her to emulate. "I would deeply appreciate your protection." She batted her eyelashes, something she'd never done in her life.

Edmund tilted his head and frowned in confusion, then blinked and arched his eyebrows with understanding. "Happy to, ma'am."

Uncle Floyd glared at the two of them as they left the parlor. Lula May held on to her mirth until they reached the barnyard, then doubled over laughing, definitely not the behavior of a Southern belle.

"Did you see his face?" She gazed up at Edmund, no longer caring what Uncle thought of her...*friendship* with her handsome neighbor. After Edmund's proposal, despite her turning him down, something had changed in that friendship. Other than Frank and her children, she'd never trusted anyone this profoundly since her parents' deaths. It relieved her more than she ever could have imagined. How easy it would be to give Edmund her heart, but only if he gave his to her.

"Yep." Edmund's expression was shadowed in the twilight, but she could hear the humor in his voice. At the same time, she read caution in his posture. "I wouldn't rile him too much. That might mess up our plan."

Her heart jumped. "You have a plan?"

"Sort of. I was thinking if I could get Floyd away from here for long enough, you could go through his things and see if you can find some sort of evidence to prove you owned the necklace. Maybe he has a copy of your grandma's will so you can see exactly what it says. Something like that."

Lula May cringed. As much as she'd felt dismayed by Uncle's searching her house, she felt more than a little uncomfortable returning the favor. "Oh, my." She chewed her lip. "Is that honest? I mean, would the Lord approve of my doing it?"

They walked toward the near pasture, where Lucas's mare now grazed close by the fence. Just as Lula May was wishing she'd brought a carrot for the horse, Edmund pulled one from his pocket. Clever man. Clever, *thoughtful* man. The mare ambled over and took it, munching noisily on the treat. Lula May imagined she could see the thank-you in her large brown eyes.

"The way I see it, it's not like you'd be breaking into his house. He's a guest in yours." Edmund chuckled. "Don't you do his laundry? You'd just be looking for things to wash."

"On a Tuesday? He knows my laundry day is every other Saturday."

"Hmm. I see what you mean." Petting the mare over the fence's top rail, Edmund gave Lula May a sidelong glance. "Your young'uns did get mighty dirty over at my place today. Might mean an extra washday." His voice held a hint of teasing, which she ignored in light of his reasoning.

"That might work." She recalled Uncle's wilted suit and shirt, for which he had at least one change of clothes. "How did you plan to get him away from here?"

"I'd thought about taking him to the cattlemen's meeting tomorrow night. I could spread the word not to discuss the posse's schedule until he and I head back here." He shrugged. "'Course, that means you wouldn't be able to go, and I think you should be there." He paused, staring down into her eyes, and once again tucked her wayward strand of hair back behind her ear. "I *want* you to be there."

Just as when he touched her earlier, a pleasant shiver swept down her neck. Oh, my. How easy it would be to love this kind, tenderhearted man. If only he loved her instead of regarding her as merely a neighbor to help, a friend to rescue.

"That means the world to me, Edmund." In the dim evening light, she held his gaze for several blissful moments, wishing against all good sense that he would bend down and kiss her.

Instead, he cleared his throat and stared away into the gathering darkness to the east. Taking a cue from him, she also shook off the intense feelings of the moment.

"His lawyer's supposed to arrive on the three o'clock train tomorrow. You could drive him to town while I do the laundry."

"Huh. There you have it. The perfect answer."

And so it was that early the next afternoon, the hottest time of day in mid-July, she found herself in the backyard scrubbing clothes on the washboard in her large tin tub...and waving goodbye to Edmund and Uncle as they drove away toward town. As soon as they rounded the hill a quarter mile beyond her property, she rinsed her last shirt and hung it to dry on the clothesline. With the younger children at Edmund's with Abel, the foreman, and Calvin and Samuel busy with the horses, Lula May headed into the house to search Uncle's large steamer trunk. She prayed with all her might that she'd find something, anything to prove her innocence.

Chapter Thirteen

"I wouldn't do that if I were you." Edmund did his best not to sound threatening as Floyd pulled a small flask from his pocket and started to pour its contents into his empty coffee cup. "Mrs. Green will throw us both out if she finds out you brought spirits into her café."

As Floyd returned the flask to his inside jacket pocket, he snorted and muttered something about backwoods Cretans. The old man would be surprised to learn Edmund knew what that word meant. In fact, the Apostle Paul had written about that race of men. "Even a prophet of their own said, the Cretans are always liars, evil beasts, slow bellies." Sounded more like Floyd Jones than anybody who lived here in Little Horn. Where on earth did the man get the idea he was better than everyone else? And where did he get the contents of that flask? According to Lula May, he hadn't been off the ranch except for attending the July Fourth celebration. Must have found a kindred spirit among the few strangers who'd shown up for the event and bought enough to last him awhile.

"Just another half hour before the train arrives." Edmund nodded toward the clock on the opposite wall.

"Yes, well." Floyd whipped his hand in the air to summon Mercy to the table. "Another one of those fine pastries, Miz Green." In spite of the compliment, his voice held an unpleasant authoritarian note. "And more coffee."

Mercy hurried to serve him. Edmund supposed she had to be nice to customers, no matter how bad-mannered they were. To soften his companion's rudeness, he gave the woman a smile and held up his cup.

"Thank you, ma'am."

"You're welcome, Mr. McKay." Mercy poured the steaming drink. "Say, did you and Lu—"

"Lucy's just fine." Edmund cut in right quick, hoping to keep her from revealing he'd been here yesterday with Lula May. No doubt Mercy had noticed Lula May's tears, but she'd had the good manners not to intrude.

"Lucy?" Mercy's brown eyes widened. Then, true to her name, she caught on to his dilemma and dropped the question. "Glad to hear she's fine. 'Scuse me. I gotta check the roast beef." She hurried away toward the kitchen.

Edmund breathed out a quiet sigh, relieved to see Floyd was too busy eating to notice the awkward exchange. He'd seemed a bit on edge since Edmund arrived at Lula May's. Edmund decided not to ask why. Let the man lead. Edmund was just along to be the driver and to get him away from the ranch so Lula May could search Floyd's belongings.

At the railroad station, Amos Crenshaw greeted both men in his usual friendly manner. "Say, Mr. Jones, I looked for you at church on Sunday. Sorry you weren't able to make it."

"Still recovering from my travels." Floyd was sweating mighty bad right now, and no wonder on a hot day like this.

"Yes, of course. A man can't be too careful about his health. I'll be sure to pray for you."

Edmund chatted briefly with Crenshaw about the upcoming roundup, when the railroad would transport cattle from the area up the line for sale in Fort Worth. When Edmund had first started out with his ranch, he'd had to drive the herd north, taking several weeks to get them to market and losing some along the way. Now the railroad got them to market in a few days with rare losses. What a blessing! While they talked, Floyd paced back and forth and stared down the tracks like he was a hungry man waiting on supper.

Right on time, the massive steam engine puffed into sight and slowed to a stop. A few passengers got off the Pullman car while Amos's son, James, traded the outgoing canvas mailbag with the incoming one. The boy then helped a porter unload luggage for the newcomers.

Edmund hadn't known what to expect as far as Floyd's lawyer was concerned, but none of the businessmen or cowboys getting off the train gave evidence of knowing Floyd. When the last person stepped down and the porter started to help departing folks into the

Pullman, Floyd rushed over and peered up through the back door of the car.

"Is that all?" He demanded of the black porter. "Check inside before you start loading up these—" He waved impatiently at the six or so folks about to get on the train as though they were bothersome gnats.

"Yessuh." The porter touched the brim of his hat in a respectful gesture Floyd didn't deserve. He climbed into the car and disappeared, coming back real quick. "That's all for today, suh."

Floyd swung around and marched over to Crenshaw, who was giving directions to a young woman carrying a baby.

"Yes, ma'am. You can hire a buggy—"

"See here, Crenshaw." Floyd came just short of knocking the woman down.

Edmund had been relaxing against the yellow clapboard siding of the train station, but this was too much. He hurried to make sure the lady was all right.

"Ma'am, I can drive you to the livery stable. Mr. Crenshaw will vouch for me."

At Crenshaw's nod, she gave Edmund a grateful smile. "Thank you. I'm making a surprise visit to see my parents, or they would be here to meet me. Do you know the Ogdens?"

"Yes, ma'am. It's not too far out of my way to take you there." In truth, the Ogdens lived north of Little Horn, while Lula May's place lay to the south of town. If he took this little lady and her baby to her parents, that would give Lula May an extra hour and a half to search for something helpful in Floyd's belongings.

Edmund hoped she would think to check under the mattress and on top of the wardrobe.

All this time, Floyd had been protesting just about everything. His lawyer's failure to appear, as though that were the fault of Amos Crenshaw or one of the arriving passengers. Edmund's offer to the young lady, despite Floyd's own former protestations that he himself was the only gentleman within miles.

Deacon Crenshaw eyed Floyd with alarm for about three seconds before his own countenance changed from accommodating public servant to protective master of his domain, the train station. "Floyd, back off." Not Mr. Jones. Floyd.

Edmund had heard Sheriff Fuller use that same tone with unruly cowboys from time to time. Now the question was, should he protect Floyd or leave him to Crenshaw? If Floyd got too riled, he might take it out on Lula May and the young'uns later.

"Well, Crenshaw," Floyd shouted, "the least you can do is check the mail to see if my lawyer sent a letter explaining his delay." He emphasized the word "lawyer," probably to strike fear into the stationmaster's soul.

"I'll get to that in good time, Mr. Jones." The stationmaster wasn't intimidated in the least. "You go on home, and if you receive a letter, I'll send it out to Lula May's place with my son."

Floyd eyed young Crenshaw with a skeptical, almost accusing eye. Which brought a harder look to the stationmaster's face.

"James frequently delivers special mail, and we've never had a complaint."

Floyd huffed out some more of his anger and then ordered Crenshaw to send a telegram for him. They entered the station to arrange it. In the meantime, Edmund helped the young mother find her luggage and loaded it into the wagon and then handed her up onto the driver's bench along with her baby.

The little fella grinned up at Edmund, bringing on a warm emotion he'd never felt before. What would it be like to have his own child? He'd never even dreamed of receiving such a blessing, but now the possibility stirred a strange longing deep inside him.

Floyd, on the other hand, wasn't the least bit happy that he had to ride in the back of the wagon all the long, bumpy way to the Ogdens' ranch.

Lula May carefully unwrapped the towels and brown paper from around several mahogany-framed portraits. She'd checked through everything in the trunk, finding at the bottom these old pictures. There was Grandma looking decidedly kinder that Uncle claimed she had been. Lula May could see her mother in the older woman's face, especially around the eyes. There was one of Grandpa, whose eyes twinkled and whose puckered lips bore witness of his toothlessness. The last picture showed young Floyd, handsome in his Confederate uniform, with the same prideful curl to his lips that he wore today. But no picture of Mama. Lula May's eyes burned with unshed tears. Poor, sweet Mama. Disowned by her family because she loved a Yankee. If only they'd given Papa a chance, they would have seen what a good man he was.

Glancing at her pin watch attached to her shirtwaist, she felt a moment of panic. Three thirty. How much time did she have left? If the train was on time, as it always was unless weather held it up, she had no more than a half hour, if that much, to replace everything in the trunk and dresser. Carefully rewrapping Floyd's picture, she set it inside the trunk. When her knuckles thumped against its floor, she heard a soft, hollow sound. *False bottom!* She dug along the edge with her fingernails but couldn't lift it. After a quick trip to her own room to fetch her nail file, she had the perfect tool to lift the covered cardboard. Underneath lay a black leather-bound portfolio and another wrapped picture, this one about sixteen by twenty inches. Curiosity drove her to look at the picture first.

"Mama." Her voice broke on a sob at the picture of her beloved mother so young and pretty and full of life, the sparkle in her eyes reflecting that of both of her parents. This must be her debutante picture, for she wore a white, scoop-necked gown of lace...and the pearl-and-diamond necklace she'd given Lula May. At the edge of the mahogany frame was etched in gold "April 24, 1861," proof without doubt that Grandma had given her the necklace. Lula May's parents married in 1865, only two months after the war ended. Lula May had been born ten months later.

Her hands shook violently as she opened the unlocked latch on the portfolio. Indeed, Grandma's will lay inside, along with Grandpa's. Lula May could hardly hold the documents still enough to read the elegant handwritten script. Grandpa had died before

Mama married, so he'd left several valuables to her, including a sufficient dowry for the union they all expected her to make with an appropriate Southern gentleman. He left a substantial allotment to Grandma. The plantation, horse farm and all furnishings had gone to Floyd, of course.

Memories blended with the written page, stories her parents had told her. After the war, everything changed. Floyd came home to find his wife, child and father dead, and all the properties in near ruin. Shortly afterward, Mama had met and married Papa, a dignified Union officer who had come to Alabama to help the defeated Southerners to heal and rebuild. No one among their friends and family saw it that way, of course, so Papa and Mama had moved north.

Which brought Lula May to Grandma's will. With the land, houses and furnishings going to Floyd, she had bequeathed various personal items to friends and servants and a gold locket containing tiny photographs of her and Grandpa to Floyd. Nowhere in the document was the necklace mentioned. Neither was Mama. Not that Lula May was surprised, but she did shed a few more tears over that.

Time had run out. She started to repack the picture and portfolio. Then another thought overcame her and she acted without hesitation. After putting everything else back in the trunk, she placed the portfolio in her desk drawer. And over the mantelpiece in the parlor, where Frank and Emily's wedding portrait had once held the place of honor, she hung the mahogany-framed picture of Mama.

* * *

Edmund followed Floyd into the house. To his surprise, they found Lula May sitting in the parlor, unusual for her in the middle of the day. While Floyd blustered to her about his ill treatment at the train station and why didn't she have refreshments ready for him after his traumatic trip to town in that useless wagon, she smiled and calmly gazed across the room at the mantelpiece. Edmund looked that way, and his heart kicked up. A new picture hung there, one of a pretty young woman who could have been Lula May a few years ago. Clear as fresh-cleaned glass in the sunshine, a fancy necklace hung around her neck. Edmund looked back at Lula May and held her beaming gaze. They'd won. Floyd couldn't harm her anymore.

"What are you looking at?" The old man whipped around, and his mouth fell open. "Where did you get that? How dare you go through my belongings?"

He took a step toward the fireplace, but Edmund blocked him.

"I hear tell you've done a bit of snooping around here yourself, Floyd." Though Edmund kept his voice even, holding on to his temper was proving to be a challenge.

"Why, nothing of the sort." Floyd looked up at him, his eyes wide. "I was merely looking for what is mine in this ramshackle excuse for a house."

There hadn't been many times when Edmund used his size to stir up fear, but right now it felt like the appropriate thing to do. From the appreciative smile on

Lula May's face, he figured he was right. "Tell me, Floyd, just exactly what *is* yours in Lula May's home?"

Floyd blustered a bit more but didn't say anything coherent.

Lula May stood up and walked to the fireplace. "I do have to thank you for keeping Mama's picture all these years. I'd like to think Grandma still had a place in her heart for her only daughter." Her voice wobbled on that last bit, and Edmund's heart ached for her. How well he knew the pain of rejection himself.

"Nothing of the sort." Floyd still acted like he was in charge. "A picture can be valid as a legal document under the right circumstance. That's why we didn't throw it out with the garbage."

Lula May started. "My, oh, my, Uncle, do you realize what you just said?"

"Whatever are you talking about, girlie?"

"Look here." She pointed at a date imprinted on the mahogany frame. "This is Mama's debutante picture, and she's wearing the necklace you claimed is yours. Not only that, but Grandma's will doesn't even mention disinheriting Mama or giving the necklace to you or anyone else, despite all the details it does include. That's because the necklace belonged to Mama. And she gave it to me."

Floyd blustered some more and shook like an earthquake, rage blazing across his round face. "I will take my supper in my room." He turned toward the hallway door.

Edmund gripped his arm. "Floyd, Lula May and I are going to the cattlemen's association meeting tonight. While we're gone, you get your bags packed, and tomorrow we'll take you to the train station." Had he overstepped? A quick look at Lula May's smiling face reassured him. "And you'd better not touch anything in this house that isn't yours. Not that picture, not anything. Don't even go in her office. You understand me?"

Unable to shake Edmund off, Floyd stared down at the hand gripping him. His posture slumped, and he raised a watery-eyed gaze at Lula May. "So this is how you treat family? Letting this Cretan manhandle me this way?"

There was that word again. Floyd really needed to hone his insults a bit more.

"I took you in when you were a pathetic, unwanted orphan, and now in my time of need, you throw me out. What is this world coming to?"

"What do you mean, time of need?" Lula May blinked those big blue eyes, and Edmund prayed she wouldn't fall for whatever Floyd was about to say.

After a brief but descriptive curse regarding Yankees and the way the war turned out, Floyd launched into a sad tale of how he'd never been able to overcome his losses. "Now those carpetbaggers have taken the last of my land and possessions." He shook a finger at Lula May. "It is your Christian duty to take care of me just as I took care of you."

"Hmm. I see." To Edmund's relief, Lula May clearly wasn't taken in by his pathetic speech-making. "All right, then. I'll give you a portion of what I have left over from the sale of Mama's necklace. You can buy a train ticket to wherever you want to go."

Smirking, Floyd pulled himself out of Edmund's grasp and straightened his wilted suit. "Very well. I shall be packed and ready to depart in the morning." He stomped from the parlor, throwing one last shot over his shoulder. "I shall expect supper in my room."

"Supper will be on the stove." Lula May stepped over to Edmund and grasped his hands. "Thank you." She chewed her lower lip, and just as he had yesterday in Mercy's café, Edmund had the urge to kiss it. One day soon he just might do that. "I'm not so sure I should leave him here with the children."

Edmund placed a hand over both of hers, enjoying the way they felt small in his grasp, and yet entirely capable. "We can take the young'uns and let Calvin and Samuel manage Floyd. They did a fine job last week."

She sighed a bit but nodded. "Yes, they did. All right, then. I'll go."

Had she noticed how he'd spoken of "we" as naturally as he felt it? The prickly little lady he'd known just over two weeks now seemed to have disappeared. In her place was an agreeable woman as comfortable with him as he was with her. Somehow he had to find a way to make that *we* official.

After supper, they loaded up the wagon and drove toward town. The closer they got, the more Edmund's thoughts turned toward other matters. With Lula May's uncle dealt with, he felt free to concentrate on the cattle rustlers. How could he and the other ranchers find out who had told the outlaws where the posse would be so they could hit a different ranch?

When they arrived at the meeting, the wind had kicked up and was shaking the canvas sides of the church tent. For the first time, Edmund decided Lula May was right about the community needing a church building sooner rather than later. Maybe she would bring it up tonight.

As Edmund joined Hank Snowden, she took her place at the lectern and asked Pastor Stillwater to offer a prayer. Then everyone took their seats on the wooden benches. Before she could bring up the first order of business, Gabe Dooley charged into the tent full of rage.

"Thirty-three head!" The man was disheveled and dusty like he'd just ridden in from the range. "They took thirty-three of my prime steers I had ready to go to market. I nearly caught one of 'em. He knocked me off my mount and gave me this lump on my head." He yanked off his Stetson and touched a raised spot near his forehead.

The men broke out in an uproar, shouting their outrage over this latest theft and injury. One of the thieves had wounded CJ Thorn, but he'd recovered. Edmund understood the indignation of the other men. He'd been furious over his own losses.

"Gentlemen!" Lula May's high, feminine voice managed to break through the noise. "We won't solve anything by being hysterical."

This brought the room to order in the blink of an eye.

"I don't need some woman to tell me not to be hys-

terical," Magnuson grumbled nearby. "Women are the
ones who get hysterical."

"And yet Lula May's the calmest person in this
room." Edmund could hear the proprietary tone in his
voice, and he didn't care who else heard it.

Hank Snowden nudged him and grinned. Edmund
chuckled. Having been a cowboy himself, he felt a
kinship with Lucas's foreman, a good, sensible man.

"Where's Lucas tonight?" Edmund spoke softly
while Lula May questioned Gabe for details about the
theft.

Snowden shrugged. "Said he got a letter from his
father and needed to deal with it." He shook his head.
"From what I can figure, the old man was pretty hard
on him. Growing up in Alabama after the war—"

"Alabama?" Edmund felt one of those prickly sensa-
tions creep up his neck. "I thought he was from Geor-
gia."

"Nope, he's from down near Mobile—"

"The one outlaw I saw was riding a paint gelding."
Gabe's nasally voice cut into their whispered conversation. "Fine looking animal. Pure quarter horse, in
my opinion."

Lula May's face turned pale beneath her freckles,
and she gripped the lectern for support. "A paint?" Her
gaze shot to Edmund.

Beside him, Snowden pulled in a sharp breath. "It
can't be."

Edmund's thoughts jumbled around in his brain. He
gave Lula May a quick shake of his head. The fewer
who put these details together, the better.

She returned a nod as she inhaled a deep breath. "All right, men. Here's what we have so far. At least one of the rustlers, if there's more than one, rides a paint gelding. Next, someone here is passing along information to the rustlers. I don't mean you intend to do it, but maybe you're putting your trust in the wrong person." She swallowed hard, and Edmund could see her hands were shaking.

"Here's what I propose," she went on. "Here's what we need to do. If you have any evidence of any kind, bring it to Sheriff Fuller instead of to the whole group." She nodded in the sheriff's direction, and he returned the gesture. "Our three posse captains will be the only ones who know where they will stand watch each night. And maybe we should have two posses out at a time."

Edmund sent her an approving smile.

Rumbles of further approval came from the other ranchers.

"Now, I know the cattle rustling is our most important concern. That's why we've formed this association." She glanced at Edmund and gave him a tiny smirk. "Once we put an end to the rustling, and I'm sure we will soon, I want you to consider another important matter for our entire community, cattlemen and townsfolk alike." She waved a hand toward the canvas wall that the wind continued to blow inward. "I don't know about you, but I think it's time we started building a real church. We ladies of the quilting bee did our best to raise money on Founders' Day…"

While she went on with her favorite argument about the men needing to provide money for the project, her mention of Founders' Day sparked Edmund's memory of the fire at the Carsons' and their cattle being stolen. Nancy Bennett had been there, but not Lucas. Lucas now had possession of Lula May's paint gelding. And the good man sitting beside Edmund had told him he reported back to Lucas every word spoken at these meetings, including the posse schedule. As if that weren't enough to incriminate Lucas, he also came from Alabama. Could he be the one who informed Floyd Jones about Lula May's life? Were the two men in cahoots? Edmund had no doubt they were, and his anger at Floyd flared up again. When he took Lula May home, he planned to threaten her uncle within an inch of his life.

Lula May used every ounce of self-control in her power not to grip the lectern with both hands to steady herself and stiffen her wobbly knees. Few of these men ever came out to her ranch, so few of them knew about her paint gelding. The cowboy Zeke did, but he wasn't here tonight. Of course there were other paint geldings, but Gabe had described hers in more detail, even mentioning that the horse appeared to have a sunburned pink nose. So Lucas hadn't taken care of the animal, as he'd promised. That alone was enough to anger Lula May. But to use it for stealing, putting it in danger if the posse shot at him—that was too much.

She did the best she could to calm the men down. Some didn't like being left out of the inner circle, as one rancher called it, especially those whose cattle had been stolen. Good thing Sheriff Fuller spoke up with his agreement to her plan. Men whose herds hadn't yet been affected, ones who hadn't lost income, were more open to her ideas about the church, but others soon joined in. She appointed Pastor Stillwater and Mr. Magnuson to look into the matter and see what supplies would be needed. In spite of his opposition to her leadership, Magnuson looked pleased at being chosen to lead this project. Of course, like the Carsons' new barn, the community would come together and build the new church.

She dismissed the meeting and joined the sheriff, posse captains Edmund, CJ Thorn and Abe Sawyer, who remained behind the others. Edmund invited Hank Snowden to remain as well, and she had a suspicion she knew why.

"Everyone who was in this room tonight was at the Founders' Day celebration." Edmund glanced around the group. "That's when the first cattle were stolen and the Carsons' barn was burned down."

"Tell me about it." CJ touched his shoulder like it still hurt from when a board fell on him during the fire and his scuffle with one of the rustlers. "If I just could have stopped him then..."

The sheriff patted him on the back. "You did your best."

CJ returned a grateful smile. Lula May knew that event had also deepened his friendship with widow Molly Carson Langley, who was now Mrs. CJ Thorn. A tiny pinch of envy touched the back of Lula May's mind. If only Edmund could love her as CJ loved Molly, she would marry him in an instant.

She listened while Edmund brought up his thoughts about Lucas Bennett. When he gave her a nod, she added, "That gelding sounds like the one I sold to Lucas just last week."

Edmund snorted. "You mean that Lucas cheated you out of."

She shrugged indifferently, but inside, her heart did a little skip. As sad as she was about the paint, Edmund's protectiveness made her feel awful good. Were his feelings for her growing, or was it just his natural sense of justice?

"I think with all of these details, we pretty much agree Lucas is probably our man." Sheriff Fuller hitched up his gun belt like he was ready to ride out and arrest him. "Anything else anyone can tell me?"

Edmund nudged Snowden, whose face grew red beneath his deep tan.

"Yes. He's been pumping me for information about these meetings," Snowden said. "Especially the posse schedule. I feel like a fool for not seeing through him." He huffed out a hot breath. "I'm going out there tonight to quit. That is, if I can find the scoundrel."

"Now, hold on." The sheriff lifted one hand in warning. "We need to make a plan. And we need to confront him as a group."

"I don't want Nancy to get hurt." Lula May's heart ached for her friend. It would be bad enough when she learned her husband was the thief. "Can you confront him someplace other than the ranch?"

They all thought for a moment.

"I know just the place." Snowden's dark frown mirrored the way Lula May felt. "There's a box canyon east of the Bennett place. Lucas has told me to stay away from there. Claims there are cougars on the prowl. Maybe he's taking the cattle there."

The group fell silent for a moment as each pondered the situation.

"Here's a plan." Abe Sawyer spoke up. "Let's put out the word on the sly that tomorrow night we're going to watch Magnuson's and Stillwater's ranches. But we'll gather near Lucas's place. If he brings the cattle back to that canyon, we'll have him."

"Not a bad idea," the sheriff said. "But we should go in the daylight. And no need to say anything to anyone else. Meet up with me at my office tomorrow morning. I'll deputize each of you, and we'll ride out together."

With all in agreement, they parted company. Edmund and Lula May retrieved the children from Mercy's and headed home.

Lula May could tell Edmund had more to say, but she wouldn't prod him. Like Frank, he'd speak his piece when he was ready. Now, if she could only wait that long.

It turned out to be less time than she'd expected. They arrived at the ranch to find Calvin, Samuel and Floyd seated in the parlor, a game of checkers set out but not played. After putting the younger children to bed, they joined the others.

"Floyd, I have a bone to pick with you." Edmund sat on a wooden chair, one leg crossed over the other in a relaxed pose.

"I cannot imagine what further indignity you plan

to impose upon me, McKay. Is it not enough that you have turned my niece, my only kin, against me?" Uncle stood from Frank's chair, which he'd claimed as his own since arriving.

Edmund also stood. "Sit down." The low, angry rumble in his chest was far different from the laugh that often generated from there.

Floyd's eyes widened, but he did as he was told. "Wh-what do you want? Do you plan to murder me?" He fell back in the chair and cast wild looks at Calvin and Samuel. "Will you not lift a hand to save your uncle?"

To their credit, Lula May's older sons refrained from showing their disgust.

"Why, Mr. Jones," Calvin said mildly, "you've made it clear as day you don't claim Sammy and me as kin, that you'd just as soon we vacate this ranch as soon as possible."

Samuel leaned one arm on his brother's shoulder. "Not that we're inhospitable, but maybe you should be the one vacating the premises."

"That's enough, boys." Lula May didn't mind Uncle getting a set-down, but it wasn't good for her sons to gang up on anybody. Beside, Edmund could manage this, whatever it was, all on his own.

"Floyd." Edmund sat back down, too. "I learned something very interesting tonight. Turns out Lucas Bennett is from Mobile, Alabama, right near where you lived. Isn't that something? One would almost have to assume you and he are friends."

"What?" Lula May gasped. "Did you know Lucas?"

Her mind reeled. So not only was Lucas the cattle rustler, he must surely be Uncle's informant.

Uncle shifted in the chair. "I may have known his family."

Calvin and Samuel gave her questioning looks. She shook her head, unable to speak. Unable to think of this horrid man sleeping in her house tonight.

Apparently Edmund had the same thought. "Floyd, I think we'd best pack you a bag and take you over to my place tonight." Rising from his chair, he stepped over to the chair, gripped Floyd's arm and hauled him to his feet. "I'll take you to the train station first thing in the morning. Let Lula May know where you set your feet down, and she can send your trunk."

Uncle sputtered and blustered, but eventually saw it was useless. He stomped from the room to obey Edmund's order.

Lula May touch his arm. "I don't know how to thank you."

"Glad to help out." Edmund gave her that appealing crooked grin she liked so much.

"I'll give you a note for Mr. Henley to withdraw fifty dollars from my account. You can give it to Floyd."

"I can do that." Edmund's eyes held a look so serious, Lula May couldn't help worrying about their other problem. "I think I'll have the pastor cart the young'uns over here tomorrow. A couple of my cowhands can help you ride herd on 'em, and you can teach 'em about training cow ponies. Would that be all right with you?"

Raw fear shot through her. As they'd decided after the meeting, Edmund and the others were going to confront the cattle rustlers tomorrow. Would she ever see Edmund alive again?

Something in her demeanor must have alerted the boys.

"Can I go with you tomorrow, Mr. McKay?" Calvin, always so perceptive, gave Edmund an earnest, eager look. "I know how to draw real fast, and I always hit my target."

Edmund placed a hand on the boy's shoulder. "I'm sure you do. We'll have to practice together someday soon. There won't be any shooting tomorrow, but I do need you to help your ma wrangle those young'uns."

She knew he didn't mean to lie. Yet Lula May hadn't the slightest doubt there would be plenty of shooting if Lucas got desperate enough. He'd nearly killed CJ, so no telling what else he would do.

After Edmund practically dragged Floyd out of the house, Lula May knelt by her bed and prayed for all of the men who planned to confront Lucas. Nancy Bennett's sweet face rose up in her mind, and she sent up many tearful prayers for her friend's safety. Yet it was Edmund's face she saw as she finally fell asleep late into the night.

Chapter Fourteen

In spite of all his prayers, as he drove to town, Edmund had to struggle to keep his temper contained while he pumped Floyd for more information about his relationship with Lucas. Using Nancy's friendship with Lula May, not only had Lucas sent news of Frank's death, he'd also sent descriptions of each of Lula May's children and what they liked, what they did. Such a betrayal disgusted and further enraged Edmund. Floyd even volunteered, bragged actually, that Lucas had supplied him with liquor, which shouldn't have surprised Edmund. He'd sometimes smelled the drink on Lucas's breath.

By the end of his questioning, Edmund had difficulty following Lula May's orders to take Floyd to the bank, but did it anyway. The old man didn't deserve this kind generosity. Still full of bluster, Floyd had no idea how close Edmund came to tossing him out of the wagon at the train station. Then he stayed to be sure the old man boarded the train.

Once the train departed, Edmund next drove to the livery stable to leave the wagon and horses. Zephyr, who'd been tied behind the wagon, tossed his head in appreciation at finally being ridden. The small posse gathered at the sheriff's office to be deputized, and soon the four men were on their way to face Lucas. They rode out to Bennett's Windy Diamond Ranch, skirting the house and barnyard where the cowhands might see them. No telling who else was in on the rustling, so they had to be careful.

The box canyon was half a mile from the house and set among craggy hills and flat mesas. If a man didn't know about the unique hiding place, he'd never think to go looking for it. Keeping to a brisk trot to minimize the noise of their approach, they made their way through the long, winding mouth of the gorge. Soon the bawling of countless cattle echoed off the canyon walls and met their ears, and the posse slowed to a walk. Boulders on either side of the ravine provided cover in case the outlaws spotted them and began shooting.

Finally they dismounted. With not even a scrub bush to tie their horses to, they voted to leave Abe with the animals. If there was a shoot-out, he could keep them from spooking.

Another twenty yards into the canyon at a passage about thirty feet across, Edmund peered around a massive rock formation. There stood Lucas, alone except for Lula May's paint gelding ground-tied some ten feet away from him. Lucas was securing barbed wire fencing to a crude wooden post. With the cattle making so much noise, he obviously hadn't heard their approach.

Edmund gritted his teeth. Here was the man who'd just the same as sold Lula May to her evil uncle by sending information only a friend would know. Once again, his anger roared up. Instead of waiting for the sheriff, he strode out from behind the rocks.

"Bennett!"

Lucas spun around, shock registering across his face.

"What are you doing, McKay?" The sheriff's voice held a warning, but nonetheless he moved up to Edmund's left side, Winchester rifle in hand.

"Hold on, McKay." Snowden stepped up on his right.

Edmund was too angry to be bothered by their objections. "I have a personal bone to pick with you, Bennett."

"That so?" Recovering quickly, Lucas took a stance that showed he meant to draw his six-shooter.

"It's bad enough that you steal my cattle. But then you sell out a decent Christian widow to her conniving thief of an uncle. You even steal her prime cow pony." Edmund's voice had risen to an angry shout. He needed to calm down, so he pulled in a deep breath. Still, if he could distract Lucas long enough, maybe they could all move in closer and tackle him.

"What are you going to do about it?" The sneer on Lucas's face held as much desperation as it did bravado.

Without warning, he drew his gun faster than Edmund expected. Edmund's own revolver was only halfway out of the holster when gunfire exploded on either side of him, a Winchester 94 to his left, a Colt .45 to his right. As Lucas slammed backward to the ground, his gun fired, the bullet whizzing harmlessly past Edmund's arm. Behind Lucas, one of the fence posts flew into pieces.

Panicked by the gunfire, the gelding took off running, while the cattle turned every which way to get away from the explosive noise. Several broke through the fence and climbed all over each other like they meant to stampede.

"Hyah! Hyah!"

Hank waved his hands to stop them, but Edmund grabbed his arm and pulled him back behind a boulder. Sheriff Fuller grabbed Lucas's arms and dragged him to the shelter of another boulder across from them just in time to avoid being trampled. As the cattle thundered past them, Edmund prayed Abe would hear the commotion and mount up before they reached him. All Edmund and Snowden could do was flatten themselves against the canyon wall and pray the stampeding animals caused no harm to any man or beast.

With the paint horse running free in front of the herd, well over a hundred head of cattle passed them before the box canyon was empty. Dust filled the air, choking the men, and bringing on desperate coughing. At last the final steer tore past them and the air began to clear, helped by a wind whipping down the canyon walls.

At last catching his breath, Edmund huffed out a sigh of relief and clapped a hand on Snowden's shoulder. Instead of the same relief, Snowden wore a sick, almost haunted expression. It only took a moment for Edmund to realize why. For the rest of his life,

Snowden would probably wonder whether he or the sheriff had killed Lucas. Edmund didn't want to know, wouldn't even ask. The only thing that mattered was that none of them had been shot. In fact, they'd done the scoundrel a favor. Now he wouldn't have to wait around to be tried and hanged. What a waste of a life!

"Let's get our horses."

They helped the sheriff carry Lucas's body up the gorge, where they met Abe, who was mounted up and leading the other horses like any smart cowboy would.

"I heard the gunshots and figured it was time to get 'em to safety." Abe eyed the body and grunted. "I feel sorry for Nancy. A sweet little lady like that getting hitched to a thieving snake."

Voicing his agreement with the others, Edmund mounted Zephyr. "Let's see if we can round up those steers and take them back to their owners."

Among the herd, which had slowed down and now wandered aimlessly, they found Lula May's horse and lifted Lucas's body onto the saddle. The sheriff headed toward town with the sad load.

Rounding up the cattle took much of the afternoon, which gave Edmund plenty of time to think things through, especially regarding what Abe said about Nancy. Like Lula May, she'd been a mail-order bride and was now a widow. But what a difference their choices of husbands had made in their lives. It didn't take much to notice how kindly Frank had always treated Lula May. Nor did it take much to notice how indifferent Lucas was toward Nancy even when they were newly married. Any casual observer could see that wasn't right, but nobody could step in and fix the matter. A man just didn't barge into another man's private affairs.

As much as Edmund had always admired Frank, something did bother him about life at the Barlow house: that expensive wedding picture of Frank and Emily had hung in the parlor up until last week. Why hadn't Frank put it away so Lula May wouldn't have her predecessor seem to watch her every move? Edmund knew his thoughts were foolishness, but he also knew what it was like to feel second-rate. Did Lula May feel that way?

Old Gad may have been a confirmed bachelor, but he'd taught Edmund that ladies were like good horses. If a man didn't want to take the time to show them they were appreciated and loved, he'd best just leave 'em alone. All those years they'd been on the trail together, Old Gad had left the ladies alone, and so had Edmund.

Trouble was, Edmund couldn't leave Lula May alone. Yet when he'd proposed, he'd made it sound like he was doing her a favor, a proposition he wouldn't appreciate if someone made such an offer to him. Now he knew better. He needed to show her what a remarkable woman she was. Needed to convince her that he wanted to spend his life protecting her and making her happy. Wanted to spend every moment of his day with her, even the times she turned prickly. Maybe that was what went wrong with his proposal. She needed to know she was loved. Well, by the end of this day, she would know, all right. He would forget Sydney

Carton's trip to the guillotine and remember Romeo's proclamations of undying love to Juliet.

He and the other men managed to get most of the cattle rounded up and driven to their rightful owners. At the first ranch, a half dozen cowhands joined them, so the operation took less time than expected. Everyone understood they might find someone else's steers among their own, but eventually honest neighbors would get them all back to where they belonged.

In the meantime, Sheriff Fuller had delivered Lucas's body to Mr. Agen, the undertaker. After that, he said he'd have to tell Nancy her husband was dead. On his way back from town, he met the men on the road.

"From the size of that herd, it's clear Lucas sold some of what he stole, so I don't think he was working alone. Somebody had to be feeding and watering them all this time. His partners will be hopping mad to learn we've outwitted them. That means we'll have more trouble."

"We'll keep an eye out." Snowden, still looking haggard, drooped in the saddle as he headed back toward the Bennett spread with the sheriff.

Edmund was glad not to be in his friend's boots. How rotten to discover the man he'd worked for was the cattle rustler. If Edmund didn't already have a fine foreman, he might hire Snowden. That was, if Snowden wanted to stick around these parts. If not, Edmund would write him a letter of recommendation to carry wherever he went. It was the least he could do for the man.

Eager to put the matter to rest, Edmund stopped in town for the wagon and team and to pick up Lula

May's gelding at the undertaker's. With her horse and Zephyr tied to the back of the wagon, he headed back to the High Bar Ranch. His thoughts turned toward the woman he would soon see, and he pondered what he should say to her.

He'd learned a heap of good things from Old Gad, had followed his example in most of them. Maybe it was time to follow the old fella's example again. Four years ago, Old Gad up and married a widow lady, and they now lived near Denver, surviving on love and a gold mine they'd discovered. If Lula May would have him, Edmund would marry a widow lady, too, a strawberry blonde beauty who already owned his heart.

Since she'd turned him down the first time, Lula May might very well get her feathers ruffled. Didn't matter. He was determined to propose again, this time expressing his love before he said anything else. That was, if he could just keep from sticking his boot in his mouth. As he drove the wagon toward her house, it seemed like an inordinate amount of dust filled his mouth and throat. How would he ever get the words out?

Around four o'clock, with the summer sun still high above the horizon, Lula May helped the last child into Pastor Stillwater's wagon and stood back to wave goodbye. Beside her, her five children noisily called out to their departing friends, promising another exciting day tomorrow. All during this day of riding, fishing, baking and horse training with the Young Ranchers' Club, Lula May had been preoccupied with thoughts of Edmund and the other men who planned to confront Lucas. From time to time, Calvin or Samuel would give her a reassuring pat on the shoulder even though they didn't know exactly what the men intended to do. Those loving touches kept Lula May from succumbing to fear or, worse, riding up to the Windy Diamond to see exactly what was going on. To see if she could help Nancy.

While praying for the safety of all involved, especially Edmund and poor Nancy, Lula May had corralled Pauline and the other girls and managed to get supper on the stove. They'd already made and iced a lemon cake, Edmund's favorite dessert, and now his favorite beef stew simmered in her largest cast-iron Dutch oven on top of the stove, and a pan of biscuits sat on the counter ready to be reheated.

Once the pastor's wagon rounded the hill just beyond her property, she told her children to finish the few chores left undone by the Young Ranchers and then to clean themselves up. Needing a few moments alone, she made her way to her office and sat staring out the window, praying as she had all day that the man she loved would return safely.

The man she loved? Yes, she did love Edmund, and she knew exactly when she'd fallen for him: when he'd given Jacob a life verse from the Bible. In that moment, not only had he given her shyest son a deep truth to instill lifelong confidence in him, but Edmund had also revealed his own depths, his own spirituality, his own vulnerability in the verse Gad had chosen for his life.

Then, in addition to inspiring her to renew her own prayer life, he had stepped in when she was at her wits' end and helped her get rid of Uncle Floyd.

Dear, dear Edmund. After less than three weeks of spending time with him, she couldn't imagine living life without him. She wanted to grow old with him, maybe even give him children, if he wanted. Could she do that, knowing he didn't love her as she loved him? Yes, she did need to be loved for herself, but maybe she could accept another comfortable marriage to a good man who would help her raise her children. She could be grateful for that. It was certainly more than poor Nancy Bennett had. More than most women had, for that matter. In time, maybe Edmund would fall in love with her.

She chuckled to herself. Silly woman that she was, she still hadn't thanked him for saving her from the flash flood. Well, that would be the first order of business when he came to give her the news of today's happenings. If he came. If he hadn't been… No, she would not fear. She might still be searching for her own perfect life verse, but the one that had stood out to her these past days was one Frank had often quoted in his last days, Psalm 56:3, "What time I am afraid, I will trust in Thee." She would choose to trust God, whatever happened.

A warm breeze blew in through the window, ruffling her hair, which had long ago fallen free from its tortoiseshell combs. She should mind what she told the children and clean up before…

The familiar rumble of a wagon sounded out in the barnyard. Edmund! She dashed through the parlor to her room and managed a quick repair of her hair. She ran to the kitchen just as Edmund walked slowly through the mudroom, hampered in his movements by her three younger children, who clung to him like little monkeys. From the grin on his face, she could see he didn't mind. In fact, he seemed to be enjoying it.

He looked at her, and their gazes locked for a small eternity. At last he cleared his throat. "Supper ready?"

With no warning of how high her emotions had risen, Lula May burst into tears and flung herself into his arms. "Oh, Edmund!"

"Mama, what's the matter?" Pauline cried, with similar cries coming from Jacob and Daniel, dear little ones who knew nothing of the drama about Lucas and the cattle rustling.

"Hush." Calvin grabbed the boys' collars, and Samuel gripped Pauline's arm. "Let's go outside." Despite the younger ones' cries of protest, Lula May's older sons half carried them out the back door.

Which left Lula May in the embarrassing position of having her arms around the neck of a man who had never even hinted he felt the slightest affection for her. On the other hand, with his arms around her waist rather than pushing her away, maybe he didn't mind it.

"You're all right."

He chuckled in his chest-deep way. "You sound surprised."

"No. No." She moved back far enough to see his appealing crooked grin. Releasing him, she cleared her throat and smoothed down her apron. "I figured a man who could pull me out of a flash flood and help me get rid of my evil uncle can safely help the sheriff arrest some cattle rustlers." Oh, dear, that wasn't really a thank-you. She started to correct herself, but Edmund's smiling expression fell into a frown.

She gasped. "What is it?"

He shook his head. "Things have been settled. I'll explain it in due time, but right now I'd like to talk to you about something else."

Lula May's heart jumped to her throat, whether from anxiety or anticipation, she couldn't tell. She grasped Edmund's hand and led him to the parlor. "Have a seat." Would he sit in one of the straight-backed chairs? Or sit in Frank's, as she hoped?

He sat in Frank's. She sat on the settee, her knees almost touching his.

"L-Lula May." He tugged at his collar. "Over the past couple of weeks, I, uh…" Shifting in his chair, he ran a hand down his cheek, where bright blond stubble held bits of dust that now sifted over his shoulder. "That is to say…" He exhaled a long breath. "I've grown very fond of…of my visits with your family."

Her heart wobbled. Did he simply love the cozy family evenings? Her cooking?

"As you know…" He suddenly sounded very formal, very unlike himself. "I never had a family, but now I feel like I've found one at last. One I'd like very much to be a part of."

"I see." All of Lula May's sweet sentiments disappeared. It was just as she feared. "And?"

"I'm not saying this right." He grimaced and gave her that crooked grin again.

"Well, try again." She would give him another chance, but only one more.

"While it's true I've always been a solitary man, preferring my quiet, er, solitude, and your young'uns sure do make a lot of noise…" He chuckled uncomfortably. "No, that's still not right." He stood and walked to the window, posting his fists at his waist.

After a few moments, during which Lula May's pulse beat twice as fast as the second hand ticking on the mantelpiece clock, Edmund scrubbed both hands through his hair, causing another shower of dust to cascade into the air.

"I'm just not getting this right." He spun around. "Lula May, I l-love you." He closed the space between them, gripped her arms and pulled her to her feet. "I love you." This second affirmation sounded firm and sure. And entirely convincing.

She melted into his arms. "Oh, Edmund, I love you, too."

"So, will you marry me?"

For only an instant, she thought about making him beg. Yet the boyish eagerness in his voice struck a chord deep within her that thrilled her beyond words.

"Yes, my dear Edmund. I will marry you."

"I know I need to make some changes. Probably lots of 'em. But if you'll have me, I'll do whatever it takes to make you happy."

"A-*hem*. I do believe I said yes."

He blinked, and his expression turned sheepish.

"You did, didn't you?" He lifted her up in his arms and twirled her around the room, coming a bit too close to knocking over her favorite lamp. Somehow, she wouldn't have minded in the least if he had.

He set her down and held her close, resting his chin on top of her head for several moments. At last, he sighed deeply. "Lucas is dead."

Lula May slumped against his broad chest. "Poor Nancy." She choked back tears. "What happened?"

"We found him at that box canyon Hank Snowden told us about. Sure enough, he had the stolen cattle, at least those he hadn't already sold. Before we could talk, he drew on us." Edmund gently released her and stared down at his boots. "It was my fault. I was so hopping mad at what he'd done to you that I practically called him out. That's why he drew. I would be dead if the other men hadn't shot him first. It threw off his aim." He glanced down at his sleeve. "That's where Lucas's bullet tore through." He grunted. "Missed my arm by a half inch."

"Oh, Edmund!" Lula May threw her arms around him again. "I told you to be careful." She wept against his chest, and he patted her back awkwardly. Poor man. He probably wasn't used to being around women who were crying. She struggled to regain control of her tears.

Tears. Oh, dear. Poor Nancy must be shedding many of them. Lula May stepped back from Edmund. "I have to go to Nancy."

"Mmm." He thought for a moment. "I guess you'd better. I'll go with you."

"No. I need for you to stay here with the children. I'll see if Nancy will let me spend the night with her. She'll need all the help I can give her."

His green eyes took on a sad but understanding look as he glanced toward the parlor window. "It's not getting dark yet, so I'll let you go. But you be careful. Stick to the main roads."

In another time, his casual way of giving orders would have annoyed her, but now it warmed her heart. Clearly it was love, not the desire to dominate her that motivated him. She could live with that.

After changing into her riding clothes, Lula May packed up some of her beef stew in a tin pail from Frank's old trail-drive mess kit. The pail had a tight lid she could secure with twine for the trip to Nancy's house. She wrapped several biscuits in a tea towel and placed the items in a canvas bag. In the meantime, Edmund saddled Lady. She met him in the barnyard, where the children had gathered with him. "I'll be back first thing tomorrow."

"If you're not, I'll come after you."

"Is that a threat or a promise?" She would indulge herself in one bit of teasing with him before embarking on her sad mission.

"Both." He managed a grin in response.

"You children mind Mr. McKay." She captured each child's solemn gaze and gave them all a smile. At their chorused "Yes, ma'am," she started to mount up.

Edmund stayed her with a touch on her arm. He bent down and kissed her cheek, then whispered in her ear.

"That's a threat and a promise, too. Something to remember me by."

A pleasant shiver shot down her side, leaving her breathless. "As if I could ever forget you, Edmund McKay."

Chapter Fifteen

Lula May arrived at the Windy Diamond Ranch house to find Hank Snowden pacing across the front porch, his boots thumping on the boards and his hat tipped back as cowboys did to cool off on hot days like today. The fading twilight illuminated the worried expression on his well-formed face. He'd been with Edmund, Abe Sawyer and Sheriff Fuller when Lucas was killed. He must feel especially shocked by his late boss's actions against their community.

"Evening, Mr. Snowden." She dismounted and took the canvas bag from her saddlebag.

"Mrs. Barlow." He touched the brim of his hat and brought it down on his forehead.

"How's Nancy?" Lula May climbed the few steps to the porch.

"I'm, uh, I'm not sure. It's not fitting for me to go inside, but—"

"That's why I'm here." She approached the door. "You go on. I'll take care of things."

"Thank you, ma'am." He hopped off the porch in one step and headed toward the barn, then turned back. "McKay doing all right?"

She smiled, a renewed relief over Edmund's safety flooding her. "Yes. He's fine."

"Will you be here long?"

"I plan to stay the night."

"Not sure where you'll bed down." He pondered the problem for a moment. "I'll bring a mattress from the barn."

"I'd be much obliged." She watched the Bennett foreman stride away before turning to rap lightly on the door. "Nancy?"

The soft shuffle of feet sounded inside. Nancy opened up, her face pale and drawn. "Lula May." From the surprise in her expression and the way she stepped back, she seemed to have erected an invisible barrier in front of herself. Did she fear Lula May would blame her for Lucas's actions?

"I'm staying with you tonight." Lula May moved into the front room and made her way to the kitchen, where she placed the food on the counter. Free of her burden, she returned to the parlor and pulled her friend into her arms, her heart breaking.

When Frank died, plunging her into widowhood, she had the comfort of knowing he'd left behind a respectable legacy. Nancy had no such comfort. From the guarded way she'd received Lula May, she probably feared all her friends would desert her. Lula May would have to show her that wasn't true, at least not for herself.

The two women held each other for long minutes, sobbing softly in a shared grief.

"Let's sit." Lula May urged Nancy toward the two chairs that sat at angles to the cold fireplace. "Can I get you anything?"

Nancy shook her head and dabbed at her tears with a man's linen handkerchief. Was it Lucas's? Lula May recalled how she had used Frank's handkerchiefs until they wore out just to have a piece of him close by.

"I didn't know…never imagined…" Nancy's eyes pleaded for understanding.

"Shh." Lula May patted her friend's hand. "We don't have to talk about that."

Nancy winced, and Lula May wondered whether she'd made a mistake. Maybe she should hear Nancy out. Talking about Frank had helped her. But again, this was a very different situation.

"I'm so ashamed about the horse," Nancy said.

Lula May shrugged. "He's back home safe and sound." She swallowed the clog of tears in her throat. Edmund said the gelding had barely outrun a stampede and had some nicks on his hindquarters and shoulders where the long horns of the cattle had broken through his tough hide. Lula May wouldn't mention it, though. Nancy had enough grief to carry. "The mare is doing fine, too. I'll bring her back. I think her days as a cow pony are over, but she'll make a good buggy horse."

Nancy waved a dismissive hand. "You keep her."

Lula May had no such intention, but she wouldn't argue.

They spent the evening talking about the quilting

bee, the plans for the church building, Nancy's new
Singer sewing machine that made such pretty, even
stitches. Lula May suspected some of the folded bits
of linen and cotton on the sewing table might be intended for baby clothes. A baby was a complication her
friend surely did not need right now. Yet if the Lord
had sent one, she needed to keep up her strength. Without mentioning her reasons, Lula May urged Nancy
to eat a few bites of stew and half a biscuit. Then she
helped her to bed.

Oddly, Lucas had slept down the hall in a separate
bedroom. Lula May couldn't think of sleeping there.
How thoughtful of Mr. Snowden to bring a mattress
from the barn. He'd left it on the front porch, and she
had no difficulty dragging it into Nancy's room so
she could be nearby if her friend needed her during
the night. The foreman had even brought the quilt he
won in the church raffle. A bittersweet pang stung
Lula May's chest. When the quilting bee had made
this one for the raffle, back before the cattle rustling
started and the Carsons' barn burned down, they'd all
been enjoying more innocent times.

Early the next morning, her own maternal instincts
called her home, but not until she'd encouraged Nancy—
forced her, actually—to eat some breakfast. With great
reluctance, she rode back to the High Bar Ranch, praying with every mile that passed that her friend would
come through this horrible ordeal…somehow.

Edmund sat at the oval kitchen table eating breakfast. He'd intended to fix the meal for the children, but

they'd beat him to it while he was out checking the stock before dawn. Calvin must have been paying attention to Lula May's cooking, because the coffee he'd made was every bit as good as hers. Edmund used it to wash down the rest of his meal. Pauline's biscuits had a dark brown crust on the bottom and a sticky middle, and Samuel's fried eggs could have cooked a bit longer. Jacob's bacon, sliced unevenly, was crisp on the thin parts and greasy on the thicker ones. Still, Edmund couldn't have wished for anything finer. It was a long sight better than anything Mushy ever cooked up because of the love that had gone into the preparation.

After they'd all finished eating, Calvin took his pa's Bible from a shelf by the table and handed it to Edmund. "Would you read a passage to help us start our day right?"

The other four children turned their full attention to Edmund, their eyes bright with interest. And maybe just a little fondness, if he wasn't mistaken. He'd grown up eating in the kitchen because Judith couldn't seem to stand the sight of him. Now it was his favorite room for eating, especially with this particular bunch of young'uns.

Unable to respond for the lump of emotion stuck in his throat, he took his time choosing a Scripture. If the oldest son in this family asked him to do this, if they all sat there so attentive, so trusting, that might just mean they truly wanted him to be their new pa. It was an honor he couldn't quite fully grasp yet. Maybe that was because Lula May was missing from the family circle. And once she came home, this was what it would be like for the rest of his life, starting his day with family—his family, sharing good thoughts for the day before they all went in different directions to do their varied chores. God truly had blessed him beyond what he'd ever thought to ask for.

Finding his voice at last, he said, "I'd be pleased and proud to read to you. Here we are. Psalm 23. 'The Lord is my shepherd; I shall not want.'" Over the top of the holy book, he saw the children mouthing the words of the familiar psalm along with him. They chimed in for the final verse. "'Surely goodness and mercy shall follow me all the days of my life, and I will dwell in the house of the Lord forever.'"

"Are you gonna marry Ma?" Daniel piped up the second they finished.

Grins blossomed all around the table. Edmund had to clear his throat again. "I'd like to, if you don't mind."

"I don't mind." From the widening of his grin, the six-year-old seemed pleased to be consulted. "So that means you'll live in *our* house forever."

Edmund chuckled at the way he'd echoed the Bible verse. "I suppose—"

"That's exactly what it means." Lula May stood in the back doorway, her face lit with some strong feeling Edmund couldn't discern.

His own emotions still high, he stood and, in two long strides, reached her and pulled her into his arms. A long sigh of relief escaped him. What was it about this woman that addled his brain, his emotions? He'd spent all his entire life shielding his heart from pain and rejection. Now his newly expanded heart could hardly contain the joy this family's love created inside him.

"Lula May." Still not used to having a woman in his arms, he nonetheless held her close, breathing in the faint smell of lilacs, his new favorite scent.

"Mmm?" She'd sagged against him and buried her face in his shirtfront. Oh, he could get used to this. In fact, had every intention of doing so.

"You all right?"

"Mmm-hmm." She lifted her sweet face and gave him a weary smile.

He knew the children were watching. Knew they all had work to do. Knew he needed to get back to his own place. Knew he *didn't* know much about kissing. But he couldn't resist placing a kiss on Lula May's nice plump lips. If her returning kiss—along with the agreeable hoots and cheers from her children—were any indication, he hadn't done too bad a job.

"Excuse me." Lula May accidentally bumped her left arm against Jacob's right one as they sat around the breakfast table, which was crowded elbow to elbow.

"You're excused." Jacob, who was all smiles these days, as were his sister and brothers, swirled a forkful of pancake in his syrupy plate and devoured the bite. His elbow, still sharp with boyish boniness, dug into her upper arm. They really needed to do something about these seating arrangements.

At the other end of the table, Edmund dug into his

stack of pancakes with an enthusiasm that did her heart good. For the past two weeks, he'd come over for breakfast several mornings a week, and with all the work they had to do on their respective ranches, any extra time spent with him made the inconvenience of the tight quarters worth it. The last time Frank had sat with them for breakfast, the younger children had been much smaller. Now Edmund's broad shoulders and her growing brood made the table a tad too small. In fact, whenever he entered the kitchen or even the parlor, the rooms seemed to shrink. Once he moved into the house after the wedding, and once the newness of their lives together wore off, would they all feel the pinch of the house's size?

Later, as the children went in different directions to do their chores, Edmund lingered over another cup of coffee.

"Lula May, I've been thinking."

"Uh-oh." Standing at the stove straining bacon grease, she sent him a mock-worried glance over her shoulder. "What now?" His deep chuckle warmed her insides deliciously.

"That night you spent at Nancy Bennett's and I slept in the boys' room, I did some thinking." He reached for another biscuit, then patted his belly and set it back on the plate. "I've been wondering how you would feel about building a bigger house for all of us, say where that stand of trees divides our properties."

Her heart kicked up a notch, and she set down the cast-iron skillet and joined him at the table. "Can we afford it?"

As if surprised by her question, he blinked those intense green eyes. She loved it when he did that. "Hmm. I guess we ought to talk about money one of these days. In short, yes, we can afford it." He snorted out a laugh. "Besides, have you seen that shack I live in? I never thought much about it, but lately I've noticed it's not much to brag about." He paused and stared down at his coffee. "Not meaning to brag at all, because every good thing I have has come from the Lord's hands, and He's seen fit to prosper me. Now I'm thinking that when we join our two ranches, we need to set an example. Need to invite folks over. Be hospitable. So we'd need a sizable house for that." He set one callused hand over hers, and a warm spark shot up her arm. "What do you think?"

"Oh, Edmund, I would love that." She glanced around the kitchen, taking a mental inventory of her pots, dishes and various utensils before another thought came to mind. "With the church building going so well, should we start another project before it's finished?"

"I suppose we could wait. We're both pretty good at waiting."

"That's what you think." She huffed out a mock-indignant breath. "Whose idea was it to wait until the new church is built before we get married?"

He took on a pensive look that didn't look entirely sincere. "Why, Miss Lula May, I do believe it was your idea. I thought our church tent was more than adequate, but you insisted we needed a building. But the tent's served a number of couples quite well. Married is married, isn't it?"

"Well…" Bittersweet memories swirled through Lula May's mind. "After the ceremony, I suppose that's true. But my first wedding was so…so plain and hurried." She and Frank had married in the parlor of this house before a circuit judge. How she longed for a church wedding this time.

Edmund stood and pulled her up into his arms. "Lula May, I love you, and more than anything, I want you to be happy. We'll have that church built in no time, and you and I will get hitched there with a proper wedding and reception afterward. Then we can think about our new house. After all, we have roundup coming soon, so I can't spend any time on it now. Why don't you draw up some plans about what you want, and we'll hire an architect from Fort Worth or San Antonio. What do you think?"

She looped her arms around his neck. "I think you're the most wonderful, thoughtful man in the world."

"That so?" He waggled his eyebrows playfully, and she let herself giggle, just like Daisy Carson did when she eyed Calvin across the churchyard.

"Indeed it is." And to prove her point, she reached up on tiptoes and gave him a heartfelt kiss. When he kissed her back with equal enthusiasm, she shut the door on her past and looked forward to a bright and joyful future with the man who loved her just as much as she loved him.

Long before she knew she loved Edmund and Edmund knew he loved her, God had planned for them to be together. When she finally decided on the Scripture verse for her life, part of John 15:16 seemed to suit her perfectly: "I have chosen you." Like Jacob's verse in Psalm 135, this one showed her how much she was loved because she'd been chosen, first by God, then by Edmund. No longer anybody's second choice.

* * * * *

Don't miss a single installment of
LONE STAR COWBOY LEAGUE:
THE FOUNDING YEARS

STAND-IN RANCHER DADDY
by Renee Ryan

A FAMILY FOR THE RANCHER
by Louise M. Gouge

A RANCHER OF CONVENIENCE
by Regina Scott

Find more great reads at www.LoveInspired.com.

Dear Reader,

Thank you for choosing *A Family for the Rancher*, Lula May and Edmund's unlikely love story, which is the second book in Love Inspired Historical's Lone Star Cowboy League: The Founding Years series. If you missed the first book last month, you'll want to look for *Stand-In Rancher Daddy* by Renee Ryan. Next month, be sure to be on the lookout for *A Rancher of Convenience* by Regina Scott, which completes our three-book series.

A Family for the Rancher is my fifth Western novel for Love Inspired Historical. Coming from Colorado, I have long wanted to write about the American West, where many of our country's values were solidified: faith, hard work and a belief in the American Dream. Although I never expected to write about Texas, I should have known the opportunity would present itself because two of my grandchildren were born in the great Lone Star State!

If you'd like to learn more about my books, please visit my website at blog.louisemgouge.com.

Blessings!
Louise M. Gouge